*****

Operation Red Dragon

Book Two of the World War III Series

By James Rosone & Miranda Watson
****

Published in conjunction with Front Line Publishing, Inc.

Copyright Information

ISBN: 978-1-957634-21-0
Sun City Center, Florida, USA
Library of Congress Control Number: 2022904114

Disclaimer

This book is fictional in nature. Any resemblance to persons or events in actual existence is merely coincidental. The views expressed in the book are the views held by the characters and are not reflective of the authors' personal views.

Table of Contents

Chapter 1
The Day that Changed the Nation

Day Twenty-One
19 December 2040, Late Afternoon
New York Harbor, New York
Freighter Zulu Warrior

Captain Omar Hammadi and his crew of eight had volunteered for this suicide mission. They would deliver the first of two of Allah's Swords against the Americans. The 50-kiloton nuclear warhead they were carrying below the deck of their ship could be set to detonate by timer or by manual control. Captain Hammadi had one of his engineers wire the trigger device directly to the bridge so that he could personally be the one that unleashed Allah's Sword on the unrighteous Americans.

They had originally planned to target Houston and the oil-refining centers, but then their orders had been changed by the Caliph himself. He'd told the men that he had had a vision and that their target should instead be Manhattan and New York Harbor.

Having served in the Iranian Navy for years, Captain Hammadi was pleased with the change in orders due to the greater tactical advantage of the new target. However, he was concerned about the increased risk in of detection before they reached their final position. He didn't want anything to stop him from fulfilling his legacy of destroying the infidels.

As they joined the queue of freighters waiting to enter the Hudson River, the crew played along with the harbor master's rules, waiting their turn to be inspected before they could proceed. After nearly three days of waiting, they had finally received instructions to move their ship into the next inspection queue. The Coast Guard announced, "Come to a complete stop, and wait to be contacted for your inspection."

Captain Hammadi started to feel nervous. They were so close to their intended target—less than six miles away, yet it felt like a million miles. Hammadi had been assured that the device was heavily shielded and should not set off any radiological detectors or other devices. It was also buried under several tons of coffee beans to ensure it wouldn't be detected by a boarding party. Despite these assurances, Hammadi's heart was still racing. If they were discovered before they were able to get close enough to their intended target and had to detonate the warhead in their current position, they would still cause catastrophic damage, but it was nothing in comparison to what would happen if they managed to reach their goal. The maximum potential carnage would be reached if they could position their ship near the I-75 bridge that connected lower Manhattan and Jersey City.

As the minutes turned into hours, they waited for the Coast Guard to board their ship. Hammadi's palpitations became one step shy of a full-blown panic attack; his palms were sweaty, his breathing became labored, and his thoughts were steadily racing. Time continued dragging along at a snail's pace while his internal urgency kept increasing. He finally decided that the boat was close enough that if he crept into the harbor and then gunned it, he could get to his intended target before anyone could do anything to stop them. The captain informed the crew of his decision, and they all said one last prayer before getting the ship and the device ready to go.

Their plan appeared to be working. They had not been hailed by the harbormaster or the Coast Guard yet, and they had just made it under the I-278 bridge. It was at this moment they received a hail from the Coast Guard. "Stop your ship and prepare to be boarded!"

The captain and his men quickly spotted the small cutter heading their way, but the men aboard it didn't appear to have any heavy weapons on them other than a 20mm cannon and a couple of .50-cals. This was more than enough firepower to disable their ship, but not if Hammadi acted quickly.

"Full speed ahead!" Captain Hammadi ordered. He prayed he would be able to get close enough before the Coast Guard ship decided to engage them or could disable their vessel.

Suddenly, an urgent voice filled the bridge, "*Zulu Warrior, Zulu Warrior*, this is Lieutenant Willis of the US Coast Guard. Stop your ship and prepare to be inspected! Acknowledge."

The ship was nearly to full speed, and they had just passed the Statue of Liberty on their left and Battery Park on their right. The radio came to life again. "*Zulu Warrior, Zulu Warrior*, stop your ship and prepare to be boarded. If you do not comply, we will fire and disable your vessel. Acknowledge!"

Hammadi continued to ignore their desperate pleas for him to recognize their warnings. He could see the Coast Guard ship repositioning itself so they could have a better angle to shoot, angling their propulsion and engine room to the rear. At that moment, the I-75 bridge came into sight. Captain Hammadi grasped the detonator in his right hand, and as he depressed the button, he let out one last, "Allahu Akbar."

****

Lower Manhattan

Jeremiah Nolen was a rising star at JP Morgan. He had made it to the "big leagues" as a trader, and over the past two years he had built his book of business to over $192.3 million. With his new promotion from senior advisor to Vice President, he felt that he had finally arrived: bigger commissions, company stock options, and a bigger piece of the action. He was handling the higher-net-worth clients now. He had earned a lot of money for his clients by buying railroad stocks, which had gone through the roof with the increased demand the war was placing on the manufacturing sector. He had also made several smart investments with a couple of companies that provided very specific component parts to the new Pershing tanks and the Razorback helicopters, the two most in-demand items of the war.

As Jeremiah looked out the window of his corner office, he reveled in the fact that he had finally moved out of cubicle land. Suddenly, the late afternoon became incredibly bright. Something powerful reflected off the building windows across from his office, forcing him to bring his hands up to his eyes to protect them as he turned his head. His metal and plastic chair quickly fell apart, dropping him to the floor. He looked down at his hands to see his skin liquefy and melt right before him, right before his body drifted into unconsciousness. The super heat generated from the nuclear device caused the structure of the building to liquefy. The structure imploded on itself and then dispersed into a million pieces of flying debris as the shockwave of the blast slammed into the expanding inferno. Jeremiah's hopes and dreams vanished into an untraceable film of radioactive dust.

****

Jersey City

Lisa Thomas was waiting in the checkout lane at the neighborhood Whole Foods grocery store with her two-year-old daughter. Like all rambunctious toddlers, her daughter was trying to pull at the candy and gum to add other items into the cart as her mother was placing her groceries on the belt for the cashier. As Lisa reached down to pick up something her daughter had dropped off the floor, a bright flash suddenly appeared near the entrance to the store. Thinking it must have been lightning for a brief moment, she placed the dropped item back where it belonged. Seconds later, the entire front wall of the store shattered, sending thousands of shards of glass flying into the store. Then the structure of the store imploded, and those at the cashier stations were thrown like rag dolls against the aisles from the several-hundred-mile-per-hour winds. Lisa was swiftly impaled on part of the structure of the building. The last thought she had before everything went black was of her daughter.

****

About four miles away from the blast site, Claudia Álvaros finished her shift as a nurse in the oncology ward of New York Presbyterian Hospital in Queens. She walked to her favorite diner, ready to eat some "breakfast for dinner" and unwind with a sudoku puzzle before heading home to her cats. Claudia knew a thing or two about the direct effects of cancer; five years ago, she had lost her daughter, Diana, to an aggressive brain tumor. The grief had been too much for her and her husband to bear, and the couple had separated. Unwilling to allow this loss to create bitterness in her life, Claudia had instead used it to fuel her change of direction in her nursing career. Before her daughter's illness, Claudia had been a school nurse, enjoying a more relaxed schedule and weekends off. After Diana's death, Claudia did whatever she needed to do in order to transition to the oncology ward; she'd had to pay her dues at the night shift on the Medical-Surgical wing, but she had finally made it. Now she spent every day helping families like hers to make it through a traumatic experience.

Every day was so rewarding, and also so painful. She couldn't help but see her daughter in the face of every patient that she worked with. However, every time a family member hugged her and said, "Thank you," with that deep gratitude that came from having someone compassionate walk alongside them in their tragedy, Claudia found the strength to keep on going. This was one of those days. As her omelet arrived, Claudia bowed her head and gave thanks to God for helping her to be a light to the patients with whom she worked.

With her eyes still shut, she was aware that there was a bright flash of some kind. As she opened her eyes, she looked out the window and saw several people behaving very strangely, almost drunk. They were holding their heads or eyes and stumbling. A loud sound, almost like rolling thunder, filled the room. Before she could process this odd behavior or the strange noise, several cars crashed into each other. She leapt up from her table to go see if anyone was hurt. As she ran outside, she suddenly saw the mushroom cloud in the distance and understood immediately what was going to happen to her and the people around her. While she didn't know everything about how atomic bombs and nuclear fallout worked, she did know a thing or two about radiation…and she was pretty sure she had received a fatal dose.

In that moment, she made the decision to simply help as many people as she could on her way out. She assessed the wounds of the car accident victims. One man's air bag hadn't activated and he had a horrible gash on his forehead. Head wounds are notorious for bleeding heavily. She grabbed the guy's scarf and quickly applied pressure to stop the bleeding. No need to worry about bloodborne pathogen exposure today. She would be dead before it could possibly matter.

She talked to pedestrians nearby, calmly saying, "I'm a nurse. I can help."

Claudia enlisted the help of several passersby to assist her in bringing the injured back to the hospital. The process was slow, as they kept stopping to help those who were most in need. One of the men who was with her was in his late sixties, old enough to remember the 9/11 attacks. He was calm and helpful, but he seemed very far away. The memories were clearly affecting him, but he was also determined to help his fellow New Yorkers.

When they finally arrived, the ER was already crowded with people. Some had injuries from falling debris, several had been in motor vehicle accidents, and a few poor souls were already demonstrating signs of radiation poisoning. They were vomiting intractably, disoriented and somewhat delusional. One woman reached up and touched her head, and a handful of hair fell out.

Given the situation, "business as normal" was cancelled at the hospital. All non-life-saving activities were cancelled. Surgeons that were scheduled for tonsillectomies were suddenly treating open fractures. Patients that were stable were enlisted to help. No one was concerned about possible lawsuits or malpractice. It didn't matter who was licensed to do what; everyone just pitched in and did whatever they were physically able to do to help one another.

Claudia hadn't started to have the nausea and vomiting yet. She calculated in her head that she could live a week or more, given the length of time it was taking for symptoms of radiation sickness to appear. She shrugged off her tiredness and selflessly began working to triage and to provide comfort wherever she could.

****

As the fifty-kiloton nuclear explosion expanded into lower Manhattan and Jersey City, it rapidly gained in speed, with temperatures quickly rising to twenty million degrees Fahrenheit. Everything within a mile and a half radius—skyscrapers, trees, cars, people—was completely vaporized. In an instant, nearly one million people were killed. Four million more received fatal doses of radiation, suffering with agonizing third- and fourth-degree burns. As the several-hundred-mile-an-hour winds swept through the city and surrounding suburbs, they blew out windows, pushed cars into each other, and threw tens of thousands of citizens on the streets of New York to the ground and into buildings like ragdolls. The impact bent dozens of skyscrapers in the neighboring boroughs beyond their tolerance levels, causing them to rip right off the lower part of the structure and fall into neighboring buildings, crashing to the streets below.

The initial blast wave dissipated, but the eerie silence that followed was not to last long. There was an immediate reversal as oxygen was sucked back into the blast cloud, and the surrounding firestorms began. The blaze from the blast created thousands of secondary explosions. A multitude of taxis, delivery trucks, and other vehicles that moments before had been traveling the bustling streets of New York burst into flames. Gas and water mains exploded, further adding to the chaos and destruction. In minutes, most of Brooklyn and Jersey City and all of Manhattan became a massive cauldron of flames and death. People were being asphyxiated from the lack of oxygen as it was sucked into the firestorm, which continued to grow and consume everything in its path.

Battery Park, Ellis Island and the Statue of Liberty were obliterated in the blast, destroying one of the most recognizable symbols of America. As the remnants of Lady Liberty fell into New York Harbor as unrecognizable hunks of melted copper, any restraint President Stein might have felt in his response was destroyed. More Americans had died in this single act of aggression than ever before American history. The Islamic Republic was showing no restraint in their war against Israel and the US, so it wasn't just time for the muzzle to come off the American military, but the leash as well.

Chapter 2
The Country Responds

Day Twenty-One
19 December 2040
The HIVE, President's Office

The President was sitting in his overstuffed leather rocking chair drinking a cup of tea, trying to relax for a short while and take his mind off the war and all the responsibilities of running the country. He was watching a movie on his tablet, trying to rest and decompress for a couple of hours. The twenty-hour days and the pressures of the war were starting to take a toll on his body; he felt every bit his fifty-five years of age, and then some. The last time his wife had seen him, she'd had a concerned tone in her voice as she'd cautiously commented, "Honey, you look like you've aged ten years in the past three weeks."

The President's head slowly drifted down to rest on his left shoulder, and he slipped into a dreamless sleep. Twenty minutes had gone by when Michael Montgomery, the President's Chief of Staff, and a few other key advisors burst into the office, startling the President. He quickly glared at the intruders.

"Monty—what the…? What in the world is so important that you couldn't even let me get one hour of sleep?" demanded the President, clearly agitated.

"Mr. President, I apologize, but you need to see this immediately," Monty replied as he quickly turned on the TV and adjusted the volume. As the President wiped his eyes to bring himself back to reality, the images of the damage from the nuclear bomb were being shown by a news drone from a news channel in Newark, New Jersey. The camera panned from where the Statue of Liberty had been to the astonishing mushroom cloud in the center of the Hudson River. The President gasped, too shocked to comment immediately. The drone continued to pan around, showing the thousands of fires spreading across Upper New York City, Brooklyn and Jersey City. All of lower Manhattan was completely gone; not a single structure was left standing, and the damage continued to varying degrees for several miles in all directions.

The next images were from a news drone that had flown into the blast zone. They were horrific. Bodies were strewn across the streets, crumpled against the sides of buildings and tossed about like discarded litter. Nearly every building was on fire. Streams of injured people were rushing out of the burning buildings. One injured woman in a business suit was carrying her severed arm with her, probably too delirious to realize that there was no way to reattach her appendage. A mother was seen cradling her young son in her arms, tears streaming down her face; he was obviously dead.

As the President sat there watching the images, he slowly sat forward in his chair in shock. His mind raced.

How could they have gotten a nuclear bomb into New York? What am I to do now? he wondered.

"Mr. President, if they were able to sneak a nuclear weapon into New York Harbor, they could have smuggled in other bombs the same way," National Security Advisor Mike Williams said with genuine fear and concern in his voice.

Mike felt like he had completely failed his president and the country. Despite his best efforts to try and protect the country, he had been unsuccessful. A nuclear bomb had destroyed the most iconic American city. Millions of people were either dead or dying. He closed his eyes for a moment, and when he opened them, a fire was lit from the inside. He was determined not to let this happen again. Whatever it took to win this war, he would make it happen.

The President, still reeling from the images being shown on the TV, turned to the Director for Homeland Security. "Director Perez, I want every ship and shipping container in our ports searched immediately for a nuke. I don't care how many resources you need, or what needs to happen. Get this done yesterday. Do you understand?"

"Yes, Mr. President. I will see to it immediately. I've already been in contact with the directors of FEMA and the Red Cross. Both organizations are mobilizing their people to New York as we speak," responded Director Perez. He was also in shock. As the images of New York continued to play, the sum total of the human tragedy before him was completely overwhelming.

The President's Chief of Staff turned to Henry and said, "Mr. President, the Secretary of Defense, Secretary Wise, and General

Branson are in the Situation Room along with the Joint Chiefs. They're insisting that you join them immediately."

"Tell them we're on our way," the President said as he stood up to follow Monty into the hall.

As the President walked down the hallway to the Situation Room, his mind was racing with thoughts of what to do next. He had wanted to keep this war conventional. However, he had also warned the Islamic Republic that any further use of nuclear weapons against Israel or the United States would result in an immediate and severe reprisal.

This war is quickly spiraling out of control, he thought.

As the President entered the Situation Room, the group lost no time in getting down to business.

"Mr. President, we're still assessing the blast site to determine if the weapon originated from the Islamic Republic," Eric Clarke said as the President took his seat at the head of the table.

"If this is traced back to the Islamic Republic, then I'm going to ask for permission to use nuclear weapons," General Branson asserted, slamming his fist on the table.

"Everyone, calm down," urged the President. "We are all in a state of shock right now. The last thing we need to do is overreact. I assure you, General, if this does trace back to the Islamic Republic, we are going to hit them hard. In the meantime, we need to identify with certainty where this bomb originated, ensure there are no other immediate nuclear threats, and begin to assist the people of New York and New Jersey."

The group seemed to take a collective deep breath. The President continued, "For now, General Branson, I want our strategic bombers armed with nukes and ready to get airborne immediately if so ordered. I also want our ballistic missile submarines to move to their global launch sites right away. We need to be prepared in case this is a coordinated attack."

"I'll send the order out immediately, Sir. We should have some information about the origins of the New York bomb within the hour," responded General Branson.

Jorge Perez informed the group, "The FEMA Director said they are initiating their contingency plans, establishing dozens of emergency aid camps outside of New York City for people to find refuge. However, it will be hours, if not a full day, before their full resources are in place."

The Director of Homeland Security was starting to feel completely overwhelmed in his position. It had been four days since he had slept in his own bed or even seen his wife and kids. Lately, he had been catching catnaps on the couch in his office, running from one disaster to another. Now a nuclear bomb had gone off in New York City; he was at his breaking point. Inside, he just wanted to curl up in a ball and cry. Of course, he could not let his staff or anyone else see that. He needed to be the image of stoic strength. He took a deep breath and steadied himself to face the next challenge and ensure his country survived the trials being thrown its way.

****

Elsewhere throughout the country, the American people had been celebrating the first major victory of the war in Israel when they were suddenly rocked to the core by the images of a mushroom cloud over New York Harbor. People gathered in coffee shops and each other's homes, silently watching the news and allowing themselves to be overwhelmed by the sheer destruction of New York and Jersey City. Virtually nothing was left standing in lower Manhattan. This was the second time that the World Trade Center had been destroyed. Dozens of skyscrapers and buildings all across the city were on fire, and others had sustained massive damage.

The indomitable spirit of the American people was bruised, but it could not be crushed. Heroes rose up to help those in need. In 2039, the DHS, DoD and FEMA had all planned for several mass-casualty scenarios—now those strategies were being put to action. An army of volunteers donned hazmat suits and headed toward the blast site. The doctors, nurses and EMTs that arrived triaged the injured into the different levels of required care and separated out the deceased; the casualties and the wounded were transferred to nearby airports or airfields and then flown to predetermined hospitals or mortuaries for follow-up care or identification.

The goal was to recover the injured and have them moved to their final triage points within twenty-four hours, before the hazmat suits would need to be cycled out for new ones. This would quickly disperse the wounded away from the epicenter to less-overloaded facilities. If this could be accomplished, there was a higher likelihood more individuals could be saved. As aircraft landed in the predetermined cities, hundreds of police, EMTs and firefighters who had volunteered in advance to assist in a national emergency would board the aircraft for the return flight to the places where they would be needed most, providing an immediate influx of emergency personnel. In the days following the disaster, civilians who had been displaced by the attack would also start to be dispersed to predetermined refugee centers, where they could be housed and taken care of until they could return home or leave to stay with family.

Chapter 3
A Caliph's Dilemma

Day Twenty-Two
20 December 2040–0100 hours
Islamic Republic
Command Bunker under Riyadh

The Command Bunker, where the leader of the Islamic Republic had moved the government, had been developed by a famous Chinese engineer who had also developed similar bunkers for the leaders of China. It was a honeycomb of various living quarters, meeting rooms and work spaces designed to sustain and support a government or run a war from several hundred feet below the surface. It also had multiple escape tunnels to ensure the occupants could exit when the crisis had passed. Caliph Mohammed and his senior staff had been quite comfortable staying there since the beginning of the war, and now that the Chinese were entering the conflict, he believed that the Americans would capitulate soon.

Mohammed sat in his war room, reading over the various field reports from General Abdullah Muhammed, his overall military commander in Jordan. The Command Bunker incorporated the latest in technology and communications systems, so the Caliph could effectively communicate with the outside world and continue to manage his armed forces from safety. Between the surveillance videos from the drones and the reports from Abdullah, he ascertained that the majority of his forces in Israel had either surrendered or been destroyed. The general estimated that they had lost close to 400,000 soldiers in a single day. Of course, there were still close to 90,000 troops fighting in Southern Israel, and General Abdullah had 300,000 troops in Amman. Another 1.2 million reinforcements were still en route.

"Caliph Mohammed, General Abdullah is requesting permission to withdraw all Islamic Republic forces from Israel and to consolidate them near Amman under the cover of our laser defense network," General Rafik Hamza said, not sure how the Caliph would respond in light of the destruction of so many soldiers in the Jordan Valley and the loss of Jerusalem.

"Do you agree with the general's assessment that he should withdraw his forces?" asked the Caliph, his voice dripping with disappointment and sarcasm.

General Hamza did not like to be talked down to. He resented the acid tone of the Caliph's words. It was his order to advance *all* their forces into the Jordan Valley, but this had made them too tempting a target, and his men had been slaughtered by massive air raids. As far as General Hamza was concerned, this military catastrophe was entirely the Caliph's fault.

"If he is allowed to withdraw his forces back to Amman, then he will be able to establish a defensive line until additional reinforcements from Iran and Iraq are able to move to the front. He is trying to buy time while ensuring the Americans are not able to launch an offensive and capture Amman," General Hamza replied, clearly annoyed at having sound military advice dismissed or questioned.

"This is a disgrace, General. An outrage. Nearly a decade of training and modernization, hundreds of billions spent on our military, and in one day, our entire attacking force was wiped out. They didn't even have to use nuclear weapons to do it!" raged the Caliph.

"If you will recall, my Caliph, you ordered General Abdullah to send all of our forces into the Jordan Valley to push past Jerusalem. General Abdullah's original attacks may have been slower than we liked, but he was grinding the Israeli and American armies into the dirt prior to sending the entire army in."

"Do not try to blame this catastrophe on me, General Hamza. I have provided everything the Army said you needed to win, and then some. We had Jerusalem, and we nearly had Tel Aviv. Now our army is destroyed," Caliph Abbas asserted, leaning back in his chair, exasperated.

"All is not lost, Caliph. This is just a setback, and once our reinforcements from Iran and Iraq start to arrive, they will be able to resume the attack. There are 1.2 million additional troops on the way, along with another three million civilian volunteers. The Russians still have forces in Turkey, and once they join the war, they will assist us in Israel. My Caliph, we lost a battle, but not the war," the general reassured him, trying to make it clear that the situation could be turned around in time.

The general continued, "I would also like to point out that we just launched our offensive in North Africa to push the American Marines into the ocean. Our navy is also setting up hundreds of small motorboats with Exocet missiles to conduct hit-and-run attacks on the American supply lines, and once the Russians join, the American supply routes through the Mediterranean will be cut off." General Hamza was confident that he could regain the initiative and trust with the Caliph.

"We also have the first of Allah's Swords about to be delivered to the Americans. We may be able to force them to capitulate to our demands as well," General Rafi interjected.

Caliph Mohammed knew General Hamza and Rafi were correct, and the smart move to make right now was to pull his forces back to Amman and regroup while they waited for reinforcements. The Russians were about to enter the war, and the Chinese had an expeditionary force on the way. Once the Russians and Chinese arrived, the IR's fortunes would change. They just needed to stay the course.

An army colonel walked into the room and immediately approached General Hamza, whispering something in his ear. General Hamza smiled and his eyes lit up.

"General, I assume you have received some good news? Please share it with us," Mohammed Abbas commanded.

"I believe we should turn on Al-Jazeera. The first of Allah's Swords has been successfully delivered to New York City."

As the TV was turned on, the council members watched as the scene unfolded. The various images showed the vast destruction of New York. The widespread devastation of the city was made complete with the obvious absence of the Statue of Liberty and the World Trade Center. Images of mangled bodies strewn along the streets flashed across the screen; throngs of wounded tried to flee the city as many more were practically piled on top of each other at overcrowded emergency rooms.

Dozens and dozens of military helicopters could be seen ferrying people from the more damaged areas of the city to numerous triage locations and regional airports. The skies were abuzz with military aircraft. Fires could be seen burning out of control in several of the boroughs and Jersey City, and blazes also plagued numerous container ships and other large ships that had been in the various harbors and piers. It was a picture of complete and utter destruction.

General Hamza smiled. Then, picking up his tablet, he decided to waste no time and started sending out additional orders. "Colonel, send word to all of our radar stations and laser defense centers to be prepared for the Americans' response. They will most likely attack us with nuclear missiles."

Mohammed Abbas looked at the images with awe and a bit of fear. If their nuclear bomb could do this amount of damage, how much damage would the Americans inflict on the Islamic Republic with their much larger nuclear arsenal? The Islamic Republic still had close to four hundred nuclear weapons. However, none of the warheads compared in size to the American, Russian or Chinese city killers (the 300-to-500 kiloton range and higher). After longing for this moment for so long, Mohammed began to wonder if attacking an American city directly with a nuclear weapon was the best way to bring terror to America.

They were supposed to coordinate the bomb going off with the second bomb quickly to follow. *They must have had to move up the timetable for some reason*, thought Mohammed Abbas. The genie was out of the bottle now. It was too late to go back. Looking at Talal bin Abdulaziz, the Foreign Minister, he ordered, "I need you to contact the American government immediately. We need to make our demand to them immediately before they launch a counterattack."

Talal looked at Mohammed Abbas for a second before responding, "I will start on that immediately. Please give me a couple of minutes to make a few phone calls." Talal picked his tablet up and then dialed a phone number that was to be the official number by which the two governments were to communicate.

As the phone began to ring, Talal tried to think of what to say. "This is the presidential switchboard, how may I direct your call?" asked a man's voice.

"This is Talal bin Abdulaziz, the Islamic Republic's Foreign Minister. I have the rest of the Islamic Council with me. We would like to speak to President Stein."

"Please hold one minute."

Chapter 4
The Phone Rings

Day Twenty-One
19 December 2040, 45 minutes post nuclear detonation
The HIVE, Situation Room

As President Stein, his cabinet and advisors were trying to determine if the nuclear bomb had originated from the Islamic Republic and what their response would be, an aide interrupted the discussion to announce that the IR Foreign Minister and Caliph Mohammed were on the phone and would like to speak with the President. The room suddenly fell silent, and all eyes turned to President Stein.

"Please put them through. We have a lot to discuss," said the President, eyes ablaze with fury.

"Mr. President, this is Talal bin Abdulaziz, the Foreign Minister for the Islamic Republic. I also have Mohammed Abbas, our Caliph, and General Rafik Hamza on the line with us. We wish to discuss a matter of great urgency with you." Back at the Command Bunker in Riyadh, Talal looked nervously back and forth from General Hamza to Caliph Mohammed. However, the anxious thoughts he was having did not translate into his voice. In a feat of great acting, he sounded as confident as any great number of dictators delivering a monologue to a brainwashed crowd.

President Stein believed the IR was either calling to claim this attack or to try and assure the Americans they'd had nothing to do with it. In either case, the President was about to ensure Caliph Mohammed knew his only choice was to surrender and end this war.

"This is President Stein. Please go ahead with whatever it is you wish to discuss, and then I have something I would like to say since we have everyone on the line talking."

Mohammed had rehearsed this conversation in his mind hundreds of times. Now he was talking directly to the President of the United States and about to make the ultimate demand.

"Mr. President, this is Caliph Mohammed. For over one hundred years, the West has propped up dictators in the Middle East and waged countless wars over our oil. America has led most of these aggressions against the Middle East, and we hold America accountable for the millions of people who have died at the expense of Western interventions in the lands of the Prophet.

"Today, the first of many of Allah's Swords was delivered to America with the destruction of New York City. If America does not agree to an immediate cease-fire and withdrawal of all military forces from the Middle East and North Africa, and surrender the Jewish State to the Islamic Republic, then additional nuclear bombs will be detonated in American cities," announced Caliph Mohammed with a steady and commanding voice.

President Stein sat back in his chair for a moment in complete shock at the callousness in Mohammed's voice and his willingness to wage total war on civilian targets. "Caliph Mohammed, you may believe that you have struck a great blow against America and that we can be defeated. If you were talking with any of my predecessors, you may have been able to intimidate them with your threats and demands. I, however, will not be intimidated.

"I want to make something crystal-clear to you. We will respond with a proportional response for this attack on New York City, but if another nuclear device is detonated against one of our cities, then I will give the order for your largest one hundred cities in the Islamic Republic to be obliterated from the face of the earth. We will use every nuclear, chemical and biological weapon if need be to utterly destroy your nation. We will completely eradicate your country and people from the face of the earth, including Mecca and the Kaaba. Do I make myself clear?" President Stein said with conviction.

General Hamza knew that if the Americans were bent on completely destroying the IR, they could do it, but it would take time. Whether or not the Americans knew it, time was not something they had on their side, especially as the Chinese moved into their second phase of their war and the Russians began their offensive in a few more days. He also believed the Russians and Chinese would intervene and force the Americans to keep the war conventional in order to keep them from using their own nuclear weapons. General Hamza whispered his thoughts to Caliph Mohammed, assuring him that the IR would take severe damage but would ultimately survive.

Caliph Mohammed felt better about the country's chances after General Hamza's brief comments. With the mute button still on, he looked at General Kalel Rafi, the IR Special Operations Commander, and ordered, "General Rafi, please have our agent with the second device detonate it immediately."

Without a second thought, General Rafi picked up his cell phone and sent a text message to his operator, who would martyr himself and detonate the second device personally. They had offloaded the device from the ship and had moved it in a specially shielded utility truck into downtown Baltimore, where it would do the most damage. Unfortunately, it was starting to get late in the evening on the East Coast of the United States, so a lot of the people were starting to leave the city.

As President Stein and his advisors were discussing the threat made by Caliph Mohammed and what to do next, a Secret Service agent walked over to the President and informed him that another device had gone off in Baltimore. One of the aides turned on one of the wall TVs to Fox News, and immediately the image of a newly formed mushroom cloud started to rise out of the downtown skyline.

President Stein could barely contain his rage and frustration at this point. With the mute button still on, he looked at the directors of the FBI, DHS, NSA and CIA and asked a very simple question. "Do you believe they have additional nuclear devices, or it possible that these are the only two bombs they have?"

The FBI Director Jane Smart replied, "We had not received any word or credible evidence that the IR had smuggled *any* nuclear weapons into the country, so I cannot say with certainty that these are the only two bombs."

Jorge Perez, the Director of DHS, explained, "We knew the IR planned on smuggling some nuclear weapons into the US via commercial shipping. As of right now, we have no idea how many they may have tried to smuggle in or have in port. It's obvious that at least two devices made it to our coast. The Coast Guard and FBI have barely had time to get organized and begin a massive sweep of the ports. I cannot confidently say they do not have additional nuclear weapons."

Patrick Rubio, the Director of the CIA, was deep in thought as the others gave their assessments. As the President looked at him, he thought about his response for a second and pulled a file up from a folder on his tablet. "Mr. President, one of our agents within the FSB had overheard from one of his colleagues that the IR intended to smuggle two nuclear devices into the US and make use of other commercial ships and natural gas tankers as improvised bombs to destroy other major ports.

"I only bring this information up right now because our agent sent this information to us this morning along with the Second Shock Army's final orders for the Christmas Eve attack." Nodding toward the NSA Director, he continued, "We were working to coordinate this information with the NSA to determine if there was additional corroborating information about the number of nuclear devices before we disseminated the threat. Obviously, since they used the devices today, we were unable to do that," said Director Rubio.

Director Perez was clearly irate and barked, "If you had provided that information while it was being vetted, then perhaps we could have pieced that together with additional information and may have prevented this from happening."

President Stein knew this could get out of hand quickly and moved to squash the disagreements before they went any further. "Jorge, if this information came in this morning, then chances are we were too late. That said, Director Rubio, you will share these types of threats in the future even if they are not fully vetted. So...before we respond to Caliph Mohammed, are you certain these are the only two devices? Should we respond with nuclear weapons of our own?" asked the President.

"We need to identify the other commercial ships that may be used as improvised bombs—they can still hurt us. As for the nukes, I do believe these are the only two they have. Our agent in the FSB is assigned to the Second Shock Army; they're currently stationed in Turkey, and one of his duties is to coordinate intelligence between them and their IR counterparts. He only learned of this information when his counterpart bragged about the Americans being forced to withdraw from the Middle East soon. He alluded to the two nuclear devices but never mentioned any additional ones. They may have slipped additional nukes in, but I highly doubt it."

Signaling for the communications officer to unmute the line, President Stein began to address Caliph Mohammed in a measured and calculated manor. "This is President Stein. I have just received confirmation, and I am looking at the video feed of a second nuclear detonation in Baltimore. I assume this was detonated by your agents?" asked the President.

Caliph Mohammed was relishing this moment, clearly thinking he had the President of the United States over a barrel. "We needed to make sure you understand that if you do not withdraw your forces from the Middle East, then we will detonate additional nuclear bombs in your cities. Your only choice is to withdraw or lose more American cities," Caliph Mohammed said confidently.

Knowing that the US needed to strike back at the IR, the President began to give his response in a cool and calm manor. "Caliph Mohammed, your regime has shown no regard for human life. Your army butchers innocent civilians while we go out of our way to minimize the loss of innocents. You have clearly indicated with these two nuclear detonations on civilian targets that you have declared complete and open war on our civilian population. Now it is my turn to tell you that we know that you only had two nuclear devices in our country. You have done as much damage as you can do. Now it is time for you to feel the complete and utter wrath of the American nuclear arsenal. I can assure you, you have no idea how much damage the US can do to the Islamic Republic, but you are about to find out."

Click. With that, the President had the connection terminated.

"Admiral Juliano, how soon can we hit Riyadh?" asked the President.

"We have a nuclear attack submarine in position, but the problem is their laser defense system. Our ballistic missiles will be destroyed quickly. We could use a cruise missile, but even those would most likely be destroyed. The cruise missile can fly under their laser defense system until just at the end, when it needs to climb to its effective altitude before detonating. It's in those last two or three seconds that it would most likely be destroyed. We could do a ground burst, but then we irradiate the area for generations," Admiral Juliano explained, a look of disappointment on his face.

"Mr. President, if you're willing to give us some time, we can install a warhead on one of the X59 cruise missiles," said General Rice, the Commanding General of the Air Force.

The President turned and asked, "I thought we had gone through our supply of them when we attacked their power grid at the start of the war, right?"

Eric Clarke interjected for General Rice and explained, "We had, Mr. President. The manufacturer said they have five missiles ready for use right now. They began full production of the X59 at the start of the war, and with the current parts they had on hand, they were able to give us five additional missiles. They should be able to start supplying us with about twenty cruise missiles a month starting in January and will ramp up to one hundred missiles a month by the end of next year."

The President turned to General Rice and directed, "I want you to pick five of their largest and most strategic cities, and I want them obliterated. What are your immediate suggestions, and how long until we can hit them?" asked the President.

General Rice thought about that for a minute. The US had secretly converted a number of mk-41 thermonuclear warheads to be fitted to cruise missiles. The yield was nothing short of amazing. "Mr. President, we will install a cruise missile variant of the mk-41, called the w-100 warhead, on the cruise missiles. The warhead has a maximum yield of twenty-five megatons, which will essentially flatten anything within ten miles of ground zero and irradiate everything within a fifty-mile radius of detonation.

"Alternatively, we also secretly developed an experimental twenty-five megaton neutron bomb. Before anyone says anything, yes, this directly violated every nuclear arms reduction treaty we ever signed. It was an 'eyes only' project with a limited number of scientists who worked on it. It was developed to essentially eliminate the population of a city without destroying it. It still produces an EMP, so there will still be damage, but it won't obliterate a physical target. We also worked out the bugs in it and raised the yield from ten kilotons to the twenty-five megaton beast I'm now talking about. The bomb needs to be detonated as an airburst, approximately 15,000 feet above the targeted area. Once it detonates, it will release roughly 8,000 rads of radiation to everyone within a ten-mile radius, killing them nearly instantly. Everyone within a thirty-mile radius of ground zero will receive a lethal dose of radiation as well," General Rice explained, reading the effects from his tablet.

The Secretary of Defense interjected, "Aside from the fact that this bomb should never have been developed, this is a particularly nasty weapon, Mr. President. No country in history has ever used a bomb with these kinds of effects before, and I'm afraid of the retaliation from the Chinese and Russians. Not to mention what our allies will say. I agree that we need to retaliate against the IR for these two attacks, but I'm just not sure if this is the right weapon to use. The million-dollar question is—what will the Chinese and Russians do? And do we risk it?" asked Eric Clarke, a bit concerned that this could escalate out of control.

The President thought for a moment, trying to determine how to respond to what General Rice had said. His brain told him not to go down this route—that this could lead to disaster—but his gut said this needed to be done to avenge the lives taken in New York and Baltimore. He was also committed to using whatever weapon necessary to win the war and bring it to a swift conclusion. With the internal battle of the mind having been settled, the President said, "Let's move forward with the neutron bomb, as it will create the least fallout and long-term damages. I don't want to destroy the global environment if possible...If I'm not mistaken, there's a portion of the IR not protected by their laser defense system—correct?" asked the President.

"Yes, Mr. President. During the blackout, we hit a number of their laser defense sites. Egypt and most of North Africa are completely open. We could hammer North Africa and their forces there. We can move forces in to secure the area once the situation in the Middle East is stabilized. If we use the neutron bombs, we'll minimize the damage and environmental fallout. When our forces move in, they should encounter little if any radiation," Eric said, offering the President some options.

"Then I want their strategic, logistical, military and high-density civilian centers in North Africa destroyed immediately by conventional nuclear weapons," Stein ordered. "One more thing, make sure our attacks don't appear to threaten Russia or China. I don't want this to escalate any further than it already has."

Secretary of State Jim Wise interjected, "Mr. President, we can inform the Russians and Chinese that our nuclear attacks are being directed at the IR. If they interfere or threaten the US with nuclear weapons, then we will not hesitate to use our nuclear weapons in retaliation."

Taking a minute to think about things, the President said, "I'm concerned about things escalating out of control. At the same time, I don't want to limit ourselves in bringing this war to a swift and decisive conclusion. That said, the Chinese already used nuclear torpedoes on our naval facility at Pearl Harbor. We retaliated by hitting their naval headquarters."

"Mr. President, with everyone having laser defense systems, the likelihood of ICBMs or submarine-launched ballistic missiles being used against each other is rather slim. Our biggest problem is materiel shortages. The war in Israel has depleted not just our pre-positioned equipment stocks in Israel, but most of our cruise missiles in the US. We burned through our entire year's production capability of war stocks in three days. We need to slow the pace of the war down," the SecDef said, almost pleading, and craftily changing the subject away from the use of nuclear weapons.

"How long until these cruise missiles could be ready with the neutron warheads to strike at the heart of the IR?" asked the President, rubbing his temples.

"Probably twenty-four hours, and another ten hours to get them in range of being used," General Rice responded.

Stein knew this was one of the most critical decision points in World War III—one that could escalate the conflict into a nuclear hot war. That was something he desperately wanted to avoid. "General Rice, continue to use the Air Force to hurt the IR and see if there's anything we can do to go after the IR laser defense system with our stealth bombers. Also, begin destroying every piece of infrastructure we can in Lebanon and Syria. If the Second Shock Army is going to invade, they'll have to go through Syria and Lebanon. There's no reason to make their passage any easier than it needs to be.

"Also, see if our stealth bombers can get through their laser defenses and start to attack their power grid again. If their grid goes offline, or those laser defenses go offline, then I want our submarines and bombers to launch a wave of nuclear cruise missiles at the IR and hit every city they can," said the President, anger burning in his eyes.

The United States had been dealt a massive blow with the effective destruction of New York City and Baltimore. Tens of millions of Americans were frightened and livid, not sure of what to do next or what to expect. The President addressed the nation that evening, letting the American people know that it was in fact the Islamic Republic who had detonated the nuclear bombs. The President assured the American people the IR would be dealt with in due time. Then he asked the American people to continue to do their jobs and go to work. The war effort counted on people carrying on with their work and doing their jobs, not fleeing to the countryside and making matters worse.

The Chairman of the Joint Chiefs assured the American people that the laser ballistic missile defense system was fully operational. The

IR could not use their ballistic missiles against the US, and neither could China. Despite the shock and horror of nuclear bombs being used on American cities, the majority of Americans resolved themselves to carrying on. America would not be subdued by a foreign power.
****

Jeff Rogers, the White House Senior Economic Advisor, and Joyce Gibbs, the Treasury Secretary, continued to do what they could to improve the American economy and ensure the financial sector didn't implode. With the destruction of New York City, a large number of the investment banks were destroyed, along with the vast majority of their staffs. This was a terrible loss, requiring Secretary Gibbs to close the stock market for the following two weeks until these organizations could reestablish themselves and determine where elements of the financial market stood.

Jeff had worked with the various American manufacturers, and they were now converting almost all manufacturing capabilities over to the production of military vehicles, aircraft, cruise missiles, rifles, body armor and everything else that the American military needed. It was going to take close to a year to retool the economy to a war footing. Once it was running at full speed, America would be producing tens of thousands of tanks, aircraft and other materiel for the war.
****

The Navy's National Defense Reserve Fleet had been activated at the start of the war, essentially reviving the Ghost Fleets. This gave the Navy an additional 120 ships (frigates, destroyers, cruisers, submarines and carriers) once the refurbishments and new weapon systems were upgraded. Among the ships being upgraded were five retired supercarriers that had originally been built in the 1990s and early 2000s. Some of these carriers were sixty and seventy years old, but once all of the renovations were completed, they would still be operational and ready to fight. Within six months, the Navy would nearly double in size, buying time until the shipbuilders could finalize construction of the new Navy.

The biggest addition to the fleet was actually the roll-on/roll-off ships and troop transport vessels. Moving vast amounts of equipment, munitions and people required a tremendous sealift capability, something the US had that the Chinese and Russians were still struggling to match. There were also twelve additional attack submarines being reactivated. Fortunately, most of the Ghost Fleet was stationed in Beaumont, Texas, and Norfolk, Virginia, so they had been relatively protected and unaffected by the war. The older fleet bases in New Jersey and California had been deactivated in the 2030s.

The various American shipbuilders had eight supercarriers under construction, along with forty-two new destroyers, thirty-eight cruisers, twelve of the newly redesigned battleships and forty-five attack submarines. The battleships of old had been massive armored floating artillery weapons. The redesigned battleships of the twenty-first century were incorporating the latest railgun technology and pulse beam lasers. These laser batteries could be upgraded later to plasma lasers once the newer energy systems could be miniaturized to fit on a ship. In addition to the lasers and railguns, the battery of 1,600 cruise missiles added significant long-range punch. The newly designed ships could effectively keep enemy aircraft from attacking the battlegroup from 400 miles away and could deliver a massive cruise missile strike as deep as 2,200 miles.

The new basic combat training facilities were starting to come on line. Each basic training course could train and graduate 72,000 new recruits a week. All of the new soldiers had to undergo a sixteen-week-long grueling training process that pushed them physically and mentally to their breaking points. Recruits were physically conditioned harder than any other military grunts in history. In addition to the standard boot camp, they also spent three weeks in simulated villages practicing house-to-house combat. Then they would progress to fighting and survival scenarios in the desert, forests, mountains, and plains. These new recruits were conditioned to be effective in combat in all global environments and were going to be the most fearsome warriors America had ever trained.

Nearly every Army Reserve and National Guard base in the country was being activated to federal service and either had or was establishing a basic training facility. Over 250,000 NCOs and officers who had retired within the last ten years were being asked to return to active duty to fill drill instructor roles—a critically short position with most of the active-duty forces deployed. Of the 310,000 soldiers completing training each month, roughly 40,000 of them were being sent for additional military training in areas such as armored vehicle operation, artillery, communications, medical, cyber, and other essential functions, while the remaining 270,000 would attend an additional thirty-day advanced infantry course before forming new military divisions or being filtered in as replacements for other units currently engaged in Asia or the Middle East. Close to 5,000 soldiers were selected to attend the elite Army Ranger School. Another 2,000 airmen were being selected for the Air Force Special Operations programs, and 3,000 seamen were being held back to attend BUDs/SEAL training. Not to be left out, 3,000 Marine recruits were also being chosen to attend Marine Force Recon and Scout Sniper schools. The growth of Special Operations Command was exponential to its regular rate of increase; however, it was going to take time to train these special operators. The typical turnaround from recruitment to being battle-ready in these jobs would be around two to three years.

Judges were once again offering certain convicted felons the choice of serving honorably in the military for four years instead of spending time in prison. This had the dual benefit of reducing the resources spent on jailing people for offenses such as robbery or assault and providing legitimate rehabilitation and job training to people who weren't beyond redemption. The recidivism rate at the country's prisons went way down, and the program was so successful that many communities saw a rise in voluntary recruitment.

The Army had reactivated several armies that had been retired since the end of the Cold War and World War II. First Army had been activated to defend the homeland, and their numbers would soon swell to over 750,000 troops. Second Army was also forming and would stay in the US for the time being as well. The goal was to get these armies established quickly and then have them train hard together for a number of months while the battles in Europe and the Middle East played out. Afterwards, the determination would be made as to where they should go.

In Europe, the US Army had activated the American Fifth, Sixth and Seventh Armies, the same armies that had helped to defeat Nazi Germany before being deactivated at the end of the Cold War. Initially, the Fifth and Sixth Army were operating at 35% strength just prior to the Russian invasion, while the Seventh was still being formed in England. General Gardner's Third Army in the Middle East had been augmented with two additional Army groups, which pushed his operational strength to over half a million troops. He had five armored divisions and six mechanized infantry divisions to counter the Russian Second Shock Army, the Chinese First Expeditionary Force and nearly two million Islamic Republic forces. General Gardner had asked to activate the American Fourth Army and position them in the Middle East as well. Once he was able to secure a breakout, he was going to need an additional Army to punch through it and fully exploit it. His goal was to finish the war with the IR as soon as possible so his forces could be fully turned on the Russians.

The challenge with the formation of all of these armies was keeping up with the demands for equipment and soldiers. Both the Army and the Air Force lacked the necessary gear to support these forces, and it would be some time until that equipment could be produced. Both services quickly turned to their boneyards to find serviceable equipment that could be brought to bear quickly. It would take nearly five months for the Fifth and Sixth Armies to reach 100% manning strength, and that would largely depend on the number of casualties the Third Army continued to sustain in Israel.

The Air Force had reactivated most of the aircraft at the Davis-Monthan boneyard in Tucson, Arizona. Nearly five hundred A-10 ground attack aircraft were being retrofitted and upgraded with modern avionics and the new railguns, replacing the venerable 30mm chain gun it was known for. The aircraft would once again resume its role of "tank buster" and close air support, with the vast majority of these aircraft being sent to Europe. There were also six hundred F-15s and seven hundred F-16s being reactivated, along with thirty-four KC-135 refueling aircraft and five additional JSTARs. These aircraft were not the most modern aircraft of the day, but compared with the fighter drones they would be going up against, they could still hold their own. Plus, their ability to attack ground targets also gave them the multifighter capability the F-22 didn't have. However, finding qualified pilots and training new ones was going to be an enduring problem.

The Army's Sierra Army Depot was hard at work refurbishing nearly 6,000 main battle tanks and over 16,000 assorted armored vehicles for deployment to Europe. With the creation of several new tank divisions, there was a huge need for tanks. The Anniston tank depot and the General Dynamics Ohio facilities could only produce so many

Pershing tanks a month. The 300 new tanks being built each month could not keep up with the demand needed to keep both the Third Army and Fifth Army supplied, let alone sustain the creation of three other armies. It would take time to build the military industrial complex to meet the wartime needs. Once fully operational, the entire manufacturing and technological capability of America would once again be pitted against the superpowers of the world.

Chapter 5
In Other Parts of the World

Day Twenty-One
19 December 2040
Tel Aviv, Israel
General Gardner's Headquarters

The bunker in General Gardner's headquarters was nearly one hundred feet underground, part of a larger bunker complex used by the Israeli Defense Forces and the government during times of war. After twenty-one days, it had begun to smell musty, permeated with the scent of stale sweat and burnt cordite. It would have been hard to completely control the odor—nearly two hundred US officers and NCOs were living in this complex, responsible for running the war in the Middle East.

An Air Force major who had been manning the air battle management section approached the head honcho. "General Gardner, the battle damage assessments are starting to come in from the final bombing raid."

"How's it looking?" asked Brigadier General Peter Williams.

"I'm bringing up the video feeds from the drones right now. The Air Force is about to send in a fourth wave of ground attack drones to hit any targets missed with the first three," said the major.

As the footage came to life on the widescreen monitors in the Command Center, the sheer destruction of the bombing was surreal. Thousands of Islamic Republic armored vehicles were burning wrecks and smoldering ruins. Tens of thousands of burnt bodies could be seen strewn all across the battlefield. There were just a few targets left that had not been destroyed by the three waves of bombers and ground attack drones.

"Order the Third Corps in. I want the entire valley secured and the IR pushed back into Jordan. General Williams, send the order to Major General Peeler to have his Second Marines pivot south and push the IR out of Southern Israel. With the loss of nearly 400,000 troops in the West Bank, the IR is going to be reeling—now's the time to press home the attack," General Gardner directed. He had a commanding voice and a look about him that only a victorious commander could project.

"I'll let General Peeler know it's time to release the Devil Dogs in the south. I know they're itching to get some payback for that Marine company that was crucified the other day," said Williams.

"We all want some payback for that atrocity," responded Gardner.

It was getting close to midnight, and the energy in the bunker was kind of quiet as various people throughout the room were taking a moment to refill their coffee in order to stay awake for the rest of the night shift. Suddenly, an NCO manning one of the communication terminals stood up and shouted, "Someone just nuked New York City!" That announcement quickly got the attention of everyone in the room. An officer walked over and grabbed the FLASH message from the Joint Staff and began to read it aloud to everyone in the room:

NUCFLASH! NUCFLASH! NUCFLASH!

Confirmed Nuclear Detonation in Hudson River near the I-75 bridge.

Manhattan completed destroyed, surrounding boroughs being consumed by firestorm.

Unknown who is responsible for nuclear device, will have confirmation within the hour.

CONUS and OCONUS Forces are to disperse and prepare for additional nuclear attacks.

All air traffic is being grounded until further notice.

Full Combat Air Patrols of all CONUS and OCONUS facilities are to begin immediately.

DEFCON Status has moved from DEFCON 2 to DEFCON 1. All Strategic Nuclear Capabilities are to be readied for immediate use.

All commanders stand by for further orders from POTUS.

Message Ends.

NUCFLASH! NUCFLASH! NUCFLASH!

General Gardner stood there for a minute, digesting what had just been read. He signaled for the message to brought to him. He needed to read it himself. "General Williams, send a FLASH message to all units in the field to immediately prepare for a nuclear attack and disperse their forces as best they can. Have their soldiers dig foxholes quickly and don

their full protective suits." Gardner didn't want to waste any time preparing his forces for what might come next. There would be anger, horror and sadness, but not today. This was the day to respond.
****

Same Time
Israel
Route 60 near Meitar

Sergeant Jordy Nelson's Platoon from the 26th Infantry Regiment, 2nd Brigade, 1st Infantry Division, otherwise known as the "Big Red One," had been slugging it out with the IR since the start of the war twenty-one days ago. Their company had set up a defensive line in the Jordan Valley near Jericho to act as a blocking force in case the IR tried to make a thrust toward Route 1. Everyone knew the IR would ultimately try to take Jerusalem—the question was how best to defend the Holy City and prevent the IR from taking it.

The original plan had fallen apart within the first forty-eight hours. Thousands of IR tanks and over two hundred thousand soldiers had crossed the Jordan-Israeli border and rushed their positions. At the outset, the 1st ID had to fall back to Mitspe Yerihom. Before long, the group was pushed back to Ma'ale Adumim, less than three miles from the Western Wall in Jerusalem. After sustaining 40% casualties in the first two days, the division was being mauled and pressed to its breaking point.

Four days of bloody house-to-house fighting in Jerusalem had left everyone in the platoon exhausted and on edge. Sergeant Nelson's platoon was once again forced to fall back to their final position in the Neve Ilan Forest, where they received enough reinforcements from the 4th ID to stop the IR from dividing the country in half. In one last move to push the Israeli and American forces out of Jerusalem, the IR started using massive human wave assaults until they overwhelmed the defenders. Had it not been for the Air Force finally establishing air superiority over Israel, the 1st and 4th ID would have been slaughtered like so many of their counterparts in the Israeli Defense Forces, who refused to fall back or surrender Jerusalem.

At the start of the war, the IR Army had invaded through the West Bank with a ground force of nearly 350,000 troops and 2,200 main

37

battle tanks. A pretty substantial force proceeded from the Golan Heights and Lebanon—around 250,000 ground troops and 1,300 MBTs. From the south, near Eilat, around 150,000 troops hit the Israeli Defense Force, and out of the Gaza Strip and the Sinai, an additional 110,000 troops joined the fray. The sheer amount of manpower drawn to this fight was unparalleled. During the following two weeks of the war, 800,000 IR reinforcements began to arrive and filtered into the different sectors.

With nearly 1.7 million troops invading Israel, the situation appeared hopeless for the IDF and American Forces. The IDF had 176,500 active-duty soldiers and 445,000 reservists to defend Israel, while the American Third Corps had a scant 48,000 troops, and the 2nd MEF consisted of 20,000 Marines just off shore in the Mediterranean. The American Fifth Corps was a few days away with their 42,500 troops.

When the IR destroyed the American Fifth Fleet with three nuclear missiles as they were exiting the Red Sea, they nearly succeeded in crippling the US Navy. However, the quick retaliatory strike of ten nuclear cruise missiles against the IR power grid reminded them (and the world) that any further use of nuclear weapons against America would not go unpunished or unchallenged. Those ten cruise missiles nearly knocked the IR out of the war altogether. Had the Russians and Chinese not intervened and begun to provide the IR with power, they would have effectively been moved back in time several hundred years. The Chinese had several nuclear-powered ships in various ports, and the Russians connected the IR power grid into their own. This breathed life back into the IR's fighting campaign.

It was quick thinking and luck that saved Vice Admiral Lisa Todd's Sixth Fleet from the same fate. Call it women's intuition; as her fleet approached Israel and the Suez Canal Zone, Admiral Todd believed the IR was up to something and ordered her air wings to provide additional cover for the fleet. Her air and missile defense ships moved into a picket position between the coast and the fleet. When the IR did launch their attack, the fleet saw it coming before it was able to get organized and immediately engaged and destroyed the oncoming forces.

With the war now on, the Sixth Fleet began to pummel the IR air and naval bases in Egypt and Libya before turning the entire fleet's attention to the capture of the SCZ and assisting the IDF in the Sinai. The 2nd Marines made their landings and quickly secured the SCZ, blocking any retreat or reinforcements to the IR forces in the Sinai and the Gaza strip. They quickly engaged the IR forces, despite being outnumbered six to one, destroying the entire IR Army in the Sinai. It was the immense air support and the use of a new ground attack and troop helicopter, the Razorback, that turned the tide of battle.

The Razorback ground attack troop helicopter was a cross between a V-22 Osprey and the old Cobra gunship. The helicopter had two small rotors encased in armor on each tilt wing, providing the helicopter with incredible speed, lift and maneuverability. Near the joint where the tilt wings connected with the frame of the helicopter was a rack of forty-two 2.6-inch antipersonnel rockets, eight Hellfire III antitank missiles, and two short-range air-to-air missiles on each side of the helicopter. Under the nose of the helicopter was a twin 30mm magnetic railgun to give the helicopter added punch. The Razorback carried a crew of four, with two pilots and two crew chiefs who each manned a .25mm magnetic railgun that could spit out 450 rounds a minute to cover the soldiers as they boarded or dismounted the aircraft. A completely new type of armor was showcased in this work of art, made from a top-secret polymer that was lighter than traditional steel armor yet five times as strong. The Razorback's shield could sustain direct hits from a 30mm machine gun without taking any critical damage. It was also impervious to current Russian and Chinese MANPADs, making this helicopter the most in-demand frontline asset in the war. It had also been in service for less than eight months before the outbreak of World War III, so it was in short supply and heavy demand.
****

As First Lieutenant Chantilly approached Sergeant Nelson's position, it became clear he was the target of the lieutenant's attention.

"Evening, Lieutenant—uh, Captain Chantilly," Nelson said.

The captain waved off the stumble over his new promotion. "I'm only captain because all the other officers are dead. Here are your new stripes...you are now Sergeant First Class Nelson, so congratulations on skipping a rank," announced the captain.

"I take it I'm the platoon sergeant now?" asked Nelson nonchalantly.

"Until another officer shows up, you're in charge. You need to get the other NCOs squared away with you running the platoon and me as the new CO. The Air Force is finishing their last bombing run in the valley, and Headquarters wants us to move in and mop up just before dawn. All I've been told is we are to move through Route 60 and head toward Hebron." He showed Nelson the directions on their tablets before syncing the route with the rest of the platoon's heads-up display (HUD) in their helmets.

"That's a long walk with no wheels, especially if we hit any resistance," asserted Nelson.

The captain shot Nelson a disappointed look before replying, "Are you really expecting there to be much in the way of resistance after the complete barbecue the Air Force just laid on them? There will be a few infantry vehicles, and even a couple of Pershing's on point—our company is to follow on foot and assist where needed, so get a few hours' sleep and have your men ready to move. We push off at 0600 hours."

In an abrupt change of pace, a NUCFLASH message suddenly came across the battle net to all soldiers. They were being ordered to shelter in place and prepare for a potential nuclear strike. Within seconds, everyone was donning protective gear and standing by for further orders.

Captain Chantilly looked at Sergeant First Class Nelson before saying, "You heard the new orders. Get your platoon ready. I need to get back to the company command post." He didn't stick around to make sure his instructions were followed. Instead, he turned quickly and ran off in the direction of the CP.
****

Time ticked on nervously, slowly and quickly at the same time. After nearly three hours of sheltering in place, no further update about the NUCFLASH message had been received. Then, finally, new orders came on the wire. Preparations for a possible nuclear attack were cancelled, and they were to resume with their original mission.

Then, a short message from General Gardner himself was broadcast across the battle net to all US forces. "It is with a deep heaviness that I am called upon to inform you that New York City and Baltimore have been hit with nuclear devices. We have confirmed that the nuclear weapons originated in the Islamic Republic and were delivered via freighters entering the Hudson River and the Baltimore Harbor. We have received no further information indicating that the IR is preparing to launch any additional weapons in our AOR. Military operations are to continue as previously planned. No enemy prisoners

are to be taken, unless they are of high intelligence value. May God have mercy on our country, and may we be a part of bringing justice to the world today."
****

0530 hours came quickly, and most of the platoon had gotten little if any sleep. They all knew someone who lived in one of the two cities that got nuked.

"So, what's the plan, Sarge?" asked one of the soldiers as he approached Sergeant First Class Nelson.

"First of all, that's SFC now, and second, we're moving out—so get your stuff together," Nelson said as he replaced his old stripes with the new ones.

Now I need to get with the rest of the NCOs and make sure the platoon is ready. I don't care what the captain says; some of those jihadis will have survived, he thought to himself.

The group rolled out promptly at 0630 with the armored vehicles. After two hours of patrolling, the platoon had only seen a trail of burnt and twisted bodies, smoldering ruins of armored vehicles and shattered homes and buildings littering the landscape. There had been some sniper fire further ahead, but nothing that slowed the advance of the Battalion on their way to Hebron.

"Sergeant Nelson," called Captain Chantilly over the HUD that was built into each soldier's helmet.

"Yes, Sir."

"Battalion wants us to move off the road and spread ourselves out as we near Route 317. They want our company to head toward Rafat and Samu'a with Bravo Company. Delta and Echo Company will be to our right as they head toward Susya if we need them, or vice versa. I'm sending the new directions through the battle net."

The new route was instantly highlighted on the HUD. In the map mode, the HUD could display not just the instructions and waypoints designated by the platoon or company commander, but also the individual identification frequency of each soldier in the platoon. This information could also be relayed to one of the tablets each squad and platoon leader carried, allowing for better coordination.

"I'll pass it over to the rest of the platoon. We'll start moving in that direction now," Nelson said, signing off.

The Army's new battle helmets had come into service with the Army and Marines at the end of 2039, so their use was still relatively new. The battle helmets (or BHs, as they were being called by the grunts wearing them) had a number of new improvements and technology woven into them. They were incredibly light compared to the traditional ballistic helmets, and unlike their predecessors, the BHs could truly stop a bullet. They also sported a ballistic visor that protected the soldier's eyes, only exposing the individual's mouth and jawline. As the platoon marched out into the Jordan Valley, their visors were adjusting from night vision mode to clear as the sun rose. When the rays of sunlight became bright enough to begin affecting eyesight, the visors automatically adjusted to darken into sunglasses. It created an incredible advantage for the US and IDF Forces.

The air in the Jordan Valley smelled of scorched flesh, burning rubber, and refuse as the battlefield continued to smolder. As the company moved through Rafat and into Samu'a, they started to meet some resistance, but the fighting was coming from small uncoordinated pockets and the men had no trouble dispensing with the ruffians they encountered. The automated targeting system in the BHs could provide a 5x zoom on any mark and would place a red dot in the visual field, indicating exactly where their weapon was aimed at any time. There was also a mini camera and mic built into the BH, allowing commanders to see what their soldiers were seeing. This tech made one US soldier worth at least ten of the IR forces because of the capabilities it provided to the individual soldier and unit.

The truth was, there wasn't much left after the bombing campaign in the Jordan Valley. The IR had massed together a large group of about 400,000 infantry and armored vehicles across the area, gathering their forces for a final push to divide the country and destroy the IDF and Americans, but they had been so clustered together that it had made for one giant easy target. The goal of the bombing mission was to destroy everything within a 675-square mile kill box, and with the 7,650 individual bombs hitting synchronized targets per bombing wave, the strategy had been highly effective. The Navy had also added their weight into the fight, firing 1,200 cruise missiles into the kill box. It was no surprise that the forces on the ground had been largely obliterated.

With the bulk of the IR Army destroyed, it was now time to push the rest out of Israel and get ready to take the fight to their homeland.

Chapter 6
Europe Changes Tactics

Day Twenty-Two
20 December 2040
London, England
Number 10 Downing Street

Despite the final fiscal and political unification of the European Union in 2026, Great Britain continued to maintain its autonomy. While the Scandinavian and Eastern European countries had folded into the EU during the Great Depression of the 2020s and early 2030s, the UK was determined to remain their own country. The free trade agreement with the US had guaranteed access to affordable food and had helped to fuel the revival of the British economy in the late 2030s. Unlike Chancellor Lowden, the leader of the EU, Prime Minister Stannis Bedford had no problem convincing the members of Parliament of the dangers posed by the Islamic Republic, Russia and China.

At the private urgings of President Stein, Prime Minister Bedford had persuaded Parliament to increase defense spending and the size of the British military several years prior. The United States had also made extremely low-interest loans available to aid Britain in their military buildup. When war had broken out with the IR, the British had not only been ready, they'd had a military force that was up to the task.

General Sir Michael Richards of the British Defense Staff walked briskly into the room. He was ready to provide his boss with the latest updates. "Prime Minister, the Americans confirmed several hours ago that the nuclear devices that destroyed New York and Baltimore did in fact originate from the IR. Caliph Abbas himself confirmed this during a brief phone call with President Stein. As of right now, the Americans have not responded with nuclear weapons, but we believe they are going to hit the IR hard in the very near future."

The prime minister was exhausted from the late-night meetings and the early-morning phone call he'd had with President Stein. He still couldn't believe the casualty estimates that indicated over four million civilians dead. He understood the need for America to respond with their own nuclear weapons but had cautioned Stein not to go overboard. He didn't want the Americans to escalate the war into a nuclear shooting exchange with China and Russia should they come to the defense of their ally. PM Bedford signaled for Sir Richards to continue.

Nodding toward the PM, he expounded, "The last intelligence brief we received from the Americans says that the Russians are going to invade the EU within 72 hours. Military intelligence and MI6 also concur with this assessment." He nodded toward Admiral Sir Mark West, the First Sea Lord, to provide the PM with the military recommendations.

"Mr. Prime Minister, after consultation with our intelligence services and the American Navy, I recommend we put our entire naval force to sea immediately. We need to ensure our naval forces are not destroyed in port or caught off guard as the American Pacific Fleet was when the Chinese launched their surprise attack," Admiral West announced with confidence. "The Russians will try to move their fleet and subs into the North Atlantic, which will cause all sorts of logistical problems for us if they are left unchecked."

"I agree, Admiral. Please have our naval forces put to sea as soon as possible. Let's also start coordinating with the EU Navy and get ready to interdict the Russian Navy in the Norwegian Sea and the Greenland-Iceland gap," the PM ordered.

The prime minister looked each of his senior military leaders in the eyes and said, "Gentlemen, the Americans have been warning us for years of the Russian military buildup. There was not a lot we could do to influence our EU partners to prepare. Now it is time to put our own preparation to the test. General Sir Wall, I want the entire Reserve and Territorial Army activated immediately. Recall all military members from leave, and cancel all future holidays. You are to have the military ready to disperse from their garrisons within 48 hours."

The British army had quietly increased their military reserve from 25,000 personnel in 2037 to 275,000 by the end of 2040. The increase was mostly infantry, military police and armor—areas that could quickly bolster the strength and capability of the active-duty force, should hostilities occur. The active-duty force had likewise been increased from 89,000 to 300,000. Similarly, the Royal Air Force and the Royal Navy had increased in size, with the Navy adding five submarines to their fleet along with additional antisubmarine capabilities.

The RAF had followed the American Air Force in developing Fighter Drone Wings to augment their piloted aircraft. The advent of fighter drones offered the RAF a unique ability to increase their air power at a fraction of the cost of traditional manned fighters. The drones could outmaneuver their manned counterparts and were for all intents and purposes disposable. If they were shot down, the pilot was not placed at risk and could activate another drone. Drone aircraft did not have to take into account the survivability of a pilot; they were smaller and nimbler, carried a good weapon load, and cost a fraction of a manned aircraft.

The Americans had perfected the manufacturing of fighter drones and were able to produce nearly 85% of the aircraft using 3-D printers. A drone could be built within two months and ready for action. The construction was still incredibly complex, and required thousands of 3-D printers of various sizes and capabilities, which is why it took so long from start to finish. It was only a matter of time until the American manufacturers were able to produce these drones in days instead of months.

Although 3-D printing had been around for decades, it wasn't until a relatively small and unknown manufacturer, the Atlas Group, had built the first combat fighter drone in 2025 that the military saw a real combat use for them beyond surveillance and pinpoint strikes. After ten years of testing and evaluation of various models, the US Air Force had finally approved the first prototype two years before President Stein had come into office. The Stein administration had exponentially increased the fighter drone programs as a means of cutting costs while improving capability.

"Air Marshal Sir Trenchard, what is the status of our air defense capability?" asked the PM as he took another sip of his tea.

"Our laser missile defense and surface-to-air missile systems now encompass all of our airfields and major defense facilities and cities. If they use ballistic missiles, we are ready to knock them down. We will move the eight mobile laser systems with the army as they disperse. We also have eighty-seven of the American mobile antiair/missile railgun systems; they will disperse with the army. I will issue orders after this meeting to begin flying air combat missions over the country and our critical facilities round the clock. The Russians may suspect we know about their pending invasion with our sudden increase in force posture, but I assure you, they will not sucker punch us," said Air Marshal Sir Andrew Trenchard with an air of confidence.

"Excellent, Sir Trenchard. We should be ready to provide fighter support over the EU when hostilities do begin. I have a meeting in two hours with Chancellor Lowden and his defense staff. I would like everyone to return to the conference room in an hour and half and be ready to participate in this meeting. We need to convince the Chancellor and his staff that they need to mobilize. With that said, everyone is dismissed to issue what orders you need to and prepare our country for war," said the Prime Minister in a stoic manner.

The European Union had also taken President Stein's advice and expanded their military capabilities during the past several years, though not as aggressively as the British. Where they differed from Great Britain was their expansion into drone technology—they had not placed significant resources into modernizing their military. They had increased personnel but continued to use equipment that was not on par with the advanced military equipment the Russians, Chinese and Americans were now using. Full modernization of their forces, to include mobile laser defense systems, railgun air defense systems and newer infantry rifles and tanks would be costly and was simply not something they were willing to do yet.

The EU had increased their active-duty army to 350,000 personnel with an additional 1.4 million in the reserves. Since the start of hostilities in the Middle East and the civil unrest taking place in cities all across the EU, Chancellor Lowden had most of the military deployed in the various cities attempting to put down the violence. They had yet to activate their reserves or deploy their active-duty forces with their full combat equipment. They were being bogged down trying to assist local law enforcement with restoring order.

As Chancellor Lowden walked into the conference room, the arguing between the Defense Minister, André Gouin, and the Minister of Foreign Affairs, Paolo Prodi, was in full swing. The two ministers had been quarreling for weeks over the war in the Middle East and the intelligence being shared by the Americans and British about the Russian troop deployments. They disagreed strongly about what it all meant.

Minister Prodi shouted at his compatriot, "The Russians are not going to invade the EU! They might get involved in assisting the Islamic Republic in their fight against the Israelis and the Americans, but they are not going to intervene in Europe. Besides, there are 350,000 US troops positioned in England, Germany, and Italy. Even *if* they decide to invade, the Americans will keep them busy long enough to allow the EU to fully mobilize."

Minister Gouin had been arguing for the activation of the reserves and making preparations in case the Russians really did invade the EU. He was unscathed by the impolite speech from his coworker. "I don't want to place all of our hopes on the American forces. You do realize that there is significant risk that the US might soon be engaged in a nuclear fight with the Russians or the Chinese, right? The Americans will certainly respond to the horrific nuclear attack on their country. When they do, this might escalate other parties to participate in kind. The Chinese have already used several nuclear tipped torpedoes, and the US has responded by destroying several Chinese harbors. That may be the extent of the nuclear exchange now, but who knows what tomorrow holds?"

"Gentlemen, please stop bickering. The British are about to come online and we need to decide what actions we are going to take." Chancellor Lowden was clearly annoyed at his senior staff.

A technician interrupted the conversation. "Chancellor, the British are ready to begin."

Lowden shifted his eyes to the holographic screen. As it came to life, he could see the British senior military leaders were all present. He nodded in acknowledgement before greeting them. "Mr. Prime Minister, it is good to see you. I am sorry it could not be under better circumstances."

PM Bedford was, if nothing else, a blunt and direct politician. He had nothing personal against the EU Chancellor, but like most Europeans, he was slow to react and quick to give in to the fringes of the EU's political parties and activist groups. "Mr. Chancellor, I will cut to the chase and keep this discussion short. We have a tremendous amount of work to do. By now, we all know the IR used two nuclear weapons against New York and Baltimore. Clearly the war is going to escalate, whether we like it or not. Are you going to mobilize your reserves and prepare to meet the Russians? Time is running out."

"We have not mobilized our reserves just yet. Our focus has been on putting down the uprisings in our cities. Not everyone in our government is convinced that the American intelligence about a Russian invasion is correct. I would also like to add that, in light of the nuclear detonations last night, the Americans are likely to use nuclear weapons of their own, and we do not want to appear to be a threat to Russia and potentially encourage them to use nuclear weapons in a preemptive strike against the EU," Lowden said, not entirely convinced of his own intelligence services' assessment of the situation.

PM Bedford was irritated but not surprised to learn that his EU counterparts weren't taking the military situation as seriously as the rest of the Allies. "If the EU is not going to take any precautions or preparation in spite of the evidence of a massive Russian troop buildup on your borders, then are you expecting the Americans to save you?" asked PM Bedford with a bit of scorn in his voice.

"If the Russians do invade, our forces will stop them. The Americans will honor the NATO defensive pact," said Minister Prodi.

"—Just as you have honored that same defensive pact when the Americans were attacked by the IR?" interrupted PM Bedford.

"We have assisted the Americans by providing our bases to launch their invasion and giving them logistical support," Minister Prodi retorted with the same level of sarcasm.

PM Bedford fixed his gaze on the Chancellor and announced, "Chancellor Lowden, we have expressed our concerns and offered to coordinate a defense if the Russians do invade. If they invade and the EU has still not activated its reserves and made preparations for the defense of Europe, then we will be forced to focus our defensive effort on protecting Britain. We are an island nation and are not equipped to defend Europe."

Without saying goodbye, the PM Bedford abruptly ended the video conference call.

"Well, that went about as well as we could have expected," said General Volker Naumann, the EU Defense Chief of Staff. Naumann was a German military officer and, as such, had received enough training from the Americans to know that if their intelligence suggested the Russians were going to invade, then in all likelihood the report was correct.

"Typical British arrogance," Minister Prodi said, dismissing the PM's warning.

Chancellor Lowden sighed deeply. "Bedford is right. We cannot rely on the Americans and British to provide the bulk of our defense. The Americans are already stretched thin; if the Americans have to choose between defending Alaska, Israel and their other interests, they will choose them over us. The British military is just not big enough to fully defend Europe. They will have their hands full with the Russian Navy.

"I want our reserves activated immediately. Our active forces need to be pulled out of the cities and prepared to meet the Russians now…Bedford is right. We have squandered precious time and disregarded the warnings the Americans have given us. Let's hope we are not too late."
****

While the central EU government began to mobilize their reserves and prepare the active-duty force to meet a possible Russian invasion, the individual member states started to activate their own military reserves and national guard forces. Chief among them was Poland, the Czech Republic, Germany and Romania. Germany maintained an active force of 250,000 soldiers, the Czechs 95,000, the Romanians 130,000 and the Poles 190,000.

The central EU government maintained a military force separate from the member states, in a similar fashion to the US with the state National Guard units. People from any member state could join the central government forces and reserves, or they could join their own country's military. The central government also had the power to draft individuals from each member state, up to the size of 25% of the member state's active duty force. Since Germany had a military force of 250,000 soldiers, they would have to provide, if necessary, as many as 62,500 citizens during an EU draft.

Chapter 7
The Great Dragon Awakes

Day Twenty-Two
20 December 2040
Da'Anshanxiang, China
Central Military Commission Command Facility

The Chinese government, like the rest of China and the world, watched the destruction of New York City and Baltimore by the Islamic Republic on their various multimedia devices and tablets, in awe of the carnage and destruction. The average Chinese citizen could not believe these great American cities had been destroyed by a nuclear bomb, and the images of the dead and dying were something the average citizen had never been exposed to before. In the past, the government would censor such images and ensure the people of China saw only what they wanted. In this case, the Chinese government wished to let the people of China know that even the great Americans could be defeated and brought to their knees. They used these images to remind their people that it was now China's time to rise up and become the dominant world superpower.
****

The fighting in the Middle East continued, drawing more and more American forces to the region. The newly created American Third Army was in the process of driving the remaining IR forces out of Southern Israel, and had retaken Jerusalem and the entire Jordan Valley. They were now in a position to strike at the former capital of Jordan, Amman.

The Chinese 1st Expeditionary Force (or 1st EF, as the CMC was calling them), had finally disembarked in Jeddah and were making preparations to move to Amman to join the remains of the IR Army group. Over half a million soldiers were on the way from Baghdad along with three million civilian militia volunteers. By the end of the year, the IR should have 800,000 regular army troops in Amman and three million civilian militia volunteers, along with 250,000 Chinese soldiers of the 1st EF. The Chinese would take over the Suez Canal Zone and assist the IR in rebuilding after they had defeated the Israeli and American forces.
****

Premier Zhang Jinping was happy with the progress of *Operation Red Dragon*. The Americans had been effectively defeated in the Pacific and posed no serious threat. Southeast Asia was starting to fall to the Red Army, and Taiwan was in its final death throes. Now it was a matter of getting ready for phase two, the capture of southern Alaska and the Canadian States.

The capture of Alaska would ensure China had the long-term oil reserves their economy desperately needed and depended upon. It would also provide them with a springboard to launch an invasion of America through their newly acquired Canadian States. The States were rich in resources, with the central provinces providing tens of millions of acres of fertile farmlands. With 2.4 billion citizens to feed, obtaining more agricultural resources was a strong priority for the Chinese. The challenge would be moving their army to North America and still keeping it supplied during combat operations.

Chapter 8
Revenge

Day Twenty-Three
21 December 2040
Mediterranean Sea near Crete, Greece

Lurking deep in the dark waters of the Mediterranean was the SSBN *Minnesota*, one of the new *Florida*-class nuclear-powered ballistic missile submarines. In 2019, the US Navy had begun a program to replace the fourteen *Ohio*-class nuclear-powered ballistic missile submarines (SSBN) with the next generation in submarine technology. The older Ohio SSBNs had been converted to cruise missile carriers and delivery vehicles for Special Forces, giving them a new purpose and mission in the Navy. The twelve new *Florida*-class SSBNs had come into service in 2034, six years behind schedule due to budget cuts during the Great Depression. They were equipped with twenty Trident III ballistic missiles, each of which would split off to hit fourteen different points through the use of MIRVs, multiple independently targetable reentry vehicles. The *Florida*s also carried 84 Tomahawk cruise missiles, making them a versatile offensive weapon.

It had been a little over thirty hours since New York and Baltimore had been destroyed, and the US had not retaliated with nuclear weapons. As the SSBN *Minnesota* waited in its holding pattern, they suddenly received an emergency action message, indicating a priority message from COMSUBLANT, or Commander, Submarine Force Atlantic. As the message was printed and decoded, the captain couldn't help but wonder if this was the order to avenge the destruction of New York City and Baltimore. The casualties from the attack were still being counted and had exceeded five million deaths so far.

The executive officer walked up to the captain and handed him the decoded message with curiosity and uncertainty written all over his face. As the captain finished reading the message, he handed it to the XO for him to read and verify it. "By order of the President, the SSBN *Minnesota* is to launch a series of ballistic missiles at targets across the Islamic Republic's provinces in North Africa and stand by to launch additional missiles against targets in the Middle East."

Further instructions ordered them to launch eight of their twenty Trident III missiles, releasing 112 nuclear warheads against the IR's largest cities, military bases, manufacturing centers and logistical hubs in their North African provinces.

As the *Minnesota* rose to launch depth, the sonar techs continued to monitor the waters around them for any potential threats. With the threat board showing green, they gave the captain the go-ahead to initiate the attack. The captain and the senior weapons officer looked at each other as they turned the keys to launch the missiles, knowing they were about to make history, for better or worse. This was only the second time a submarine had ever launched a nuclear attack against another nation. The vessel shuddered briefly as one missile after another ejected from the tubes and was sent to their targets. As the first rocket broke through the water, its booster ignited and it raced for the sky, slowly starting its arc toward a point about one hundred miles in the air, where it would release its MIRVs for maximum effect.

****

In a bunker one hundred feet below the surface of the Creech Air Force Base in Nevada, five B-5 stealth bomber drone pilots were hooked into their controls, guiding drones that were flying 40,000 feet above the Mediterranean Sea. The bomber drones were on their way to deliver the first of the most destructive weapons ever to be used by one nation against another.

Approximately two hundred miles west of Israel, four of the five stealth bomber drones launched their X-59 scramjet cruise missiles, carrying the largest neutron bombs ever developed. Tehran, Baghdad, Riyadh, and Cairo were all targeted; they represented the largest industrial and logistical nodes of the IR. They also represented the largest population centers outside of Asia.

A single B-5 flying over Italy launched their lone X-59 at Istanbul. The purpose of these neutron bombs was not to destroy these historic cities; it was to kill the population in a thirty-mile radius while causing as little destruction and environmental damage as possible. Unlike the 112 cities in North Africa (and thirty more in the Middle East), these five cities could be repopulated with virtually no residual radiation left to clean up.

The bomber crews watched as the scramjet cruise missiles hit their maximum speed of Mach 10. Numerous antimissile lasers and missiles reached out to try and knock them out of the sky, desperately trying to defend their country. Dozens of lasers in Turkey, Jordan, Iraq and Saudi Arabia were frantically trying to destroy these fast-moving missiles with no luck. Horror began to spread across the defenders as they realized they could not hit the missiles. Several Russian and Chinese ships were in the area and began to use their antimissile systems to try and engage the American missiles by launching their own missile interceptors and lasers, but it was all to no effect. The missiles were traveling too fast for the lasers to hit them long enough to cause them to explode.

The first missile detonated 15,000 feet above Istanbul. Within a fraction of a second, everyone within a ten-mile radius was hit with over 8,000 rads of radiation and died almost immediately. Their organs began to liquefy, and blood poured out of every orifice of their body, until they died minutes later. Everyone within a thirty-mile radius of Istanbul received a fatal dose of radiation and would die over the following thirty days. Their hair and teeth would begin to fall out within hours or days, and then their internal organs would fail. Finally, blood would ooze from eyes, ears, nose and mouth until finally their bodies would give out. Their death would be long and horrific. The first neutron bomb used in combat effectively killed 14 million people, including several hundred thousand IR soldiers.

As the missile detonated, the EMP immediately fried the electronics across the thirty-mile radius of the city, blacking out the live news broadcasts that millions of people across the Republic had been watching. Within an instant, an emergency alert was being broadcast all across the Republic, urging everyone to make their way to the nearest bomb shelter or basement. The IR immediately let the people know the Americans were launching a nuclear attack against them. The Islamic world erupted in anger and angst at the thought of American nuclear missiles heading toward them, not sure if their city was one of the targets or not.

Once the first missile detonated above Istanbul, the laser operators realized there was nothing they could do to stop the four remaining missiles closing in on their targets. The bombs detonated above Cairo, Riyadh, Baghdad and Tehran, effectively killing fifty-one million, two hundred and fifty thousand people instantly. Another thirty million more received a lethal dose of radiation. The power grid all across the Republic began to fail as the EMP blasts ravaged the IR's critical infrastructure, which routed the majority of the nation's power through substations that operated within the major cities.

The simultaneous missile strikes by the SSBN *Minnesota* killed another fifty-six million and, in time, would kill thirty-two million more from radiation. In a single day the IR had lost 110.25 million people and another sixty-two million more would perish in the coming weeks. Within the hour, it was determined the IR had lost 128 cities in total, along with all of their major military installations, industrial, logistical and communication centers. The Americans' attack had effectively plunged the country back into the dark again as their power grid went down.

The *Minnesota* launched a second wave of nuclear missiles an hour later and hit thirty additional sites across the Middle East to include Mecca, detonating just above the Kaaba. Within twenty minutes, a TV drone was showing raw footage of the mushroom cloud still lingering over what had once been Islam's most holy site and House of God. Muslims across the globe exploded in anger toward the US. So many could not believe the Americans had just destroyed the most cherished symbol of their religion. Riots erupted in various parts of the IR, throughout Indonesia, Malaysia, the entire Middle East and Northern Africa.

Fortunately for the IR, the Russian and Chinese warships in the Arabian Gulf had managed to shoot down seventy-six of the 106 nuclear warheads, minimizing the damage the IR received to several of their military facilities, cities and port facilities in Kuwait, Iraq and parts of Iran. The thirty missiles that did get through hit every major power station in the country, along with critical logistics and transportation nodes. The exception was the Kuwait area, which was heavily protected by both Chinese and Russian warships. Together, they were able to successfully intercept the American ICBM MIRVs directed at that target.

Chapter 9
Mobilization

Day Twenty-Four
22 December 2040
Newark, New Jersey
FEMA Field Headquarters

Within hours of the nuclear bomb going off in New York, FEMA had immediately gone into action. They had run several tabletop drills and exercises in the past, simulating what they would do if a nuclear bomb ever went off in a major city. Now those drills were being put into practice as thousands of FEMA workers were directed to one of the two disaster zones. FEMA also alerted all of the cities that had been designated as disaster and medical relief centers and activated their FEMA disaster relief volunteers.

Thousands of police officers, EMTs, firefighters, nurses and doctors had volunteered to be a part of a reserve force of FEMA personnel in case of a historic natural disaster. These individuals would immediately head to a designated airport and be ready to fly to the affected area to provide what support they could. Hundreds of hospitals across the US were placed on alert and told to expect injured people from the disaster sites in the coming hours and days. National Guard armories and school gyms were also being readied to receive displaced people from the blast.

The nondeployed members of the New York, New Jersey, and Northeast National Guard units were immediately activated and ordered to head to the blast zones to begin assisting in the evacuations and recovery efforts. FEMA requested hundreds of aircraft from the airlines to begin the massive airlift of equipment, injured and displaced people, and all of the volunteers from across the country. All flights into Newark, LaGuardia and JFK were redirected to other cities. All outbound flights were allowed to leave to make room for the incoming aircraft that were bringing additional rescuers and much needed equipment.

Fortunately, the EMP blast from the nuclear bomb was contained to around five miles from the epicenter, so it had not affected the airports, though it had seriously damaged the telecommunications and transportation system as many routes traveled through parts that were affected. The Air Force began to shift several of their communication drones to head over New York and Baltimore to provide immediate 4G wireless capability over the affected areas until communication systems could be reestablished.

FEMA had organized their rescue and recovery response into three stages, the first being as close to the affected area as possible. These sites would begin the triage of injured people and identify those that needed to be flown out immediately to one of the local hospitals, and those that could be driven to the second stage of treatment and local hospitals. Once there, patients' injuries would be tended to, and then they would be scheduled to be flown to one of the disaster relief cities for further treatment and free up the local hospitals for the more serious patients.

Everyone being treated by FEMA was being biometrically enrolled and then given a wristband with a RFID chip to identify the injured person and to keep track of where they were being treated. This function was going to be critical to ensuring family members stayed together and, if separated, could be found and reunited quickly. The third staging point was for displaced persons and refugees who could no longer go back to their homes. The government immediately established a five-mile perimeter around the blast site, preventing people from going back into the hot zone.
****

Claudia Álvaros had had the wildest, craziest 48 hours of her life. She had managed to stay awake without sleep for the last couple of days, moving from one patient to the other without ceasing and, in true nurse fashion, barely stopping to use the restroom at all. When the FEMA agents arrived at the hospital to help transport all of the patients to safety, she had stayed behind until there were only a handful of people left to move and she was basically ordered to get on a plane. She didn't realize until she was in the flight, but she hadn't had anything to eat or drink since the bomb had gone off. The result was that she had actually gotten incredibly dehydrated and had managed to throw her electrolytes way off balance. She was forced to become the patient for a little while as she was hooked up to IV fluids to stabilize her condition.

Claudia had a brother in Houston, so she had requested to be transferred there. Once she arrived, she learned that she actually had *not* been exposed to a fatal level of radiation. She had gotten indoors before the fallout had really started to come down, and although she had been exposed to some additional radiation that emanated in through the entrance, her condition was still treatable. The hospital had also given everyone who wasn't acutely dying a dose of potassium iodine. She went through the full decontamination process before being transported. She was scrubbed within an inch of her life with a special solution and given new clothing to wear. Now they were giving her new medications that had recently been developed to treat and prevent damage to her bone marrow and internal organs. It would take her a little while to process the fact that she had another chance at life.

****

The only individuals allowed to enter the contaminated area were rescue workers, firefighters and paramedics. Police were assigned to go door to door and search for injured people and to evacuate everyone in the danger zones. Radiation was going to be high within the perimeters, and unless people began to move out of them, they were going to receive a lethal dose of radiation in short order. All police and rescue workers were required to wear a radiation counter, and once the readout reached a certain level, they were no longer allowed into the hot zones.

As FedEx and UPS cargo aircraft landed at previously identified airports, they were loaded with prepositioned pallets configured to transport injured people in double-decker beds. Other parts of the planes' cargo holds were set up for people with more severe injuries. The Boeing transports could move sixty non-critically-injured people and up to twenty-four intensive care patients, along with all the medical equipment and personnel needed to care for them.

While the aircraft were being readied for their new medical mission, helicopters arrived at the airports from the stage one and two triage centers, bringing hundreds of injured people to the waiting aircraft. As the planes were filled with the wounded, they began their takeoffs to the next destination. Most aircraft would fly to a city within a two-hour radius and then return for another trip. FEMA had the aircraft spread out their trips to different cities so one city wouldn't suddenly get overwhelmed. As medical, police and firefighter volunteers showed up at those airports, they were loaded into the aircraft for the return flight.

Within sixteen hours of activating the disaster relief plan, thousands of seriously injured people had been flown to dozens of cities across America. Those who couldn't return to their homes were being loaded into trucks and taken to Fort Dix or flown to Fort Drum, where field tents and barracks were being made available for people to stay in until they could be flown to their next of kin in another city or state. Because it was in the throes of a cold Northeast winter, establishing adequate shelter for the tens of thousands of refugees was imperative.

By the end of the first day, FEMA had their disaster recovery system fully operational and running at 100%. People were being treated and relocated to other cities for further care or tended to by their extended family. Those who had nowhere else to go were being provided with housing and food on various of military bases and in local hotels near those military installations until something more permanent could be arranged.

******

Emma Shultz was one of the ER nurses who had volunteered for the recovery effort; she lived in Richmond, Virginia, which happened to be one of the major hubs for many of the patients from the Baltimore area. Emma had seen 'em all in her twenty years in the emergency department—gunshot victims, drug users and those with run-of-the-mill broken bones, so in some ways this was all routine for her. She really was a natural, not just for the profession but for that specific type of nursing. When a true emergency arose, it was almost as if a switch inside her would flip and she would be able to shut out her emotions. Some people would panic in this chaos, but to her, the next task was always clear.

Emma had rarely been overwhelmed by the emotional side of her job, except for when she'd worked at a hospital that had a lot of drama and in-fighting between the nurses on the staff. She'd only stuck it out there for about a year before she moved on to greener pastures. At first, this disaster seemed just like any other day at the office. She moved steadily from patient to patient, providing efficient yet compassionate care. Her job was to stabilize patients as they flew in, getting them ready to be admitted for longer-term care, and she had a set of protocols that she could follow for treatment without constantly asking a doctor for orders. IV fluids, standard medications, and injury management—one after the other, things were falling into place.

Then, out of nowhere, they flew in an entire classroom of second graders. The children's hospitals were completely overwhelmed, so every hospital had to take on their share of the pediatric patients. This was Emma's weak spot. She could easily handle the standard injuries that always happen in childhood; she had certainly seen her share of playground accidents. However, whenever there was a case of child abuse or neglect, her stomach churned and she would feel sick over it for days. As the innocent, beautiful seven-year-olds kept piling in, she was suddenly overcome with emotion. What kind of monsters could do this to children, for no reason at all? What misguided delusional philosophy would lead someone to this kind of depravity?

She hadn't gone to the bathroom in a while. She slipped away into the restroom and had a cry for a few minutes. Then she splashed some water on her face and did her best to hide the signs of her little emotional outburst before rushing back onto the floor. This was going to be a long day.

Chapter 10
New Commander

Day Twenty-Four
NATO Headquarters Brussels, Belgium
22 December 2040

General Michaels had been the US European Commander and the NATO Supreme Allied Commander (SACEUR) until two days ago; he had been dining with his wife at a restaurant in Brussels when he'd suddenly suffered a heart attack and died. His expeditious demise was still under investigation, but it was believed he had been poisoned, causing his heart to fail on the eve of the Russian invasion. President Stein knew he had to get a new commander in place who had combat experience. General Branson would be ideal, but his counsel was needed with the President. Plus, he was the organizational genius behind the rapid mobilization of forces in the US.

That left General Wade—he had overseen Operation Brimstone in Mexico as the senior military commander and then had moved into command position at US Central Command (CENTCOM). Now he would take over as Supreme Allied Commander NATO. The President wasted no time in announcing his choice.

General Wade didn't waste any time either. His first task was to get the American and NATO forces ready to take on a Russian army that number in the millions of men and tens of thousands in tanks and drones. As soon as he accepted the new position, he immediately began to disperse forward elements in Poland, Hungary and Romania, getting them ready to meet the Russians head on. Their mission was to conduct a series of delaying actions and give ground as required, but most importantly to make sure their forces were neither surrounded nor destroyed. They needed to buy time for the reactivated American Fifth, Sixth, and Seventh Armies to constitute.

General Aaron Wade was a very competent commander, but he was an unknown to Europe and NATO. He had never served in a European or NATO command or staff position, instead spending all of his military time either in the Middle East, Asia or South America. He had little time to move to a theater of operation and take over command of a multinational force he knew very little about. The NATO countries had historically been more of a social club than a military organization. The only countries that really maintained a military close to the NATO standards were Germany, Poland and England. French Special Forces were still on par with the US and others, but the rest of their force was using outdated equipment from decades of neglect and lack of modernization.

The European Union attempted to take over control of the national military forces, and to a large extent, they had. Each country's active military force became a National Guard force, like the ones that the American states each maintained. The exception was Germany's force; theirs was as strong and large as the entire EU military force, of which Germany provided nearly 40% of all the military members. Germany was by far the industrial and military backbone of the EU. The question was—would Germany's strength be enough to save Europe from the Russian hordes, or would the EU collapse?

With the situation temporarily stabilized in Israel, the American Fifth Army was not going to open a second offensive front into Turkey. They were now redirected to form in Northern Germany and be prepared to defend Western Europe. The American Sixth Army was forming in Southern Germany and would move into Hungary and Romania, with their fallback position identified as Serbia and Hungary's western border once they were ready. NATO would slowly allow lost ground in order to buy time for the rest of the EU Army to mobilize and reinforce the Americans.

General Wade's combined American Force consisted of 575,000 soldiers, with another 200,000 set to arrive over the next five days. The biggest problem facing him in the EU was equipment. They were in desperate need of tanks, armored vehicles, munitions, artillery and aircraft. The vast majority of the available equipment had been shipped to Israel to replace the horrendous losses General Gardner had taken. The American economy was quickly retooling for war, but it would be months if not a full year before the economy could produce enough equipment to replace the current losses prior to the Russians invading. It was going to be a fight against time. Truth be told, General Wade was not confident he could win.

****

Major General Dieter Schoen was the Commander of the German 10th Panzer Division Bundeswehr, which consisted of approximately 12,200 soldiers spread across two armored brigades, a grenadier brigade (mechanized infantry), an artillery brigade and a mountain infantry brigade. His division had 680 Leopard 3Cs main battle tanks, the most advanced European battle tank available. Unlike their French counterparts, these tanks were on par with anything the Russians had. The disadvantage they had was their numbers. The Russians would be advancing into Poland and the rest of the EU with 8,000 or more main battle tanks and light drone tanks. As good as the Leopard was, it wouldn't last long against numbers like this. General Schoen knew his best chance of success was to see if he could get an American Pershing battalion to integrate with his tanks division.

Schoen was a rising star in the German Army. He was young, just 39 years of age, and the absolute picture of what you would expect a German general to look like. Tall, blond hair, blue eyes, muscular, and good looking, but under the extremely polished and well-starched exterior, the man was also a military genius. He had trained with the Americans at the Army's Fort Benning Armor School and participated in numerous armored training exercises with the Americans, both at the Fort Irwin National Training Center and at the US Army Joint Military Training Center in Hohenfels, Germany.

Word had it that Germany was building a new battle tank using the American advance armor and railgun technology. The question was, would it be completed in enough time to make a difference? Intelligence also said the Russians had a new tank that might make its own appearance in the near future.

General Schoen directed his division to start heading toward Warsaw. Once there, they would offload their tanks and other armored vehicles and begin moving them to various marshaling points, where he could quickly deploy them against the Russians. He wanted to get his scouts and antitank units deployed as soon as possible; the key was going to be identifying the likely enemy approaches so that the engineers could determine the best-prepared positions to send the tanks and grenadiers.

The EU leadership might not believe the Russians were going to invade, but after hearing General Wade's speech and seeing the intelligence himself, Schoen wanted to get his division into the field and deployed as soon as possible. This would be the first time the German

Army would be deployed in Europe to fight against another army since World War II. General Schoen was determined to show the world and the Russians that, despite not having been involved in any recent wars, the German war machine was something to still fear. The Fatherland was retooling for war, this time as America's ally.

The 13th Panzer Division was moving toward Rzeszow to the south of General Schoen, which was approximately 45 miles west of the Ukrainian border. This was one of the two most vulnerable points for Russian attack—the other was the Lublin-Warsaw gap, which was where Schoen concentrated his forces. The 13th Panzer Division consisted of two extra brigades of grenadiers (mechanized infantry) and light antitank drones instead of the heavier Leopard 3Cs. This was a good equipment setup for the area they were guarding, which was loaded with mountain ranges, impassible ridges and rock formations. Combat in this area would certainly turn into close-in fighting. On the other hand, the Lublin/Warsaw gap was relatively flat country, ideal for fast-moving tanks. General Schoen placed carefully plotted tank traps in this area, preparing for the first of several tank battles. In addition to controlling the Lublin-Warsaw gap, Schoen was the area commander and was directing the 10th and 13th Panzer Divisions in order to stop the Russian armored advance.

The Polish Army was going to focus their defense in the north near Bialystok on the Belarus border. Their army was heavily equipped with German-made military equipment, including Leopard 3C tanks, so integrating with the German divisions in Poland was not going to be a problem. The Poles and Germans knew they could give ground for a time, but they were determined to make the Russians pay for each kilometer of ground they took and ensure they kept the Russians out of Germany. If they failed their mission, the industrial machine of Germany, which was the backbone of the EU, would likely fall. Then there would be no hope of producing the tools of war needed to win the ultimate victory.

There was still no sign of the French or Belgian units yet; they were supposed to join the Polish forces in the north and provide them with additional support. In addition to the 10th and 13th Panzer Divisions, Germany was moving three divisions of infantry to shore up defensive positions in and around the major cities in eastern Poland.

Chapter 11
Tipping Point

Day Twenty-Four
22 December 2040
Northwest Virginia
Presidential HIVE

The President and his advisors had been monitoring the political situation in Asia and Europe intensely since Stein had ordered an overwhelming nuclear response against the IR. The Chinese media came out with an official statement, insisting that the war remain conventional and agreeing to no longer use nuclear torpedoes or any other form of nuclear weapons. They also said that if the US hit China with a neutron bomb, they would respond with their own colossal nuclear response. The war of words continued to heat up as President Stein had the Secretary of State convey that any nation who used nuclear weapons against the United States would face a similar response to the retribution the IR had just received.

The leaders of the European Union were still in a state of shock at the sheer destruction that the IR had inflicted on New York and Baltimore. They were then further aghast at President Stein's response; over one hundred and ten million people had been killed, and more than a hundred cities were decimated. They felt that the Americans had responded too harshly in retaliation, not to mention the environmental catastrophe they had just unleashed—thousands of tons of dust particles were being thrown into the upper atmosphere. In an effort to keep his allies appeased, President Stein made it clear that the United States would refrain from further use of nuclear weapons in the war, unless one was used against America or American forces again.

In addition to the possibility of further use of nuclear weapons, the President was still very concerned with the domestic attacks. The IR had masterfully infiltrated Special Forces and intelligence agents into the country, and they had recruited thousands of American Muslims and Muslim immigrants to conduct terror attacks against the country. This had unfortunately led to more American Muslims joining in to be a part of what they thought was a real chance at a revolution in the country. As a result, hundreds if not thousands of reprisals began against American

Muslims, the vast majority of whom had absolutely nothing to do with the terror attacks. The violence between the Muslim and non-Muslims in the country had risen to the point where the President had addressed it directly in several briefings. He was hoping to get the American people to calm down and to trust the justice system to handle the threats. Stein encouraged those who were concerned to report suspicious activity to the authorities and let them deal with it.

In the HIVE, the senior advisors were meeting to discuss the recent developments. The President sat down across from the DHS Secretary and jumped right into business. "Director Perez, have we identified any additional IR or Chinese cells in the last couple of days?" The President was hoping they had finally rooted out the last of them.

"Within the first two hours of the Trinity Program going live, we apprehended forty-six suspected IR operatives in Dearborn, Michigan. We caught them prior to their execution of a massive attack. One of the prisoners said their goal was to encourage a Muslim uprising in Dearborn and Detroit and then support them with weapons and explosives. We captured over 1,200 assault rifles, nearly 8,000 pounds of Semtex, fourteen MANPADs, and three dozen explosively formed penetrators, or EFPs—the kind that punch right through our armored vehicles. It was a huge success for DHS and the Trinity Program," reported Director Perez.

Breathing a sigh of relief at finally catching a big break, the President replied, "This is a big deal. I want this brought up during the press briefing. See if there is some footage we can release as well. The public needs to know that we're apprehending these terrorists and seeing real results. Has the Trinity Program identified any other significant threats yet?"

Secretary Perez continued, saying, "We have. There were sixty-seven Chinese nationals identified that had been working in a variety of jobs in the energy and utility sector. We now believe they may have been directly involved in the massive communications blackout with the Uninet routers and switches. The program also identified 1,385 military officers and NCOs across all branches of the military that have ties in one fashion or another to the PLA, Russia and the IR. All of these individuals had Top-Secret clearances and worked in sensitive areas within the military—"

General Branson interjected, "—We're going to put them on trial for treason as well. Sorry for the interruption, Director Perez."

The Director nodded and continued, "In addition to the military members, 3,456 government civilians and 856 government contractors have been arrested. Not all of these individuals had ties to the PLA; some had ties to the Russians and the IR. Everyone detained is going to be charged and tried for treason once all the evidence has been collected." Director Perez smiled with pride, feeling vindicated after having pushed so hard to make this controversial program operational.

"Where do we stand on getting the communications grid fully restored?" asked the President's Chief of Staff.

Director Perez brought up another slide with some additional information regarding the various status updates and explained, "As of right now, we have about 75% of the grid operational again. There are still some issues with data speed, but that will get resolved as more of the routers are replaced and upgraded. We're finally starting to get the parts we needed from the UK. It's now more of an issue of replacing the burnt-out switches and routers throughout the grid. It's going to take some time. The aerial drones and aerostat blimps are helping to plug the holes and gaps in the grid for the time being."

The President smiled. He was impressed by the ability of his staff to see the problem and find a way to quickly solve it. This close collaboration between the private sector and Allied and partner nations was key to getting the country's communication system back in operation.

Leaning forward, the President praised his team. "Director Perez, your team has done an outstanding job getting the communications network back up and running. I'm also glad you put forth a strong case for going live with Trinity. I was skeptical about using such an intrusive surveillance program, and I know others in the room were as well. However, no one can dispute the results, or the speed with which it found these traitors within our midst. I want this program to stay 'eyes only' and keep the circle of people that know about it small. The less people that know about this the better."

The President's Chief of Staff asserted, "We need to get these successes in the press. Lord knows the people need something; they're still reeling from the destruction of New York and Baltimore. That said, people are pretty pumped up about our nuking the living daylights out of the IR. Everyone knew someone who died in the vicious attacks," Monty said, surveying the group.

"Jim, how are the Europeans taking all of this?" asked the President, wanting to get a sense of the political situation with his allies.

"Like everyone else, they were shocked by the IR nukes in New York and Baltimore. They were also horrified at our response. They are saying we went overboard and should have shown some restraint. They are also crying foul about the environmental damage this is going to cause," Jim said, knowing the President would have gone further if the others hadn't insisted on limiting the conventional nuclear attack. Stein had wanted to unleash more than a thousand nukes, hitting the entire Islamic Republic from North Africa and the Middle East to Asia.

The President *was* concerned about the environmental damage the nukes had caused but found himself saying, "Perhaps they can show restraint when one of *their* cities is nuked. Are they mobilizing their forces yet? Will they be able to provide any sort of defense?" The President was clearly not expecting a satisfactory response.

General Branson moved to answer the question. "Mr. President, they've mobilized their entire reserve force. Germany is really stepping up. They just announced the conscription of three million additional soldiers, not that they'll make a difference for at least six to twelve months."

A holographic image of General Wade came to life. From his European post, he had been participating in the meeting via conference call. Now he interjected, "The EU is still in the process of pulling their active forces out of the cities and reequipping them with their combat equipment. The only units that are ready right now are the German 10th and 13th Armored Divisions and the Polish Army. Both German divisions have the latest Leopard 3C model tanks and will be more than a match for the Russians. The Germans are also mobilizing three infantry divisions to begin setting up defensive positions in and around some of the major Polish cities. The Poles, for their part, are moving most of their armor and mechanized forces to the north and trusting the Germans to hold the center. The EU forces in Poland, Hungary and Romania have all been placed on alert and moved to their marshaling points. For the first week, they will be on their own until the Fifth and then later the Sixth Army are ready."

The President butted in to ask, "Will the German divisions be enough?"

"These are their two best divisions. General Schoen is the area commander, and he's by far their best field general. I'm confident they will hold the Russians for a few days, long enough for us to get at least part of the Fifth Army to the German border and ready to fight," General Wade replied, his face set like flint.

Changing maps on the holographic display, General Branson began showing the North Atlantic and the British sector. "The Brits are going to secure Iceland and Norway. They will focus heavily on interdicting the Russian Navy and ensuring the sea lanes between North America and Europe continue to stay open. They're also going to be providing a large portion of the air support over Europe, since most of our airpower is still in the Middle East."

Eric Clarke, the SecDef, interrupted to add, "We have 1,200 fighter drones fresh from the factory. They're being formed into new fighter wings and will be sent to Europe within the next three days. It's still going to be close to a month, maybe two, until we have most of the aircraft from the boneyards ready to go. Even then, we lack trained pilots. We've shortened the training period for our pilot program, but that means our pilots will be less trained and experienced when they go into battle. We are also calling back into service a lot of retired pilots who used to fly these aircraft when they were still on active duty."

General Branson was used to the SecDef adding information during his brief and continued on as if it never happened. "They will get their experience, just like the infantry will—through direct combat. The additional fighter drones and aircraft from the boneyards will help, especially the 500 A-10s. Those are incredible tank busters. My concern is that we have heard rumors that Russia has a new fighter, the MiG40. We're not sure of its capabilities, but from what we have heard, it uses some sort of new technology that makes the aircraft virtually invisible to the naked eye. If that's the case, then this new fighter is going to cause us some major problems."

Sighing deeply, the President felt another migraine coming on. "Gentlemen, what I need to know is—do we have sufficient forces to hold on to our gains in the Middle East and prevent Russia from capturing Europe? If not, then this is the time to bring up any issue."

Everyone in the room sat silently thinking for a moment about what the President had just asked. It was a good question that needed to be addressed before hostilities with Russia really started. Eric sat back in his chair and exhaled forcefully, then leaned forward, surveying everyone at the table before responding.

"Mr. President, we're at a tipping point right now. We've just stabilized the situation in the Middle East, and that could change quickly if the Russians or Chinese decide to throw more troops into the mix. We have North Africa and the Strait of Gibraltar that still need to be secured, and then we have Europe."

The world was finally at a critical moment where the dictatorial regimes finally had the military and economic advantage over the democratic governments of the West. The decline of the US as a global influencer and the rise of China, Russia and a united Middle East had given them the edge they had longed for. After nearly seventy years of planning, China finally had the technological and military might to not just challenge the US but potentially strip them of their superpower status. As China secured Southeast Asia, their attention would likely turn to mineral-rich Alaska and the fertile farmlands of the American West Coast.

The Secretary of Defense spoke up for the group, saying, "Unless some miracle or an act of God happens, and the EU Army is able to mobilize and stop the Russians, I don't believe we'll be able to hold Europe for more than six months. It's going to take us close to twelve months to field an army strong enough to defeat the Russians, and that assumes those forces won't be needed to reinforce the Middle East, Australia or our own West Coast."

The President knew Eric was right—there was only so much the US could do with the current forces and equipment they had at hand. The military boneyard near Tucson was already being scavenged for equipment that could be reactivated, and so too was the Navy's Ghost Fleet. The President needed time—time to allow the American economy to deliver the tools of war needed to win. However, it was time that the democracies of the world did not have.

"You bring up some good points Eric. We can only defend and win if we prioritize our theaters of operation," responded the President. He looked down at his tablet for some information before continuing. "What we need to do right now is to determine which combat zones we will divert most of our resources to, and then focus on establishing a delaying action in the others."

General Branson saw this as his opportunity to step in and provide his military opinion. "Mr. President, I recommend we finish operations in the Middle East. The Russians and Chinese have forces there, but that theater isn't going to be their main area of operations. Let's secure and stabilize that region so we can relocate those forces to Europe.

"Next, I recommend that we move Asia to the backburner. I hate the idea of abandoning Asia, but until our carrier forces are built back up and Japan joins in, we're not going to be in a position to take China on and win. With that said, I recommend we continue to build up a defensive force in Australia and move to withdraw all forces from Japan and relocate them to Alaska. The Klondike is incredibly vulnerable to both Russia and China, and those forces in Japan could be the difference in deterring or preventing an attack there.

"I also recommend that we begin a full evacuation of the Hawaiian Islands. The Chinese will certainly make a move for them. Once cut off, the civilian population on the island would begin to die off. The island also has limited military value because the naval and air facilities there have been wrecked by the Chinese sneak attack there. We are preparing our military forces to fight a guerilla war on the island and establish a continuous surveillance operation of the facilities once they do fall to the Chinese, but there's nothing we could do for the civilians. I recommend we begin a forced evacuation of the residents immediately, while we still have time."

Secretary of State Jim Wise spoke up. "This is not going to look good in the public eye, Mr. President. I understand the need to prioritize the various theaters of operation, but it will appear that we are abandoning Asia and essentially surrendering to China. Is there some way we can continue to keep some sort of military pressure on the Chinese?"

Eric understood Jim's concern as well and added, "He's right, Mr. President. It will appear that we are surrendering to China and ceding Asia to them. However, if we keep our submarine forces and the Navy involved in Asia, sinking Chinese shipping and going after other soft targets, then we can keep the public and the Chinese from believing we have ceded Asia to them."

General Branson concurred. "These are good points, Mr. President. I have to agree with their assessments. It is important we make the Chinese believe we haven't completely surrendered the fight to them, especially in light of our withdrawal from the Hawaiian Islands, if we do in fact move forward with that plan."

The President knew the next two weeks were going to be critical to the direction of the war and its outcome. The decisions being made right now would have a profound impact on the future history of the world. "Then it's settled. Asia will be moved to the backburner until we can defeat the IR and Russia. I want everything done to secure Israel and knock the IR out of the war immediately. Find a way to cripple them— starve them into submission if need be—but make sure that we bring that war to an end, or at least to a point where they're no longer a threat.

"I also want a decision from the Japanese. Are they going to honor their defense pact with us and get involved in the war or not? If they choose not to honor the agreement, then I want General Branson to move forward with the full withdrawal of US forces from Japan to Alaska. We will not protect Japan from China if they aren't willing to honor their defense agreement, nor will we allow the Japanese to intern our forces for the duration of the war," the President said emphatically.
****

Following what was probably the most important meeting of the war, the Secretary of Defense and the Chairman of the Joint Chiefs immediately began to get things moving. Sixty thousand soldiers who had just completed training were being transferred to Australia to add to the 48,000 troops already stationed there. They would comprise the bulk of US forces in Australia. 11,000 Marines were sent to Alaska to aid the Army in defending critical naval and land points that could be used by either Russian or Chinese forces, and they began to build a host of defensive forts and positions all throughout the Klondike. All other US forces shipped to Israel to assist General Gardner's Third Army.

Chapter 12
The Lion Licks His Wounds

Day Twenty-Five
23 December 2040
Islamic Republic Command Bunker beneath Riyadh

The Islamic Republic had been hit hard by the American nuclear response. The damage was still being assessed and communications across the Republic were sporadic at best. They had communications with their army in Amman, but little else was functioning.

"What is the status of our military? Do we still have a combat-effective force?" asked Caliph Mohammed.

Zaheer Akhatar, the Caliph's personal advisor, laid out the news. "Our forces in Amman were unscathed by the American attack. We still have nearly three million regular and civilian militia forces ready for combat, though we lack the supplies for a long campaign. The rest of the Republic is in tatters. Our scientists, along with those from Russia and China, determined that the Americans used some sort of new bomb called a neutron bomb. When it detonates, it causes very little in the way of damage to the target. Rather, it emits a lethal dose of radiation to everyone within a thirty-mile radius, and of course emits a massive EMP. Near as we can tell, the Republic was hit with five of these devices. They hit Istanbul, Cairo, Riyadh, Baghdad and Tehran. These attacks were quickly followed up with 143 nuclear strikes, hitting every power plant, hydroelectric dam, major seaport and logistical node in the entire Republic. The one exception was the province of Kuwait; the Chinese and Russian warships destroyed the American MIRVs targeting that area. The Americans also destroyed our largest one hundred cities.

"On a good note, the Chinese and Russian Navy was able to destroy forty-two nuclear missiles before they hit their targets. They are also connecting slave cables from their ships to our electrical grid to start providing localized power in parts of Iran, Iraq, Saudi Arabia, UAE and Oman."

Caliph Mohammed sat in his chair for a minute, trying to digest what he had just been told. He stood up, motioning for everyone else to stay seated while he paced back and forth for a couple of minutes to try and decide what to do next. As he returned to his chair, he turned to his advisors and asked, "What options do we have left? Is the war still winnable?"

General Rafik Hamza, the overall commander of the IR military, knew the only option left was surrender, but he dared not suggest it. They had taken a calculated risk that the Americans would back down in light of the destruction of two of their cities. The introduction of a neutron bomb to the equation changed things immensely. Also, these missiles that the Americans used appeared to be the same as the ones that had hit them at the outset of the war. Their spies had told them that those were experimental missiles and that the US did not have any more…they could not have been more wrong. If they were now mass-producing these missiles, then the Republic did not have much time left to either win the war or surrender. They had also not taken into consideration the potential loss of their top one hundred cities and their entire infrastructure.

The room was silent for a few awkward moments. Knowing someone had to deliver the bad news, General Hamza began, "Caliph Mohammed, we can continue to attack the American and Israeli forces through Jordan with our remaining forces and the supplies that we have left. When the Chinese and Russian forces move into position, we can begin a second offensive with them."

"I gather from the tone of your voice that this is not how you would like to proceed?" asked the Caliph.

All eyes turned toward General Hamza to see what he would say next.

Rubbing his temples briefly, he said, "Caliph, we made a calculated risk that we could survive a nuclear strike by the Americans. We were wrong. We did not anticipate the use of a neutron bomb or the destruction of our top one hundred cities. Our entire infrastructure— dams, power plants, bridges and roads—are being systematically destroyed by American drones now that our laser defense system is offline. We have no power practically anywhere in the Republic. Worse still, in many places, we have no water."

He took a deep breath, knowing that he was about to risk his life with his next statement. "Caliph, I recommend that we pursue a cease-fire—not a peace agreement, a cease-fire. We can continue the war in a few months once the Russians attack the Americans and the Chinese continue their expansion. This will buy us time to pick up the pieces of the Republic and retain control of the country we have fought so hard to create."

The Caliph sat back in his chair for a moment before responding. "Thank you for your direct and clear recommendation. We did make a calculation, and we were wrong. I happen to agree with you. I believe we should pursue a cease-fire. However, what do we do with China and Russia? The Chinese already have an army group moving toward Amman, and Russia will have the Second Shock Army move down through Syria. What should we tell them?" asked the Caliph with a bit of uncertainty.

"This is an interesting question. I am not sure how they will respond. The Chinese will demand that we continue the war; the Russians will as well," General Rafik acknowledged.

"There is an alternative. We can continue the war and go along with them, but just not commit our forces as aggressively as we have. Rather than continue to attack with our full force, we use the most minimal amount of forces possible while we focus on trying to hold on to the land we have. We are still allowing the Chinese and Russians to use our land as a launch point, and we will be supporting them, but our focus will be on rebuilding our infrastructure and country," said Talal bin Abdulaziz. He was hoping everyone else understood his point.

Muhammad bin Aziz, the Minister of Industry, interjected, "Caliph, the Chinese have several ships in port right now in Kuwait. The Americans have not attacked them, and the ship captains have agreed to provide us with short-term power. We still have a laser defense battery operational there, and I would like to get it back online and then get the power plant nearby repaired. Once it's repaired, we can have our additive manufacturing plants, the 3-D printing plants, operational. They can start producing the parts we need to get our power grid back online and get our laser defense systems running. The Russians are also sending dozens of their advanced S500 surface-to-air missile systems. They are going to start establishing them throughout the country to try and help us get the American drones and fighters off our backs. Then we can prepare the area for their forces as they move into our lands."

The Caliph got up and began to pace once again while he thought about what his advisors had suggested. If they did not restore power to the country and reestablish order, the entire Republic could spiral out of control and they could lose the country. "Talal and General Rafik, please get in contact with the Americans and see if we can get a 96-hour cease-fire while we work out the details of a truce. I also want you to get in touch with the Chinese and Russians. Let them know that we are going to sue for a cease-fire to buy ourselves some time. They are welcome to continue to use our facilities and access our territory. Any assistance they can provide to us would be greatly appreciated."

Following the meeting, the Islamic Republic asked the Israelis and Americans for a four-day cease-fire while they worked out the details of a longer-term truce. The IR used this time to get several of their laser defense and SAM systems back online and secure a small bubble so that their manufacturing could start to replace destroyed power and transmission equipment. It was going to be critical to reestablish their power grid and restore order within the country. The Russians also began to provide the IR with several dozen mobile laser defense systems, reducing the effectiveness of Allied cruise missile and air attacks against the remaining IR infrastructure.

The Chinese First EF and the Russian Second Shock Army began to move toward Israel and the Allied forces, setting up the second battle for Israel.

Chapter 13
A Very Un-Merry Christmas

Day Twenty-Six
24 December 2040
10 Downing Street, London
Underground Command Bunker

Prime Minister Stannis Bedford and the Allies knew the Russians were going to launch their attack against the EU on December 25. What they did not know was what time of day the skirmish would start. Rather than waiting for the hammer to fall, at midnight on the 24th, the Prime Minister ordered the military to initiate a covert attack against the known Russian positions before they were able to begin their aggressions.

In the deep dark trenches of the ocean floor, the submarines of the Royal Navy launched torpedoes toward eight Russian submarines that they had been shadowing the last several days since leaving their port in Murmansk. The Russians had been moving their subs into the North Atlantic in preparation for their invasion of the EU; their goal had been to attack the Allied shipping lanes and stop additional troops and materiel that were being moved from the US to Europe. However, within minutes, the Royal Navy had destroyed a total of fifteen Russian submarines, completely dashing their hopes of launching their own surprise assault.

At the same time, the Royal Air Force JF35 stealth fighter bombers and B5 stealth bomber drones began hitting Russian fixed-based laser defense and S500 SAM systems, along with sixteen forward airfields. The Russian air defense systems were able to shoot down twenty-nine of the forty-five B5s and twenty-one of the eighty-six JF35s, but not before they successfully destroyed their targets, creating a temporary wide hole in the Russian air defense.

With the newly created gap in security, the Americans fired 4,300 cruise missiles at the Russian First and Third Shock armies and targeted dozens of power plants across Western Russia. They also hit a dozen more laser defense systems, along with one hundred and thirty-two mobile laser defense vehicles. The Russians managed to destroy nearly half of the cruise missiles and two-thirds of the attacking drones;

however, several hundred tanks and other armored vehicles were destroyed by the American missiles.

The Russians, eager for revenge, immediately launched their offensive. Three thousand Spetsnaz soldiers began destroying bridges, dams, dikes, power transmission nodes, and cell towers throughout the EU and Great Britain. One-third of the Netherlands and Belgium began to flood as the dikes keeping the seawater at bay began to wreak havoc on the country. With one phone call, the Russians also activated all of their assets to engage in targeted assassinations. One thousand, three hundred and twenty-one EU government officials were murdered within the first several hours.

The first four hours of Christmas saw some of the most intense combat that Europe had seen since the height of World War II. Thousands upon thousands of manned fighters and fighter drones were engaged in aerial combat, vying for control of the skies of Europe. While the battle in the clouds was taking place, nearly five thousand Russian main battle tanks and twelve thousand light drone tanks began to move across the borders of Russia into Romania, Hungary and Poland. In total, four million Russians advanced across Europe, led by the famed General Kulikov.

****

When the Russian Third Shock Army crossed the Polish border, they immediately ran into heavy resistance from the German 10th Panzer Division. General Schoen had prepared his positions well, knowing exactly where the Russians would advance. With the cover of Allied drones and air support, he struck fast and hard.

The main tank battle took place at a crossroad between Highway 63 and Highway 19, just south of Lukow at a city called Radzyń-Podlaski. General Schoen had moved 430 Leopard 3C main battle tanks and 530 Puma antitank infantry fighting vehicles to this position. Each Puma carried eight antitank guided missiles, a 30mm autocannon and six infantrymen. The Germans fought courageously and with all their might against the Russians and blunted their initial assault. The German infantrymen savaged the Russian armored vehicles as they advanced near any of the Polish cities. During the 24-hour running tank battle, 1,124 Russian tanks were obliterated. In comparison, the Germans lost just 243 tanks and 343 Pumas before they fell back to the city of

Garwolin, ten miles south of Warsaw. The German Army was once again proving to be a formidable foe.

****

General Wade still hadn't unpacked his bags when the fighting had begun. The British had presented their plan to him to hit the Russians hard and blunt their preemptive strike. With war a near certainty, there was no need to wait to be attacked. General Wade had agreed and persuaded President Stein to give the go-ahead. When the British had attacked, General Wade had hit the Russians with nearly every cruise missile he had available. They had the element of surprise, so there was no reason to hold anything back.

As General Wade looked up from the desk he was sitting at, Major General Bryant from the British Royal Army walked in with a battle damage assessment (BDA). "Were the raids successful?" asked the SACEUR.

Major General Charles Bryant was the NATO liaison officer for the Royal Army and was responsible for coordinating the RA and USA ground and air forces in Europe. He was also General Wade's new XO. With the death of the previous SACEUR CG, General Wade had been relying on General Bryant a lot.

"We hit them hard. BDA shows we destroyed three hydroelectric plants and five other power plants. Another six were heavily damaged. It's going to cause some rolling blackouts and wreak havoc on their communications and logistical networks. We also hit their rail and bridge networks pretty hard. Twelve of their airfields are temporarily taken out as well."

"Excellent. At least we scored some immediate hits before everything kicked off. How are we faring in the air war?" General Wade asked cautiously.

Bryant glanced down at his tablet and cycled through a few slides to get to the information he was looking for. "It's still touch-and-go right now. We are starting to see those new MiG 40s we've been hearing so much about, and the Su-37 is as fearsome as we thought it would be. They are tearing through us right now."

General Wade had been afraid the new MiG and Sus might do this. "How bad are they hitting us?"

"We've shot down three MiGs and ninety-two Su-37s, at a loss of seventeen JF35s and one hundred and twenty-three of our F-38 drones."

General Wade knew these types of losses were not sustainable, particularly if the Russians had a large quantity of these new MiGs. He thought to himself, *How many of these do they have?*

Putting his thoughts into words, he said, "These are not maintainable losses. Do we know where the aircraft are flying out of? Is it possible for us to try and launch a raid on the airfields?"

"No, Sir. We have not identified where they are flying out of yet. The issue that the pilots and intelligence are having is that the MiG is technically invisible. As in, they literally cannot see the aircraft."

"I remember reading about that in one of the intelligence briefs. What are we doing about it?"

"The one weakness to the MiG is its heat signature. The rest of the aircraft operates at such a low temperature in comparison to its exhaust that it stands out when using a specialized Doppler radar system. Unfortunately, we don't have a lot of these specific types of instruments in Europe, nor do we use them in our missiles."

"I want more of these radars brought in from the States immediately. Also, get in touch with some reps from the manufacturers and see if they can figure out a way to get them incorporated into our heat-seeking missiles. Get on the horn with whoever you need to, and get more of these radars in theater immediately."

"Yes, Sir."

"How is the rest of the air war going with the drones?" Wade asked.

The Allies had nearly 12,400 fighter drones and 1,900 manned fighters in Europe. At the start of the war, the Russians had nearly 17,000 fighter drones and 3,600 manned aircraft. The primary advantage the Allies had was their railgun defensive systems. Both sides had fixed and mobile laser defense and missile systems, but only the Allies had railguns.

"It's too early to determine how the air war is shaking out. Right now, the First Shock Army is rolling over the Romanian and Hungarian armies. We've directed both armies to fall back to their defensive positions as we speak. The Third Shock Army is being slowed down by General Schoen and the German 10th and 13th Panzer Divisions at

Rzeszow, Lublin, and Radzyń-Podlaski. During a running 24-hour tank battle, they destroyed over 1,200 Russian tanks before falling back to just 10 miles south of Warsaw.

"The bigger concern we're seeing with some of the drone fighter squadrons is cyber-attacks. Not all of the squadrons are being affected, but in one instance, the entire squadron's fighter drones simply went offline and crashed before the technical folks could figure out what was happening," General Bryant said, a bit concerned with the report.

General Wade was very concerned about cyber-attacks as well. The IR had used them in Mexico and caused a lot of communications problems for his forces there. Those issues were supposed to have been fixed, and thus far, it appeared that the secured military communications grid "battle net" hadn't gone down. However, the Air Force apparently still had some vulnerabilities in their drones that would need to get sorted out.

"I'm also getting some reports from the civilian sector of massive cyber-attacks taking place all across the EU. Water treatment plants are being turned off, or in some cases destroyed. Some of the power plants are going offline and there are all sorts of other issues hampering daily life. But this issue with the Air Force drones is concerning. If we don't fix that, we may not have anything left to save. Any word from the Air Force on what they're doing to fix the problem?" asked General Wade.

"Before I came in here, I spoke with a colonel in the cyberwarfare division who said they believe they have identified the problem and are working to close the vulnerabilities as we speak. He also said we should expect many more cyber problems as the war progresses."

"Great," Wade replied sarcastically. "Well, stay on this. Actually, assign one of your deputies to make this his top priority. I need you focused on helping me run and coordinate the ground and air war right now. Make sure your deputy gets in touch with our NSA LNO and tell them they need to get this fixed, or the Russians will be all over our tanks." General Wade sat back down and signaled for General Bryant to sit as well. An aide walked in a second later with a cup of tea for General Bryant and a cup of black coffee for General Wade.

Wade knew things were going to get dicey. He also knew the EU Army had to hold the line for at least two weeks before the American

Fifth Army would be at 100% strength and able to take the Third Shock Army head on. They were stripping the Sixth Army of all of its equipment and personnel in order to get the Fifth Army operational immediately.

Bryant and Wade continued to discuss the ground war and how it was impacting the civilian populace. "I know it may seem like things are falling apart quickly, but I assure you they will start to stabilize over the next forty-eight hours as the Russians start to run out of steam. The Reds are explosive in their attacks, but they lack the ability to sustain them. We just need to hold the line for a couple of weeks. The Fifth and Sixth Armies are coming."

The US had rerouted ninety Pershing tanks that had originally been heading toward Israel to reinforce the Fifth Army. General Gardner was not happy about losing such valuable MBTs but understood the need for them in Europe if Fifth Army was going to have a chance at stopping the two Russian Shock Armies. The US had also agreed to a 96-hour cease-fire with the IR after the nuclear attacks; the halt had given General Gardner's Third Army a chance to consolidate their gains in Israel and gave his forces a chance to rest.

Chapter 14
Korean Peninsula

Day Twenty-Seven
25 December 2040
South Korean Presidential Briefing

With the withdrawal of US forces from South Korea, the Koreans were feeling a bit apprehensive. The North was saber-rattling again. China had been gobbling up the entirety of Southeast Asia; it was only a matter of time until they decided to finish the Korean War. South Korea had to act, and act soon, if they were going to secure their future.

Young Hee Guen-hye had been President of South Korea for less than two years. In that timeframe, she had directed the military to prepare for a preemptive military strike against North Korea. Knowing that China was going to make a move against Asia at some point, she wanted to make sure they could prevent Seoul from being destroyed in the opening hours of a war with the North. North Korea had positioned over 15,000 artillery pieces aimed directly at South Korea's capital. If the artillery weren't taken out in the opening hours of a conflict, then the city and the people that lived within it would suffer horrific casualties.

When the Americans had withdrawn, all 495,000 South Korean active and reserve troops had been called up and placed on ready alert along the entire border with North Korea. The South Korean Air Force was flying additional fighter aircraft over the country, and the Navy had moved most of their ships to sea. The nation was as ready for war as they were going to get.

Since South Korea didn't possess nuclear weapons like the North, they had developed a small stockpile of chemical and nerve agents, geared toward a specific type of offensive operation. The preemptive strike would involve South Korea hitting the entire North Korean lines with artillery shells and rockets filled with VX nerve gas and sarin. The goal was to overwhelm the defenders quickly with a chemical attack. While they were dealing with the initial shock of such an attack, the Republic of Korea Air Force would begin to napalm all known artillery and rocket positions, destroying the equipment. This would quickly be followed up by the ROK Army advancing in their own chemical suits across the front lines and securing the enemy positions, removing the threat of the North's artillery against Seoul.

This attack would require an immense amount of VX and sarin gas to be used quickly. The ROK artillery barrage would last for five minutes before the Air Force would swoop in with their own payload. The ROK Air Force would also hit every known nuclear weapons site in an attempt to destroy the North's ability to launch their nuclear missiles. This would be the largest chemical weapons attack since World War I, and President Young Hee Guen-hye hoped they would be able to destroy a large enough portion of the North's army to get them to surrender quickly. It was risky using chemical weapons; her hope was they could knock the North out of the war fast enough that they would not be able to use their nuclear weapons against the South.

After much deliberation and discussion, it was agreed that the attack would begin on December 26. This would give them twenty-four hours to get everything ready, and hopefully keep the North from finding out until it was too late. The longer they delayed in launching the attack once it had been agreed upon, the higher the likelihood of the plan being discovered.

Chapter 15
Decision Point

Day Twenty-Seven
25 December 2040
Presidential HIVE, Northwest Virginia

It was Christmas in the underground bunker, and the President wanted nothing more than to visit the troops in Israel or Europe. However, it was deemed far too dangerous for the President to travel. The recent political assassinations by Chinese intelligence agents and Special Forces against American elected officials had been very successful in the initial days of the war, until the Trinity Program was activated. With the Russians now in the war, there was a lot of concern of potential Russian direct-action units trying to assassinate the President, or worse, take him hostage. Seventeen US senators and eighty-four Congressional leaders had been assassinated over the last three months—this was just at the federal level. The Chinese, IR, and now the Russians were trying to sow as much chaos, confusion and fear as they could by going after the American leadership structure, waging complete and total war on the US and its way of life.

As the President walked through his quarters and into the underground presidential offices of the HIVE, he couldn't help but notice that, despite the world being at war, the presidential staff had still found time to decorate the facility for Christmas. The President invited the troops guarding the facility perimeter to be rotated in for a Christmas lunch and dinner served by the President, his family and his staff.

After serving the last round of soldiers their Christmas dinner and talking with as many soldiers as he could, the President walked into the Situation Room for the scheduled briefing at 2000 hours and took his seat at the head of the table. Once he was situated, he signaled for the meeting to begin. He glanced at the agenda in front of him, which included the cyber-attacks to the country's communication infrastructure, the Trinity Program, the civil violence problem, and disaster recovery efforts underway in New York and Baltimore.

Director Jorge Perez from DHS began, "Merry Christmas, Mr. President, and to everyone here. I have a brief update on the cyber-attacks we have been experiencing and an update on the fixes that have been made. With a lot of help from both the UK and Australia, our major phone, internet and data providers are once again operational. There were some brief rolling blackouts from the utility companies that had been affected, but they're shorter and less frequent now as we bring more power plants back online. We expect to have the power grid back to 100% capacity within the next the month. The internet, phone and data exchanges are also back up and running at 100%. We attribute about 12,300 deaths to the cyber-attack. We arrived at this number by looking at the number of 911 calls during a similar timeframe that would have resulted in a death had emergency personnel not been able to get to a patient or respond to a car crash, break-in, etc. We also added in the number of people who died at various hospitals and nursing home across the country from the rolling blackouts. This number could conceivably have been much higher."

The President just shook his head in disgust.

Director Perez continued, "We have replaced the destroyed routers and switches to get everything back up and running, but it will still take many months to replace and repair everything. With AT&T and other phone and internet providers operational again, we have returned operational control of Verizon back to the company. The government has successfully switched our service provider over to Verizon as well and will diversify that service once the other companies' infrastructures are fully repaired. As for the utility companies, by and large, they were not affected by the current wave of cyber-attacks. Similar cyber-attacks continue to originate from China, but not nearly in the volume they had been. We attribute that to the cruise missile strike in Shanghai that destroyed the PLA's main cyberwarfare headquarters.

"We are seeing an uptick in cyber-attacks from Russia now that they're in the war. Presently, none of the cyber-attacks are penetrating anything vital, and they're being shut down as soon as they're detected. I'm sure the NSA can give you a better picture of our offensive cyber-attacks and how effective they are—I'll leave that for their brief. It would appear our concerted efforts to reinforce our cyber defenses and harden the power grid against cyber-attacks have really paid off."

Changing images on the screen, Director Perez went on, "Mr. President, the recovery effort in New York and Baltimore continues to run relatively smoothly. We continue to relocate the injured people to various hospitals and cities around the country, just as the plans called for. People whose homes are in the hot zones and are too close to the blast site to return are being relocated to a city of their choosing, and assistance is being provided. We've expended $600 million NAD in the last week. We will need another $16.2 billion NAD for the remainder of the year for the resettlements, and another $52 billion NAD for recovery and cleanup operations."

The President interrupted, "—Monty, ensure Speaker Fultz knows Director Perez is going to be contacting his office for a supplemental budget increase. Make sure they get the funds they need and let's get an oversight group involved to ensure the money is getting to the right people."

"Yes, Mr. President. I'll send him a message following the meeting," Monty responded, tapping a short note on his tablet.

President Stein was pleased at the incredible response time with which FEMA and DHS had deployed to the disaster zones. The planners for this type of disaster had really put a lot of thought into how people would be evacuated and treated, and they hadn't neglected to plan for what to do with refugees and resettlement. Obviously, people who lived in the hot zones couldn't go back to their homes, so some sort of compensation plan needed to be developed. FEMA had established a process that would take the fair market value of an individual's home and then add $75,000 for personal belongings and pay that to the affected person, minus the mortgage on the property. This enabled the banks to recover their loans, freed the displaced families of debt for homes they could no longer use, and gave them enough cash so that people could purchase the necessities to start over.

"Please continue, Director, and thank you for keeping us up to date on the recovery. It is important that we take care of our people," the President said with sincerity in his voice.

"As of twelve hours ago, when we updated the search parameters, the Trinity Program had identified 496 individuals with ties to Russian intelligence. We have FBI units detaining them now for questioning. Our main concern is the intercepts we decoded a few hours ago. Several Spetsnaz teams located in the US have received orders to begin carrying out attacks. We have no idea what the targets are or how many people are involved; that's why the FBI is detaining those individuals I mentioned earlier," Director Perez said.

The President was concerned about this last statement. America had already suffered enough domestic and political attacks. The last thing the country needed was further nasty surprises. "Director Perez, please continue to do whatever is necessary to apprehend these individuals. I want the CIA, DIA, and NSA to identify some potential targets, then quickly draft a plan to beef up security at those locations. We need stability while we focus on the recovery of New York and Baltimore and the war overseas.

"What is the status of our operations in Europe?" asked the President, changing topics.

General Branson stood up. "Mr. President, the situation in Europe is tense and fluid. The Russians have moved their army groups into Hungary and Romania and are pushing EU forces to their fallback positions faster than we had planned for. The Poles and Germans are holding the line a little better. They've managed to stop the Third Shock Army near Warsaw. The EU is pouring tens of thousands of troops into Poland."

Changing some images on the holograph, General Branson continued. "We're starting to see those new MiG40s and Su-37s, and they are tough. Right now, no one has full air dominance over the battlefield, but it's not looking very good for the Allies."

General Adrian Rice, the Air Force Chief of Staff, broke in to add, "The MiG40 is a tough aircraft, but they're limited in number. Right now they're taking control of the high-altitude fight; however, when they come down closer to the ground, that's when we have scored a few hits with our railguns. We found a weakness in the aircraft's stealth system—it's the heat it emits. The problem is, we can only spot them using a specialized Doppler radar, which we are short of on the battlefield and have never integrated into our air-to-air missiles before."

"Well, if that's the case, let's definitely get more of these specialized radars to Europe. Whatever we need to take control of the skies, let's get it done, gentlemen," dictated the President.

"Yes, Sir," came the response.

"How much longer until the Fifth Army is ready to kick the Russians out of Poland?" asked Stein.

"Soon, Mr. President. We have redirected 90 Pershings to them, and another 210 will arrive within the next month. Right now, they'll make use of the M1A5s we still have in circulation. We've brought another 2,200 M1A4s out of mothballs and hope to have them combat-ready within the next 60 days," General Branson said.

General Wade's holograph came to life as he said, "One important item to note, Mr. President, is a recent cyber-attack against some of our fighter drone squadrons. My Air Force and NSA LNOs have told me they've identified the problem and are working on a solution, but this could become a serious issue if the Russians or the Chinese can find a way to bring down more of our drone operations."

General Rice, the Air Force Chief of Staff, jumped in. "We are aware of the problem, Mr. President, and we're currently working on a new software patch and incorporating some additional network security protocols. We believe they gained access to the drone networks via an insider threat. One of the senior NCOs and two officers who worked in the drone program network security branch were recently apprehended as a result of the Trinity Program. Now that we know how the attacks originated, we are confident we can permanently fix it."

The President was relieved to know they had identified the problem and it was currently being resolved. He also knew there wasn't much that could be done in Europe just yet—troops, battle plans and defensive operations were all underway. The only course of action right now was to let things play out and give his generals the latitude they needed to make their military decisions.

"General Branson, General Rice, I'm not going to micromanage the air war. I want my generals to have the ability to make the choices on the ground. I *do* want to be informed and kept in the loop. I may offer a suggestion or advice here and there, but just as in Mexico and Israel, I will leave the actual tactics and strategy to you."

As the President looked at his commanders, he could see the apprehension leaving them. Henry continued, "General Wade, we're going to switch to the Middle East theater now. If you need to leave, we will understand."

"Thank you, Mr. President, for your vote of confidence, and I will step out now. I will continue to keep the Security Council and General Branson apprised of our operations." Then his holograph disappeared.

General Branson changed the maps and slides over to the Middle East. "General Gardner, are you still with us?" asked General Branson before continuing.

"Yes, Sir. I'm still here and ready to provide my update," General Gardner said as his holographic image appeared.

"Very well, please continue," requested the President.

"As you know, Mr. President, the Second Shock Army has moved out of Turkey and is transiting through Syria and Lebanon as we speak. Our air forces continue the battle for the skies; neither side has really taken a decisive advantage in that area as of yet. We anticipate our ground units making contact with the Russians within the next 24 hours. I've moved half of my Pershing tanks to meet them, and I'm confident we will hold them within the ten-mile buffer zone we've established between the Lebanon and Syrian borders with Israel." Images were shown of US, Israeli and Russian units as they were moving toward a convergence.

"The Chinese First Expeditionary Force has arrived near Ammon. They're under a blanket of mobile laser and SAM defense systems, so for the moment, the Air Force hasn't been able to attack them much. They appear to be getting ready to make their own offensive push, which will most likely coincide with the Russians. We believe they're going to try and go after the port facilities in the Red Sea and will also try to make a play for Sinai. We're unsure of whether or not the IR will launch another offensive into the Jordan Valley with their remaining forces in and around Amman. Right now, intelligence is actually suggesting that they may, but the attacks won't be very serious. Intelligence intercepts are showing that the IR is desperately trying to disengage while they work on reestablishing power to the country in order to regain control of their remaining cities," General Gardner explained. He placed his tablet on his desk and looked up for questions.

The President was intrigued by this last statement and asked, "So you believe the IR may attack and forgo this peace agreement, yet they wouldn't put their entire effort into attacking like they did in their previous offensive operations?"

"Yes, Mr. President. Our nuclear attack hit them hard, apparently harder than they're letting on or want to believe. Right now, only a small portion of the Republic actually has a functioning power grid. With most of the country in the dark, they've lost communications, and essentially control of large portions of the Republic. Unless they're able to reestablish that control soon, the rest of the country may fall into anarchy as both food and water shortages become critical to nonexistent," General Gardner said in response. More images were shown of Chinese and IR military units and areas of the IR that were currently without power.

Jim Wise, the Secretary of State, saw an opportunity and jumped in, adding, "Mr. President, with the country in disarray, this could give us a limited opportunity. Most of the IR is broken down into governing sections with a regional deputy Caliph that reports to Mohamed Abbas. If we were able to establish contact with the regional deputy Caliphs, we could offer them a separate peace agreement if they break away from the central government and form their own country."

The President sat back in his chair for a moment while a few others in the room discussed the possibility of such an event happening. It certainly did present a unique opportunity, and one they should explore. After some thought, he replied, "I believe there is some merit to this idea. If we can somehow divide the IR and get the governing regions to break off from the central government, then perhaps we can get the entire Republic to collapse. It would eliminate one of the Axis powers."

Secretary Wise added, "I can have my people begin reaching out to them immediately through various back channels. If any of them are amenable to an agreement, I will let the group know."

"Excellent, then please move forward with your plan, Jim." The President smiled for the first time during the meeting.

Stein wanted to know what the situation was with the rest of Israel and with their government, and asked Secretary Wise to bring them up to speed, along with General Gardner.

Secretary Wise spoke first. "The Israeli government is still working out of Tel Aviv; they actually never left, staying put even during some of the heavier fighting taking place outside the city itself. They're still evacuating people from the country that aren't part of the reserves to Cyprus and Italy.

"Of note, several pro-Israeli paramilitary camps have sprung up in the US and Europe. In Europe, nearly 25,000 people have signed up to join these groups and receive military training before heading to Israel to help fight. Similarly, in the US, there have been an overwhelming number of people wanting to volunteer to go fight in Israel. Close to 200,000 have volunteered at these camps so far. Right now, DHS is keeping them under a close watch but isn't actively saying they cannot support Israel in this manner."

Before this conversation could go further, the President interjected, "—Jorge, I want these groups left alone. If American Christians or American Jews would like to join these groups and fight for Israel, then please let them do so. I do want a full registration of who they are and when they leave, but no action is to be taken against them. Israel is a strong ally of ours, and if people wish to come to their aid, then they're free to do so. I would like to encourage them to join our military if they want to fight, but I will not have the government stand in the way of them joining Israel if they so choose. Is that understood by everyone?"

"Yes, Mr. President," came the response in unison.

"However, we will let the Israelis worry about how they're going to move them to Israel; that's something we will not divert our military efforts from to help," the President added.

Changing gears again, the President asked, "General Gardner, what's the status of the Israeli army?"

General Gardner's holograph appeared again and spoke. "They're still fighting. Once their entire reserve force was called up, their numbers swelled to over 600,000. They lost nearly 260,000 in the Jordan Valley and the fight for Jerusalem and Tel Aviv. We have most of their forces deployed now in Southern Israel on our right flank and in the center against Amman. The only Israeli units in the North in any serious numbers are several armor brigades. We want to crush the Russian armor units first, and then redeploy our armor units to the South to handle the Chinese. With the IR not looking like they are going to get really serious right now, it relieves a lot of pressure on our center.

"With the additional reinforcements I've been receiving, my force now stands at 560,000. I still have 460 Pershing tanks and another 1,454 M1A5 tanks. I'm facing 4,500 Russian tanks and another 4,000 Chinese tanks, so the odds are a bit long, but I think we can hold. Our equipment is better," he added with confidence.

"General Gardner, do your forces have everything you need to defeat the Russian and Chinese army groups?" asked General Branson.

"Yes, Sir. We have everything necessary to hold Israel. If you want me to defeat them, I'm going to need close to double the number of troops. As the Air Force is able to wrestle control from them, the situation will turn out a little better. Our big concern is making sure our supply lines aren't cut off. The Russian Navy is going to start to run havoc on our shipping lanes if they break out of the Bosporus and the Aegean Sea. Before the Russians move into Istanbul, I want to drop an airborne brigade to secure the straits and then fill it to the brim with sea mines."

Stein liked the idea of sending an airborne unit in to secure Istanbul. If they could secure it and mine the straits, they could bottleneck the Russian Black Sea Fleet before they would be able to break out and do some real damage. "I agree, General Gardner. Have a brigade secure the city, and drop as many mines as we can spare into the straits. Let's see if the Greeks will send some troops in and help us secure these targets," the President ordered.

****

During the following three days, the battle lines in Europe and the Middle East changed dramatically. The Russians had secured most of Romania and laid siege to Bucharest. They'd captured the majority of Hungary and were preparing to invade the Balkans. The Poles and Germans continued to hold the Russians around Warsaw, forcing a bloody house-to-house fight on the outskirts of the city. General Schoen was proving to be a worthy adversary for General Kulikov. The suburbs around Warsaw were being heavily destroyed as German and Polish soldiers fought for each house and block of the city. The Russian offensive had ground to a halt for the time being while they continued to advance around the city and try to cut it off.

With Istanbul being a virtual ghost town after the neutron bomb attack, US forces and 30,000 Greek soldiers quickly secured the city before the Russians or the IR were able to get any serious forces there. Within 24 hours, the Allies were in complete control of Istanbul and began to heavily mine the straits. Dozens of railgun systems were also strategically placed in and around the city and the waterways. Unfortunately for the Americans, while the loss of Istanbul did hurt the Russians, the Reds already controlled several large ports on the Black Sea, so the defeat didn't cripple their operations in the Middle East.

After moving in and securing Istanbul, the Greek soldiers began to clear the city of the dead. Every house and street was littered with dead bodies that were well into the decomposition state. The Greeks began to dig mass graves outside the perimeter to bury the dead. The soldiers tried to identify people as best they could. The ones that could be named were given separate graves; the ones that couldn't be were lumped into mass grave sites. It was a terrible job, but something that had to be done before disease began to run rampant throughout the city. Forty-five thousand additional Greek soldiers arrived in Istanbul to assist in both establishing new defenses for the city and the clearing of the millions of dead bodies.

Greece also initiated a massive draft and moved to arm roughly 500,000 men and women. They were going to receive two weeks of basic training—just enough to learn how to shoot, identify rank and engage in basic infantry tactics—before they would be sent to shore up defenses in Turkey and their border with Macedonia and Albania. Serbia also began to arm tens of thousands of their civilians in an effort to defend their border with Hungary and Romania as the Russians continued to advance toward them.

As the Reds continued to move their army group through Syria and Lebanon, they eventually ran into the American Third Army. General Gardner's troops were tired, but they were battle-tested and ready when the Russians arrived. Despite being outnumbered, the American Pershing tanks proved their weight in gold. The Reds controlled the high-altitude air war, while the Americans controlled the lower-altitude fight. This was both a blessing and a curse for the Americans; they were able to provide better ground support than the Russians, but the MiG40 was still able to drop precision bombs from high altitude, hitting critical targets and remaining largely immune to Allied air defense systems for the time being. They managed to destroy a number Pershings, turning the ground war into a war of attrition rather than the fast-moving mobile tank war Gardner had hoped for.

With the situation being bogged down in the North with the Russians, the Chinese launched their invasion of Southern Israel. Despite the heavy losses the Israelis had sustained, they were holding the line. The Chinese had not fought a serious foreign army thus far, so their troops were simply ill prepared to fight a determined and battle-tested foreign army like the IDF.

The Israeli and American forces stopped the Chinese just outside of Eilat, keeping them from gaining access to the critical port facilities nearby. The problem faced by both the Russian and Chinese forces was that they simply didn't have enough troops to properly exploit any breakthroughs or opportunities. The Chinese started their operation with 250,000 soldiers, while the Russians had 350,000. With the IR not fully committing their entire army to the fight, the Axis powers did not have enough troops to push the Americans out of Israel once General Gardner had been fully reinforced.

The Israelis also had 25,000 Jews from Europe join the IDF militia forces, and close to 200,000 more volunteers had been raised from the US. The Israeli Air Force was working through the logistics of how they were going to move these additional people from the US to Israel, where they could be integrated into other Israeli units.

Chapter 16
WMD Unleashed

Day Twenty-Eight
26 December 2040
Seoul, South Korea

At 0400, in the early hours of the morning, the ROK Army launched their surprise attack on North Korea. Five thousand artillery pieces and hundreds of rocket launchers began to fire their deadly cargo of sarin and VX gas all across the North Korean front lines. They chose to hit the North Koreans with two different types of chemical attacks, as each one acted slightly differently than the other. It was hoped that the dual attack would be more effective and harder to defend against. Though the North Koreans were known for their stoic nature, screams of agony echoed across the quiet of the early morning. The ROK Air Force immediately began to engage North Korean radar sites and surface-to-air missile sites, punching holes in their air defense system for the bombers to fly in and drop more chemical and gas bombs. This enabled the ROK bombers to swoop in and deliver a death blow to the second echelon of soldiers—they hit them with thousands of sarin and VX laden bombs, from the front lines to as far back as fifty miles.

In the first ten minutes of the attack, the ROK Army had effectively disabled nearly 70% of the enemy artillery crews while the Air Force began to drop cluster bombs and napalm on the equipment, utterly destroying it. As the North Koreans tried to respond to the opening salvos, they found themselves completely immersed in sarin and VX gas. The vast majority of soldiers either were unable to don their chemical protective gear or lacked the gear entirely. Then the ROK Air Force began to pound them from the air, destroying their air defense systems and further diminishing their ability to respond to this surprise attack.

At the end of the first hour, the ROK Army began to advance all across the front lines, encountering little in the way of resistance. What they saw was horrifying. Tens of thousands of twisted and disfigured bodies of those who had not been able to secure their chemical protective gear lined the battlefield. What minor conflict the ROK Army encountered was uncoordinated and lacked sufficient force to stop their advance.

****

With the army advancing across the front lines and deeper into North Korea, the air force immediately began to attack every known and suspected missile site that might house the North's nuclear missiles. Hundreds of bunker-buster bombs and missiles were used against these positions in an attempt to neutralize the North's only real trump card, their nuclear arsenal.

By 1800 hours, the ROK Army had advanced to Pyongsan, nearly 30 miles inland from the border. Slowly, the North Korean Army was responding to the invasion and tried to mount a defense. However, each time the North would amass their forces, they were immediately attacked by artillery and air force units, which dropped more sarin gas on their positions. One of the true weaknesses of the North Korean Army was that they had not actively planned or trained to fight in a chemical war because they had nuclear weapons. The South had, because the Americans always trained as if it was a certainty that chemical warfare would occur.

Despite the relentless human wave attacks by the North, they could not stop the ROK Army from advancing toward Pyongyang. The South was relentless in their use of chemical weapons, and by the end of the first day of the Second Korean War, the South had utilized the same quantity of chemical weapons that had been employed during the first year of World War I. Nearly 300,000 North Korean soldiers were killed by the chemical attacks.

By the third day of the Korean War, the ROK Army was at the outskirts of Pyongyang and showing no signs of stopping. The North Koreans were desperate and indeed had attempted to launch their nuclear missiles. However, due to the quick thinking of two ROK pilots in the area, they were able to identify the silos as they were being opened and engaged them. They demolished both silos before the missiles could be launched. After blasting Pyongyang with sarin for nearly four hours, the ROK Army moved in and secured the capital as the North Korean government fled to China. What tattered elements were left of the North Korean Army quickly surrendered.

While the world was appalled at the massive use of chemical weapons by the South Koreans and the sheer loss of life, which, including civilians, had grown to over one million—there was no denying that they had effectively blocked the use of nuclear weapons by the North. Essentially, the Korean War had ended within 96 hours. The South quickly sued for a separate nonaggression pact with China, who agreed, so long as South Korea provided no military assistance or support to the Americans in the Chinese war against the US. After consultation with the Americans, the South Koreans agreed to the Chinese terms. For the first time in nearly 90 years, the Korean Peninsula was once again united.

Chapter 17
Southern Negotiation

Day Twenty-Nine
27 December 2040
Brasilia, Brazil

Secretary of State Jim Wise and Secretary of Defense Eric Clarke arrived in Brasilia in a small unmarked private jet for a meeting with the president of Brazil, Michel Rousseff, and his national security staff and senior military leaders. President Stein had spoken with President Rousseff at length about their country joining the war and furthering their economic integration. Eventually, the Brazilian president agreed to meet with Secretaries Wise and Clarke to discuss what role Brazil and the other South American countries might have.

The harsh winter in Washington, D.C., had been taking a toll on the aging body of Secretary Wise, so as he stepped out of the plane, the warm weather of South America felt like a sweet kiss upon his face. The armored SUV and escorts arrived right on time to take them to their meeting. After a short thirty-minute drive, they arrived at the President's home to address the awaiting group.

Brazil had benefited greatly from the Grain Consortium, selling large amounts of food products to Asia prior to the war starting. With those trading partnerships terminated, they were starting to see the ill effects of this bad news in their first quarter GDP numbers. The United States had stepped in, placing massive manufacturing orders for steel, copper and manufactured goods that they used to purchase from Asia. This shift would help grow Brazil's manufacturing base, and with any luck would turn the tide of the country's economy.

The President of Brazil was waiting for his American guests at the front door when their vehicle arrived. He walked down the path to meet them and with genuine warmth said, "Welcome to Brazil." He extended his hand to shake each of theirs. "Please come with me. We have some food and drinks set up for you in the library. The others are already in there waiting for us." The President led his visitors through the spacious mansion to the library, which was equally grand. The room had vaulted eighteen-foot ceilings, with rows of bookshelves and paintings of famous Brazilian artists and other national icons all along the walls.

After everyone exchanged pleasantries and had some appetizers, President Rousseff motioned for everyone to find a seat around the large table that had been brought into the library for their meeting. A technician finished setting up the holographic presenter in the center of the table, and Secretaries Wise and Clarke both uploaded their briefings.

"Gentlemen, I appreciate your traveling to Brasilia to speak with us. I know both of you are incredibly busy men. Please, if you can begin, tell us what it is that President Stein is requesting from Brazil," said the President graciously.

"Mr. President, ministers and generals. We appreciate your willingness to speak with us and thank you for all that Brazil has done to help the United States in perhaps our greatest hour of need. As President Stein has conveyed to you, we are in need of assistance once again, and we are turning to you as an ally and friend." Secretary Wise gauged the room for their initial reactions to his statement, trying to identify those who might pose obstacles.

"As you know, last week the Islamic Republic detonated two nuclear bombs on American soil. While you have likely seen the footage of the devastation on the news, there is still information about the extent of the damage that we haven't shared with the American public. We will be explaining the following in a press conference this evening, but we've determined that the structural damage to most of the skyscrapers, harbor, bridges, and surrounding boroughs, both in New York City and in Baltimore, is completely beyond repair. For safety, the remnants of any surviving structures will need to be torn down and bulldozed. There is no salvaging what was left."

As the videos showed the extent of the structural and human losses, Jim could see on their faces their shock and horror at the damage that they were witnessing.

"The casualty numbers right now stand at close to four million dead, with nearly eight million more injured and homeless. As you can see, the damage is nearly catastrophic. The cities of New York and Baltimore will have to be abandoned and sealed off until the radiation can be cleaned up and cleared. This may take a decade or more to complete."

President Rousseff interjected, "America has our deepest condolences on the loss of life. This truly was a barbaric attack against a civilian target. What can Brazil do to help America?"

Jim cleared his throat before continuing. "America cannot fight this war on our own any longer. As you know, Russia just declared war on the Allies the other day and has begun a massive invasion of Europe. The Chinese continue to conquer one country after another in Asia, and right now there's little that can stop them. We are asking that Brazil, along with the other South American countries, join the European Union, Great Britain, Israel, Australia, Canada and others in this war against tyranny."

The Minister of Foreign Affairs jumped into the conversation. "Brazil is already producing massive amounts of munitions, weapons and other materiel that America and the Allies need for the war. What more can Brazil offer America that we have not already given?"

The Minister of Defense interjected, "Troops, the Secretaries of Defense and State are here to ask Brazil to start to participate militarily, am I right?"

Eric Clarke, the SecDef, answered, "Yes, that is what we are here to ask. We need soldiers, sailors and airmen to help us defeat the Axis powers."

President Rousseff nodded slowly and then surveyed his advisors and ministers before saying, "Secretary Clarke, while we certainly wish to assist you, Brazil does not have a large military right now. We also do not have the support structure to manage a large military right now. We could provide armed support, but it would be limited."

"We recognize this, and we have a proposal we would like to make. First, we would like to request what forces you do have available be immediately sent to support NATO in Europe. Second, we would like to request that Brazil begin an immediate mobilization within your country for war—"

Before Secretary Clarke could finish his sentence, several ministers began to grumble, and the Minister of Foreign Affairs interrupted, "—Sir, the Axis powers are not directly threatening Brazil or South America. If we start a countrywide mobilization, they may perceive us as a direct military threat. Brazil does not live under the antiballistic laser missile defense bubble that America and Europe have."

Eric tried to regain control of the meeting before he lost it completely. "We recognize that. We would immediately begin construction of over two dozen fixed-site missile defense systems in South America, and would augment them with numerous mobile laser defense systems and a series of railgun defensive systems. America would extend our same missile defense technology to Brazil and South America."

The President signaled for everyone to quiet down and let him speak. "Assuming we went along with this plan—exactly how many soldiers are you requesting of Brazil?"

"Mr. President, America is asking for an expeditionary force of 600,000 soldiers," the SecDef said.

For a moment, the room was completely silent. Then, suddenly, it burst into loud conversation among the various minister and advisors, with the President trying to gain control of the room. After nearly ten minutes of a heated discussion, Clarke and Wise signaled that they would like to address the group again.

"Gentlemen, we realize this is a large commitment, and that it represents a lot of young men and women we are asking your nation to place in harm's way. This war is a turning point in history. The Axis powers have a military force of over twenty million soldiers; if we don't band together now, then it may be too late to stop them. If the Allies in Europe and America are defeated, there will be no one to help South America when the Chinese and Russians come for you. We must unite now, before it is too late."

"We understand the threat. This is just a lot you are asking of us. I do not believe we have the ability to train and support such a large force," said the President, looking to his military advisors for support. They nodded in agreement.

"We have thought about that as well, and President Stein has some ideas on how to address that. The US would send you 7,500 military trainers and advisors to help establish five new military training bases here in Brazil. Each new training base would have 1,500 military advisors who would train this expeditionary force. We propose that the training for these soldiers would last ten weeks and be focused on specific military professions. One base would be dedicated to training men and women who will be filtered into various military support functions. Upon completion of their basic training, they would be sent to the US to attend their specific military support duties—medical, supply, administration etc. Three of the training bases would focus on training combat arms career fields. The fifth training base would be designated for officer and senior NCO training. They would attend the same combat training everyone else receives. However, their final three weeks would be geared toward leadership and command training." While SecDef Clarke spoke, he was showing them via holograph the various types of training facilities that they had envisioned.

"Each week, a new class of 5,000 recruits would start training, and as the pipeline of trainees starts to fill, the bases would churn out 5,000 new soldiers at the end of ten weeks and each week thereafter. At this pace, it would take six months to train the 600,000 soldiers for the expeditionary force once the training begins. We would frontload the training for the soldiers who will need additional military training in the US so that they would complete their advanced training by the time the rest of the force is ready. Following the six-month train-up period, the expeditionary force would receive thirty days of leave and then report back for a series of two-week training exercises. After that, they would then be prepared for deployment."

The President and his military advisors continued to examine the information Secretary Clarke presented before the Brazilian Minister of Defense asked the question, "Where would this expeditionary army be deployed to?"

"Right now, we're not 100% sure. It will be the middle of August before they're ready to deploy. A lot will depend on what the situation looks like in Europe, the Middle East and Asia. They could be deployed to the Middle East as an occupation force so that we could transfer the American Third Army to Europe or Asia, or they could be deployed to Europe to assist NATO. We'll have a clearer picture as we get closer to that timeframe. President Stein is also open to suggestions for where you would like to see them deployed as well," the SecDef said.

"Let me ask a more practical question. How are Brazil and the rest of South America supposed to equip or pay for this expeditionary force?" asked the Minister of Finance.

"The President has authorized me to provide the export/import and manufacturing licenses to build the myriad of armored vehicles and other military equipment that will be needed. This will create tens of thousands of high-end manufacturing jobs for your country. In addition, because of the cost required to support and sustain this expeditionary force is substantial, the US Department of Defense will be responsible for paying the salaries of the force and will purchase the required military vehicles and aircraft being produced by Brazil at 15% above cost," Clarke finished.

"I assume there will be a similar training program for the pilots for these aircraft as well?" asked the Chief General of the Brazilian Air Force.

"The individuals identified for pilot training will be sent to the US for training at our facilities; they will be integrated into the American Air Force for the duration of the war and will be transferred back to Brazilian national control once the war is over. We will not train a separate Air Force or Naval Force in addition to the ground force. The ground force will receive all of its air and naval support from the US. Essentially, Brazilians who want to join the air or naval arm of the expeditionary force can do so; they will just be integrated into the American air or naval forces for the duration of their enlistment or the length of the war, whichever comes first," Clarke said, hoping this addressed their concerns.

"How long will this expeditionary force be required to serve?" asked the Minister of Defense.

"They will be required to serve for the duration of the war, or for four years, whichever is shorter," Secretary Clarke answered.

"Is this same offer being made to the other South American countries as well?" asked the Minister of Foreign Affairs.

"Yes, we're seeking a total of one million soldiers to form the South American Expeditionary Force. We'll be asking the other countries to contribute a similarly sized force, though most of the manufacturing of the equipment needed would take place in Brazil, pending your joining the Coalition."

"So, if we do not join and Argentina does, then the manufacturing goes to them?" asked the Minister of Foreign Affairs.

"That would be correct. Brazil is our biggest supporter, and we wanted you to have the first chance at this offer," said Jim Wise.

"Gentlemen, we need some time to discuss this privately. I would like to ask that you take a break to freshen up or get some sleep and then meet us for dinner in four hours. We will have an answer for you after the meal," said the President, concluding the meeting.

****

As Clarke and Wise left the room, they walked to an outside patio so that they could soak up some sun while they drank a glass of fresh tea. "Do you think they're going to join?" asked Eric, looking to get another perspective.

"I believe so. That is, unless the Chinese have already approached them and made a better offer. However, I believe that at this point, South America is too heavily tied to the American and EU economies to just cut ties and join the Axis powers," Jim replied, though it sounded like he was trying to convince himself.

"If they do, it's going to be a herculean effort to get this expeditionary force trained. Not only do they not have the facilities built, they would still have to draft the needed soldiers," Eric said, not sure if they had bitten off more than they could chew.

Jim thought for a moment before responding, "We can bring in more private military contractors to help augment your soldiers."

"That only works to a certain extent. Besides, the PMCs are already stretched thin. It's not like people's enlistments are ending while the war is going on. We've stop-gapped everyone for the time being," said Eric.

"You know that's going to become very unpopular if this war continues for several more years," Jim retorted. He remembered what it was like during the Iraq War in the 2000s when the Bush Administration had put a stop loss in place to keep the Army numbers up.

"I know. Our plan is that for anyone whose eight-year active and inactive reserve enlistment is up, we offer them a $50,000 tax-free bonus per year that they reenlist, plus a one grade promotion. The number of people who are nearing or are at that actual enlistment mark is actually rather low. Several years ago, we phased out the two- and three-year enlistment and went to a four-year enlistment with four years in the National Guard or Reserves. The Guard and Reserves activations have also been increased from eighteen months to thirty-six months, until we have enough active-duty units to fully replace them." Eric took a long drink of his tea before he added, "This was a problem during the Iraq War in the 2000s as well. Too many National Guard and Reserve units were being activated, and it was seriously impacting the families of these men and women, not to mention their employers. The situation is not lost on us. As a corresponding active-duty unit completes their training and receives their combat equipment, we are rotating those citizen soldier units back to the US. It's just going to take some time, like everything else."

"I'm glad to hear that you are taking this issue seriously. My grandson, Tyler, is in the Wisconsin Army National Guard; my son says he is doing good, but he's not sure when their unit will be rotating back to the US."

Eric looked at the man sitting next to him as if for the first time. "Jim—I had no idea your grandson was in the military. Where is he currently stationed? What does he do?" Eric asked, genuinely concerned.

"He's a staff sergeant in the 126th Field Artillery Battalion, part of the 57th Artillery Brigade. They're currently deployed in Israel. His unit arrived there a few weeks after the war started," replied Jim with pride in his voice. He pulled out his cell phone and showed Eric several pictures of Tyler. There were a number from his wedding and a few of him with some of the soldiers from his unit in Israel.

"Do you talk with him much?"

"He called me once a few weeks back to say happy birthday, and to let me know he's doing OK. I offered to help him get reassigned to the US, but he said he couldn't leave without his unit. He said it would look bad, and he couldn't just leave them when they needed him." Jim's eyebrows furrowed while he talked—he couldn't hide his concern.

"If you want, I can look into having his unit reassigned. Since they're an artillery unit, I'm not sure I could pull them off the line entirely. We're desperately short when it comes to artillery." Eric sat there thinking for a few minutes. "Tell you what—if the Brazilians do join the Coalition, we're going to need to pull some combat units to do all of the training down here. I could arrange for his unit to be one of the ones pulled if you'd like me to have him moved to a less dangerous place."

Jim sighed before responding, "I appreciate the offer…maybe. You know the President has been pretty adamant about making sure special favors aren't being pulled for senior officials and their family members. I would hate for him to find out I had my grandson's unit pulled for my own selfish reasons," he said.

"He certainly hasn't been making friends with the ultra-wealthy and politically connected people in the country. He had me personally ensure that every member of the Congress and Senate who has an eligible son or daughter was drafted and placed in a line unit. During one of our planning meetings, he said this would be unpopular, but he was determined that every eligible citizen, including the wealthy and politically connected, must serve in this war. You should see the emails and phone calls I get from some of my friends who still work in banking and business. They all ask if I can get their son or daughter a deferment or at least ensure they won't see combat."

"What do you tell them?" asked Jim. He was curious now.

"I tell them what the President told me—everyone must serve, especially the wealthy and politically connected who have benefited so much from our country. The President promised that this war would not be fought on the backs of the lower and middle classes of the country."

"I'll bet that goes over really well," said Jim as he chuckled.

An aide walked up to Jim and Eric and asked if they could please join the President and his staff in the library again. They both got up and followed him back into the mansion and to the library.

"Secretary Clarke, Secretary Jordan, please come join us for a toast if you will. We have discussed your offer, and though some of my ministers and advisors disagree, we have come to the conclusion that you are right. It is time for South America to do its part and join the Allies. We also want to thank you for choosing Brazil to head up the Coalition. We are honored to be a part of this chapter of the world and on the side of the Americans and those who love freedom," President Rousseff said with a smile on his face as he raised a glass of champagne.
****

The Secretaries of State and Defense flew on to meet with the Argentinians, Peruvians, Chileans and Colombians, gaining their acceptance to join the Coalition and participate in the newly created South American Expeditionary Force. In time, this expeditionary force would swell to a little over one million soldiers and could grow significantly larger if need be. It would take close to ten full months before this new army was ready to deploy.

Chapter 18
Crash Course

Day Thirty
28 December 2040
Southern Israel—US Marine Positions

Gunnery Sergeant Thornton had just finished cleaning his M5 AIR when one of his junior sergeants walked into the tent with a handful of new replacements. "Sergeant Thornton, I was on my way back from headquarters when I was told these ten Marines were our replacements. This is Corporal Lewis; he's the senior guy with the replacements. The rest are outside the tent, if you want to speak with them," Sergeant Miller said.

Sergeant Thornton sat there for a moment. "Corporal Lewis, have you or any of the other guys with you seen any combat?"

"No, Sergeant. I'm a reservist. The rest of the guys are either fresh from boot camp or were working noninfantry positions before we were all shipped out," Corporal Lewis said, knowing that wasn't the answer Sergeant Thornton was hoping to hear.

"I appreciate your candor, Corporal. Take a seat, and I'll bring you up to speed a bit before handing you off to one of the other sergeants. I'm going to filter your replacements evenly among the squads. I'm not sure if you know or not, but our platoon had a 63% casualty rate. We were part of the first wave to hit the Suez, and then we spent the next three weeks fighting the IR north of Eilat." Corporal Lewis's face looked nervous, and a bit scared. Sergeant Thornton remembered feeling that same way, right before they'd left the troop carrier for the Suez.

"The most important thing that I can tell you is to stay alert and listen to those who have been here longer. These IR guys aren't taking any prisoners, and neither are we. They attack in massive human waves when they do attack, so be ready when that happens. Now they say we're facing the Chinese. Well, I've never fought the Chinese before, so I can't give you any words of wisdom with them. Just remember your training. Fight like a man possessed, and remember, there is no surrender. They will crucify you," Sergeant Thornton said in an icy tone. He could see on Corporal Lewis's face that he was still digesting what he had been told and didn't care for it one bit.

"Word has it we're going to be moving back to the front lines around midnight. There's supposed to be a possible Chinese assault sometime tomorrow, so they want us to reinforce the Israeli positions. Once you get to your assigned squad, get your fire team ready for action and try to grab a couple of hours of sleep. If you have any further questions, ask your squad sergeant, and they'll provide you with whatever information they know," Sergeant Thornton concluded. He dismissed the newly arrived corporal, who was still in a state of bewilderment.

By 0500 the following morning, Gunnery Sergeant Thornton's platoon had been filtered into a short network of trenches and foxholes that the Israelis were using. His group of fifty-four Marines had been integrated into an Israeli company holding this part of the Eilat line in the ruins of Aqaba, a city that had been mostly turned into rubble with the back-and-forth fighting between the Israelis, Marines and IR forces. When the Chinese had attacked, the Allied forces had fallen back to the ruins and turned them into a defensive network and trap to prevent the Chinese from moving into Eilat or the rest of Southern Israel.

At 0530, the Chinese began to bombard the ruins of the city and the Allied positions with artillery and rocket fire. The explosions were kicking up a storm of dust and smoke; however, through the haze, Gunny Thornton could see Chinese infantry units moving forward toward their lines. When his eyes focused a little harder, he could make out that the advancing infantry was fortunately not equipped with the new exoskeleton combat suits. He breathed a sigh of relief, knowing that at least they were going up against the regular PLA infantry. Those suits would have given the advancing horde a huge physical and technical advantage over the Allies. Luckily, only a limited number of the Chinese Naval Infantry units had them, and so far, they had only been used in the Pacific. Gunny Thornton found himself wishing that he had an exoskeleton suit—rumor had it that the Army and Marines were going to be bringing their own suits to the fight soon.

Thornton began issuing orders to the rest of his men. "Stand by to engage the enemy. We need to wait until the new targets have been acquired in our HUDs."

The Gunny linked the images his heat imaging scope had identified with his HUD so that the rest of the platoon could see what he was seeing.

Grabbing the attention of the appropriate Israeli counterpart, he instructed, "There's a pending infantry attack. Follow our lead when we start to engage the enemy. Since you guys don't have the HUDs, we'll be showing you where the targets are." Although the IDF was starting to receive the same HUD and M5 AIRs the US was using, not all of the units had them yet.

"Acknowledged," was the only reply. This particular IDF fighter was not exactly the conversational type.

There were a few tense moments of waiting. As the Chinese infantry came to within 200 meters of their positions, Gunny Thornton shouted, "Open fire!"

Within seconds, sixty-plus Chinese infantry collapsed dead in their tracks. The M5 advanced infantry rifle was an incredible killing machine; it had a range in excess of 2,000 meters and fired a .25mm projectile at speeds of Mach 5. It was the only tactical infantry railgun rifle in the world. The power pack attached to the buttstock of the rifle could provide enough power to fire 2,500 projectiles, or ten magazines, and had a digital counter on it that could help a solider keep track of when the battery pack needed to be replaced. The projectiles traveled at such a high speed that they were able to penetrate all forms of body armor and lightly armored vehicles.

Once the Marines opened fire, the Israelis joined in, adding their own weapons to the fray. While dozens of Chinese soldiers were being mowed down, half a dozen light drone tanks started to move forward from around the rubble of what used to be the Radisson Blue hotel. The tanks stopped briefly and began to fire high-explosive rounds at the Marines and IDF while more Chinese infantry moved forward.

Gunny Thornton saw in his HUD that several of his Marines had been killed by one of the light drone tanks. "Someone get those AT6s and take out those tanks!" yelled Thornton to his antitank team. The AT6 was the sixth generation of antitank rockets used by American infantrymen; it was three feet in length and fired a one-shot, high-explosive antitank rocket. It could destroy most main battle tanks and was extremely effective against light drone tanks and infantry fighting vehicles. It was the perfect antitank weapon for the light infantry.

Whooossshhh…three rockets raced away from the Marine lines and headed straight for the Chinese light tanks.

BAM!...Boom!

All three rockets struck their targets, and the tanks immediately began to explode as their ammunition started to cook off.

Red and green tracers and thousands of bullets flew through the air, crisscrossing back and forth between the Marines, IDF and Chinese as the infantry continued to advance. Slowly and steadily, the Chinese soldiers pushed forward until the two groups were within fifty meters of each other, throwing grenades and shooting each other up close and personal. While the Marines and IDF soldiers were heavily engaged with the Chinese soldiers to their immediate front, a massive human wave of soldiers was forming further behind the Chinese lines.

The whistling of artillery could be heard as the Chinese began to land additional high-explosive rounds amongst their own soldiers in an attempt to kill more Marines and Israeli soldiers. Their horde rushed forward. Somehow the Marines and Israelis had managed to recover from this latest round of attack. They started killing off the remaining Chinese soldiers in front of them. Before another minute had gone by though, they looked up to see a massive swarm of new soldiers screaming at the top of their lungs, headed right for them.

Thornton immediately got on the radio. "This is Gunny Thornton. We need artillery and mortar support now! Engage in predetermined pattern Bravo," he shouted to the company's artillery LNO.

Hitting the button on his BH, he switched over to address his men. "Engage them from maximum range, and be prepared for hand-to-hand combat if necessary."

Just as the Chinese got to within 200 meters of the Marines position, dozens of artillery and mortar rounds started to land all around the Chinese soldiers, decimating their ranks. Bodies were being flung around like rag dolls as 155mm artillery rounds and 81mm mortar rounds continued to rain down on the Chinese. As the fighters got closer to the Marine positions, it quickly became apparent they were really going to have to fight them hand-to-hand.

During the equipment refit several weeks ago, the Marines had been issued World War I-style trench knives, which amounted to brass knuckles with a six-inch blade for close quarters fighting. The trench knives were strapped to the left or right boot of the Marine, depending on which hand was dominant. Some Marines even carried one on each boot. As the Chinese neared their positions with their bayonets fixed, the

Marines parried their lunges and reached for their trench knives. The fighting quickly devolved into primal bloody combat as the Israelis and the Marines grappled for their very lives.

After nearly three hours of fighting and ten minutes of hand-to-hand conflict, the Chinese fell back to their old positions under the cover of a short artillery barrage. Up until now, the PLA hadn't fought against a well-trained and determined enemy. They were starting to find out just how tough the Americans and Israelis really were as thousands of their fellow countrymen lay dead, wounded and torn apart all across the ground between their positions and the Americans.

By the time the battle was over, Gunny Thornton could see he was down another nine Marines killed and nineteen injured. Of the nineteen wounded, twelve had to be moved back to the aid stations and would not be returning. His platoon had just gone from fifty-two Marines to twenty-four. He reported his losses to headquarters and requested additional reinforcements or a replacement platoon be sent forward. The Israelis still had close to a hundred able-bodied soldiers, though they had taken close to ninety casualties as well.

Gunny Thornton's platoon was ordered to fall back to battalion headquarters with the rest of the company. Another platoon was moving in to their position. One of the three remaining officers in the company had been killed, while another had been wounded, leaving the newest officer, a second lieutenant who had only been with the company for five days, in charge.
****

As Thornton sat with his platoon cleaning their weapons after the morning fight, a major walked toward him. He realized the man was his old lieutenant, Jack Lee. "Sir, it's good to see you. Congratulations on the promotion. A major now, eh?" Gunny Thornton said with a warm smile and a handshake. No one dared salute an officer near the front lines. It identified them as someone important and made them a target for snipers.

"It's good to see you too, Joe…I'm glad you've made it through all this. Our company has taken so many losses since we arrived here last month," Major Lee replied.

"It has been rough, but we're still here. What brings you over to my platoon?" asked Thornton.

"Well, I have some good news and some bad news. Which do you want first?" asked Major Lee.

"Ah. Give me the good news. I've had plenty of bad news lately."

Smiling, Major Lee said, "Congratulations, you've been given a battlefield commission. You've officially been promoted to first lieutenant."

With a look of surprise and eyes wide as saucers, he managed to stammer, "What? I was just promoted to gunnery sergeant."

Knowing Thornton might not be happy with a commission, Lee went on to explain the decision. "The Marines have taken some terrible losses, and you know that as well as anyone else. We've also lost a lot of officers. Your company is a case in point. You should have five officers in your company; instead you only had three, and all were replacements. Now you're down to one, and he's a brand-new guy fresh out of officer training school. You are a damn good Marine, Thornton. When asked who I would promote to officer out of your company, you were top of my list. That's why you're being promoted to first lieutenant. You'll be taking over command of the company. I'm promoting two more senior NCOs in the company as well. We need more officers and NCOs...right now, we're short on both," Major Lee said. There was just a hint of sternness in his voice, enough to convey that he didn't have a choice in the matter.

Joe could see that Major Lee might just be a little annoyed at him for not being more excited about this promotion. He had probably stuck his neck out to get him moved up the ranks, and now it might appear that he had been wrong. Joe moved to correct the direction of the conversation. "Thank you for the promotion, Sir. I didn't mean to come across as ungrateful. I was just a bit surprised."

Major Lee was relieved Thornton wasn't going to make a bigger issue out of this and continued, "It will be an adjustment, but I'm confident you'll rise to the challenge and lead your company. You'll need to make sure you attend the daily command briefings or send someone in your place. I'm transferring a senior first sergeant to your company to help you out with the administrative part. He knows you've just been promoted, so you don't need to explain anything to him. I also wanted to let you know that you've been awarded three medals: a Silver Star for combat action during the battle for Be'er Sheva, a Bronze Star for action during the capture of the Suez Canal, and the Purple Heart for that shrapnel you got in your arm during the battle for Be'er Sheva. We'll try to hold a ceremony for everyone being awarded medals in the near future."

"Wow, thank you, Sir. I'm not sure what to say to that, other than I was just doing my job, and so were my Marines," First Lieutenant Thornton replied.

"A lot of Marines did their duty, and a lot of them are going to be recognized for it. Before I leave, I have one more piece of bad information I need to give you. Our battalion is being moved to the rear to be reinforced. Once we've received our replacements, we'll be shifting positions and moving north as an antitank unit to support the army as they fight the Russians."

"Well, it's not as bad as I thought—fighting Russians or fighting Chinese doesn't really matter. Either one can kill you just the same," Thornton said, resigned to their fate.

With the business of promoting Thornton done, Major Lee moved on to find the other two NCOs he was turning into officers as well. The Marines had lost close to 5,548 personnel and another 12,321 were too injured to fight since the start of the war in Israel. Senior NCOs and officers were in short supply, which was why battlefield promotions were being awarded quickly as new replacements continued to arrive. Lieutenants who showed promise and initiative were being promoted to take over companies, or in Jack Lee's case, his battalion.

Chapter 19
The Coming Freeze

30 January 2041
Poznan, Poland
General Schoen's Headquarters

General Schoen's 10th Panzer Division had held the Russians for over a month. They had conducted attack and counterattack operations against the Russian Third Shock Army and successfully slowed the Russians down but not stopped them. The 13th Panzer Division had been mauled pretty badly in the south of Poland and was being consolidated into the 10th under General Schoen. The German and Polish armies had lost control of Warsaw and Krakow, along with two divisions of German light infantry in the process.

The Polish had lost most of their army near Bialystok when the Third Shock Army was able to break through the German 4th Infantry Division and had surrounded 82,000 Polish and 32,000 German soldiers. They held out for five days of heavy fighting before surrendering to the Russians, collapsing the Polish northern defensive positions. The Russians were now less than twenty miles from the German border, with only the 13th Panzer Division left between them and Germany. The American Fifth Army was still consolidating east of Berlin to go on the offense but had detached the 12th Armored Division to reinforce General Schoen. The 12th Armored Division was the one American division that was made up solely of the new Pershing tanks. These tanks were beasts and more than capable of engaging a numerically superior force and defeating it. The division was also augmented with an artillery brigade, which consisted of the M109A6 Paladin self-propelled 155mm artillery, and the M270 Multiple Launch Rocket System (MLRS), which could fire twelve rockets in less than forty seconds. One M270 vehicle could saturate one square mile with high-explosive cluster munitions or antitank bomblets or mines. With one battalion of MLRSs and two battalions of M109A6 Paladins, the division had a serious punch to it.

With the addition of the American 12th Armored Division, General Schoen had been able to stop the Russian advance for the moment. Then the winter storms had blown in with a flurry and shut down all military operations.

****

Over the past decade, the global climate had changed due to the Indian-Pakistan nuclear war. The conflict had blown an immense amount of dust particles into the atmosphere. This caused global temperatures to drop three full degrees Fahrenheit and increased the size of both the north and south polar caps. It had changed the weather enough that some once-fertile lands now had shorter growing seasons and others had longer growing seasons with the shifts in the jet stream.

During the Indian-Pakistan war, there were over 150 nuclear weapons used, each in the 10-kiloton to 30-kiloton range. Most were ground-burst detonations, which sent far more dirt particles into the air than a traditional air burst. New York and Baltimore had each been hit by 50-kiloton warheads, both ground bursts, throwing tremendous amounts of dust into the atmosphere. The United States had responded by hitting North Africa and the Middle East with over 130 nuclear warheads in the range of 100 to 300 kilotons, all of which were air bursts, since the President had wanted to minimize damage to the environment. Fortunately, the neutron bombs didn't leave any fallout beyond their initial lethal radiation, considering these were significantly larger nuclear weapons.

The increased fallout from the American bombs had thrown an enormous volume of particulates into the upper atmosphere. The results were even worse where they had been used over desert and more arid land. This soon began to wreak havoc on the environment and actually dropped the global temperature another five degrees Fahrenheit. Where it used to be in the upper nineties in Florida during the summer, it was now in the upper eighties. This drop in temperature and change in the jet stream, in addition to the immense amount of moisture thrown into the atmosphere from the New York bomb as it detonated in the harbor, had caused dozens of blizzards across the Northern hemisphere.

In February and March of 2041, numerous epic whiteout snowstorms struck the battlefields of Europe, in many cases forcing the battles to grind to a halt. Most of the Allied and even Axis equipment could operate in a blizzard, but the logistics of trying to coordinate large-scale armies through blinding snow that was accumulating at speeds making it nearly impossible for supply vehicles to move forced the warring parties to hunker down and wait out the weather. Fortunately, the meteorological conditions were giving the Allies the time they needed to continue moving armored forces and equipment into southern France and England.

The Sixth and Seventh Armies were still forming and using the blizzards to their full advantage. It would still be near the end of summer before these two armies were at 100%, but they could be used significantly sooner if need be. Alaska and the Pacific Northwest were also getting hammered with snow. This was slowing down the Army Corps of Engineers' ability to build the intricate defensive network they needed to repel any potential invasion by China or Russia.

Chapter 20
Spetsnaz

Three Months Later
26 March 2041
Boeing Aircraft Plant Kansas City, Kansas
Vice Presidential Speech

Vice President Michael Kern had been on a public speaking tour across the US, rallying support for the war and encouraging the American people. Kern had known Henry Stein for nearly twenty years before they had run for public office together. Kern had been a partner at a law firm that worked with President Stein's corporation as it evolved and grew over the years. Stein had made most of his money in real estate and urban development, turning blighted neighborhoods into family friendly locations with lots of parks and green spaces. He had also become quite adept at investing and had started a private equity company that was separate from his real estate business. As one business grew, so did the other, until Stein's PE company reached $4.8 billion in holdings. He'd timed the market right during the economic collapse in the 2020s, and while everyone was selling their stocks off, his PE company had gone on a buying spree, and so had his real estate company. When the economy did turn around, he had netted his investors a whopping 428% return in two years.

President Stein had picked Kern to be his VP because he wanted someone with a business law background. One of the first priorities and responsibilities given to VP Kern was to streamline the government rules and regulations governing the economy. Overregulation had stifled economic growth and made it harder for businesses to remain profitable; it was a jobs killer that needed to be corrected. Kern was a charismatic man and an exceptional public speaker, with an ability to connect with people, even in a large crowd. With the war moving into its fifth month, the President wanted his VP out among the people, growing the Freedom Party's reputation and cultivating a positive environment despite the war and the high casualties.

VP Kern had been making a televised speech at the newly expanded Boeing aircraft plant in Kansas City, KA. Boeing had added 4,600 new high-paying manufacturing jobs to the city and had plans to double that number by the end of the following year. With the horrific aircraft losses occurring in the Middle East and Europe, the demand for F22s, JF35s, and the entire suite of fighter and bomber drones was enormous. Lockheed Martin and Northrop Grumman couldn't handle the demand either, even though both companies had begun expanding their own manufacturing capabilities. This particular Boeing plant was going to be responsible for producing the latest Boeing fighter drones. The government had recognized that drones were faster and cheaper to produce, so they had placed an order for 16,000 units to be delivered as soon as possible.

****

While VP Kern was making his televised speech, a team of eight Spetsnaz soldiers began to set their ambush site for the VPs motorcade. The VP was traveling with the Secretary of Transportation, so being able to kill them both was a bonus. The night before the motorcade was to travel this particular route to the airport, one of the Spetsnaz members had attached several blocks of C-4 plastic explosive to the manhole covers along the VPs route. The explosion would destroy the lead vehicle and blow a hole in the road, making it impossible to pass. Then a second detonation 50 yards behind the first would occur, completely trapping the motorcade.

Once the motorcade was trapped, the plan was for several members to engage the vehicles with RPG7s and two heavy machine guns. If all went according to plan, the attack should take three to five minutes, tops. This particular Spetsnaz team had been designated to conduct political assassinations. They had already managed to kill a US senator and one Supreme Court justice. They had nearly been captured during their last mission and had barely escaped. They spent the last five weeks lying low at a country farm in Missouri, until their handler had contacted them and given them the details for the VPs trip to the Boeing plant. They had exactly three days to move to the target location, identify how they would attack Kern, and figure out how they were going to get away.

It was a tough assignment—one they were not sure they would survive. Then again, the opportunity to assassinate the Vice President was too big not to take the chance. That was after all, the height of their glory and their legacy, to hit the most influential target possible. After surveying the routes to and from the airport, they determined that the Secret Service would most likely use the frontage road along the interstate on their way to the airport because the interstate had had one lane closed for construction. Too many dangers could be hidden in a construction site for the Secret Service to take a chance driving along it; they would opt for the frontage road.

This smaller parallel route was flanked with some small industrial buildings and a forest preserve on the opposite side. This window provided them with the best position from which to launch an attack, hopefully allowing them to escape via the heavily wooded area. With the attack mapped out, now they just had to wait.

****

"That was a great speech, Mr. Vice President," said one of his aides as he took the VP's jacket from him before entering the SUV for the airport.

"Thank you, Richard. I sometimes wonder if my speeches get repetitive," said the Vice President as he ducked his head and entered the limousine. "Is the plane ready to go?" Kern asked the security detail in the vehicle with him.

"Yes, Mr. Vice President. We should be at the Lockheed plant by 4 p.m. We're still on schedule," replied one of the Secret Service agents. The convoy then left the Boeing plant and began to head toward the airport. The procession headed down a frontage road, just off the highway that ran along a densely wooded area. The Secret Service wanted to avoid the construction along the interstate.

As VP Kern was looking at his notes for the next speech, he began to change a few things around. Suddenly, he heard a loud explosion, and the vehicle abruptly stopped, causing him to scratch over his notes. Looking up, he saw the lead vehicle in their motorcade was on fire and there was a huge hole in the center of the road. Less than a second later, a second explosion happened, this time behind them. Just as the vehicle started to accelerate for the sidewalk in front of a small industrial building, they began to take heavy machine-gun fire. At first, the bullets didn't penetrate the vehicle, but within seconds, that soon changed; the engine and the front seat section of the vehicle were riddled with bullets. One of the agents quickly opened the side door of the vehicle and pushed the VP out of the vehicle to the sidewalk. Seconds later, the Secretary of Transportation's body was barraged with bullets, killing him instantly.

Whooshing sounds could be heard as RPG rockets flew into several of the support vehicles in the motorcade, causing them to explode and killing the occupants. More machine-gun fire came from several of the Secret Service agents, intermixed with what sounded like two heavy machine guns and several assault rifles. The VP tried to stand, following one of the agents to the door of a building near them, and was hit by several rounds to the chest and legs. He quickly fell in a heap and, to the eyes of the Spetsnaz team, appeared dead. Just as quickly as the fire fight had started, it ended. The team quickly abandoned their weapons as they disappeared into the woods they had been hiding in and made a run for their getaway vehicle.

Fortunately, the VP had been wearing a bulletproof vest under his suit. The vest had stopped the rounds—the VP had collapsed from the sheer concussion of the rounds hitting him and the pain of the two bullets that had torn through his right leg. One of the shots had nicked an artery; he lost a lot of blood before the Secret Service agent nearby was able to tie a tourniquet, saving his life.

Kern was quickly flown to a local area hospital, where he was treated for his injuries. After a week in the ICU, another week at a stepdown unit, and a month at a rehabilitation facility learning how to walk again, he would make an almost complete recovery. However, he would always have to use a cane from here on out.

Despite massive police canvassing of the area, the Spetsnaz team that carried out the attack was not found. The attack on the VP's motorcade reinforced the threat the various Spetsnaz teams posed and the need for their immediate capture. Unlike the Islamic Republic, the Russians targeted only military and government officials, not the general public.

Chapter 21
All is Not Quiet on the Western Front

31 March 2041
HIVE, Northern Virginia
National Security Briefing

The war in the Middle East ground to a halt shortly after the New Year. Several governing districts seceded from the Islamic Republic, taking Egypt and all of the African provinces and regrouping them to form the North African Confederation. The new country was led by a liberal Muslim leader who wanted nothing to do with the Caliph and his radical brand of Islam. Their leader denounced the actions committed by Caliph Mohammed and bemoaned that the world had been led to war, that 300 million Muslims had died, and that the Kaaba had been destroyed.

The new North African Confederation immediately sought a separate peace agreement with the United States and Israel, and they were granted one. Their new focus was on restoring order and communications throughout the country and reestablishing food supplies to their starving and dying nation. Tens of millions of people had been left homeless and destitute from the nuclear attack America had rained down on them. Fallout was everywhere, and the transportation system was a mess. Most of the region had also suffered from electromagnetic pulse damage as well, further complicating their recovery.

Millions were being relocated to Cairo now that the radiation from the neutron bomb had dissipated, alleviating some of the displacement crisis. Aside from the EMP damage, the infrastructure in Cairo had been largely left intact. Of course, there were over ten million dead and decomposing bodies throughout the city that needed to be removed and either buried or burned. The city had been abandoned for nearly a month after the bomb had gone off. Now it was being repopulated as refugees poured in from around the country.

The rest of the IR continued the war, along with the Russians and Chinese. Neither side wanted to commit additional forces to capturing Israel and removing the Americans from the region, nor did they want to admit defeat. The war had settled into static lines, with trenches and fixed positions being developed. Israel had regained its original territory, plus a ten-mile buffer zone inside of Lebanon, Syria, Jordan and the Sinai, along with the Suez Canal. The Chinese reinforced their position and maintained 290,000 troops in the region, while Russia had withdrawn troops and left 310,000 in place while they focused their efforts on Europe.

The US continued to maintain a force of 560,000 troops in Israel and assisted the Israeli Defense Forces in training the hundreds of thousands of volunteers from around the world that had joined the IDF militia forces. As the militia units became more proficient, they were integrated directly into the IDF. The US had also been providing the IDF with thousands of older military vehicles and equipment from the various Army boneyards. The equipment wasn't modern by any means, but it was free, armored, and still functional enough to shoot and kill with it.

The IR still had nearly one million troops in and around Amman. The civilian volunteers that had swelled their ranks to nearly three million a few months prior had been transferred into the regular army and were in various training facilities spread throughout the Republic. The IR was still committed to the war; they just weren't actively fighting or looking to advance conflict until they were able to rebuild their army and air defense capability.

Through the help of the militias, the IDF had swelled to over 800,000 soldiers. The Allies' plan was to restart offensive operations at the end of spring, allowing the Israelis enough time to fully equip and train their forces. This time, they would defeat the IR and finally knock them out of the war entirely.

Europe, on the other hand, was a complete mess. Aside from nearly two months of blizzards, the Russians had captured Romania, Hungary, Serbia, Bulgaria, Macedonia, Kosovo, Albania, Bosnia, Slovenia, half of the Czech Republic and nearly all of Poland. The fight now was centered in Austria, Germany and Croatia. The Americans had finally been able to get enough troops sent to Europe to aid the EU in stopping the Russians, but they lacked the military equipment to push the Russians back and liberate the captured territory. Britain had succeeded in stopping the Russians from capturing Iceland or being able to push their fleet out into the North Atlantic but had been unable to do much to stop them from capturing the Scandinavian countries of Finland and Sweden. They were still fighting the Russians in Norway with the Norwegian military and had managed to bog the Russians down. The

British had also transferred two armored divisions to Europe to help in the defense of the continent.

China had captured all of Southeast Asia and was invading Malaysia and the Philippines. They had left the Koreans alone, according to their agreement, at least for now. Japan remained neutral, despite their insistence they were going to join the war. American human intelligence sources had learned that Japan planned on staying out of the war for at least another six months. They had drafted two million conscripts who needed training; they were also finalizing the completion of a dozen missile cruisers and two additional carriers. President Stein was not convinced and had ordered the military move as much armor and heavy equipment as they could from Japan to Alaska. The goal was to relocate close to 70% of US forces from Japan to shore up the Alaskan defense.

Under the advisement of his national security team, President Stein began to build up the defenses in Alaska and the Pacific Northwest. China had successfully captured everything they wanted in the Pacific, with the exception of Australia. It was believed by the intelligence community that they might turn their sights toward Alaska and the Pacific Northwest instead of Australia. The Chinese needed oil, natural gas and mineral resources to fuel their economy. These were all items the US had in abundance in Alaska and the Pacific Northwest. The military had moved the newly created American First Army (which would consist of 750,000 troops once they completed their military training) to the Pacific coast of the country. As more soldiers completed their military training, they would form the Second Army, which would also consist of 750,000 soldiers and would move to cover Alaska and the Pacific Northwest as a deterrent to any potential Chinese aggression.

The United States as a whole was still recovering from the loss of New York City and Baltimore. Most of the residents that needed to be relocated had been moved to new cities around the country or to various temporary lodging established by FEMA to help the victims. The weather, of course, was causing all sorts of logistical and recovery problems. Despite the challenges, the government and the American people were determined to help each other and to recover from this horrific attack.

The economy was one of the few bright spots. The US had reached as close to full employment as possible with the massive rebuilding of the armed forces and the thousands of infrastructure and construction projects across the country. With the loss of Manhattan and large chunks of New York listed as a hot zone, a new city needed to be built. Several sites were being considered for "New Manhattan," but nothing had been settled upon just yet. In addition to the thousands of construction projects, the military was still recruiting heavily and would swell to over eight million personnel, with another three million more to enter service by the end of the following year.

Wall Street had moved its operations to Chicago, consolidating with the Chicago Mercantile Exchange. More importantly, people had jobs, and overall, they were high-paying jobs as the economy continued to roar. With the loss of trade between the US and China, there was an enormous demand for products and consumer goods that used to be produced in Asia and now needed to be produced at home in the US (and, to a large extent, South America and England).

As the boom continued, the provinces in Mexico began to return to normal and stabilize. There were still incidents of violence and guerrilla activity, but the Mexican people had good high-paying jobs due to the numerous infrastructure projects, and as a result, they really began to see an improvement in their own communities. This made it more difficult for the insurgency to continue as more and more people realized they didn't want to go back to the way things used to be prior to the Americans getting involved. Their lives and the lives of their children were now significantly better than they had been under the old Mexican regime.

The FBI, US Marshals Service and the DOJ had completely revamped their entire police training program and, with significant assistance from several private contracting companies, were training 10,000 new police officers per month in Mexico. These new police officers were given mentors from American law enforcement to help guide them, and they learned how to develop a good community presence and a working relationship that was absent the corruption that had been so rampant under the old regime. There were large rewards issued for individuals that the intelligence community had identified as criminal and insurgent leaders, which placed additional pressure on those causing trouble.

Throughout the recovery, the US government continued to operate underground until the threat of a potential Russian nuclear attack was defused. President Stein and President Fradkov agreed to keep the war conventional. However, just as the government was about relocate back to the White House, several Spetsnaz teams began to attack older presidential bunkers and even managed to kill a number of high-ranking Congressional leaders.

The attack on the Vice President had infuriated the American public. The US had had enough of the attacks against their political leaders and civilians. Most people had now resorted to openly carrying firearms, making it more challenging for law enforcement to determine if an attack was about to happen or there was just a group of armed citizens protecting their families as they went to the mall. With assistance from the Trinity Program, several Spetsnaz teams were rooted out and eventually captured or killed. Now that the threat was reduced, the President wanted the government to relocate back to Washington, D.C., on April 1. It was time to return the government functions back to the capital.

The administration's secretive Trinity Program was proving to be the most complex and intrusive surveillance program ever developed. It had identified over 12,000 foreign agents operating in the US in one capacity or another and enabled the FBI and DHS to apprehend these individuals, limiting their covert actions. The level of crime across the country had also dropped immensely as police were now receiving accurate and timely shared intelligence from the Trinity targeting data for specific high-crime activities across the nation, such as murders, rapes and gang-related violence.

As the President walked through the hallway on his way to the last national security briefing in the HIVE, he couldn't help but think to himself how silly it had been for him to have initiated the COG and moved the entire government underground. Between the political assassinations and the terrorist attacks, it had seemed like the right decision at the time. Perhaps it had been the right call, but maybe they should have returned to Washington sooner. President Stein walked into the Situation Room and signaled for everyone to remain seated while he walked around and took his seat at the head of the table.

"Let's get this meeting started. Where do things stand in Europe?" asked the President, looking at General Branson.

"Yes, Mr. President. General Wade is currently on track to start his spring offensive. He's received 2,500 M1A4 battle tanks that we took out of mothball and refurbished, adding to the 4,000 he currently has. He also received our latest supply of Pershing tanks straight from the factory. He now has 900 Pershing tanks, which should be more than enough for his army groups to push the Russians back," General Branson explained.

"Our latest round of basic training recruits has also arrived in Germany. Our troop count in Germany now stands at 1.2 million, divided into two armies, although we're still extremely short on combat vehicles and other war materiel. The bulk of those soldiers are being leveraged as light infantry for the time being."

The President smiled and realized that for the first time in the last three months, they were finally going to hit the Russians and push them out of Western Europe. This war was devastating the EU, and so was the war with China. Global trade and shipping had all but stopped, with all sides sinking each other's shipping. "This is excellent news, General. Please let General Wade know he's to begin his offensive as soon as he believes they're ready. I want the Russians pushed out of Poland by the end of summer," commanded the President.

Secretary of State Jim Wise jumped into the conversation to add, "Mr. President, I have news about Japan that I believe we should discuss. It may change some plans in Europe."

Everyone turned to look at Jim and then to the President. "Ok, then please go ahead Jim, and let us know what you've heard from them," the President said.

"Mr. President, the Japanese told me they have a high-level agent in the PLAN, and this agent passed along some information about a future operation the PLAN is preparing to execute. Their agent said the PLAN has relocated most of their amphibious assault craft and troop carriers to the East China Sea for a big amphibious assault."

"Are the Chinese finally going to move against the Japanese?" inquired the President. He was thinking it would be poetic justice if Japan was invaded and then asked for help just as the US had demanded that the Japanese abide by the mutual defense pact, which they had so far failed to do.

"No, Mr. President. The Chinese have explicitly told the Japanese they would be invaded if they did not remain neutral in the war. Right now, the Japanese are content to remain neutral, and the Chinese are content to let them stay that way for the time being. What their agent said is that the Chinese are planning a massive naval assault against

Alaska and the Pacific Northwest," Jim said, a bit anxious about the information he was sharing.

General Branson jumped in and asked, "Do we know where in Alaska they're planning to invade or how many troops will be involved?"

"Before I answer that, the news does get worse. The Russians will be sending an expeditionary force of 250,000 troops as well. The Chinese, on the other hand, are going to be invading with an army of five million soldiers. They told me the primary target for the Russians is Nome, Alaska, while the Chinese will be going for the port facilities at Seward before advancing on Anchorage and then on to the state of Yukon, British Columbia, and Washington State."

General Branson sat back and thought for a minute about what had just been said, as did the President. "This does change the picture in Europe, doesn't it, General Branson?" inquired the President.

"Yes, Mr. President, it does. General Wade's offensive will need to rely on a steady supply of reinforcements from the States as recruits finish basic training. He will also require a steady supply of armor and other military vehicles. If we're shipping everything from the production line to Europe and his forces, then we won't have the equipment or force needed here to defend the homeland," General Branson said, ensuring he looked everyone in the eye to confirm that they understood exactly how bad this threat really was.

Sighing deeply, the President asked, "How much time do we have before this planned invasion, and what's the CIA's assessment of this?"

Director Rubio spoke up. "The CIA does believe the information to be credible. The various troop movements, ships and so on are consistent with preparations for an invasion. As to the timeline, the Japanese source says it'll happen within the next thirty to forty-five days. Our sources also believe that timeline is accurate."

"Then we don't have much time, do we?" pondered the President aloud. "What are your suggestions, gentlemen?"

General Branson signaled to speak first, saying, "Mr. President, I recommend we move quickly to get as much of our equipment and troops out of Japan and to Alaska as possible. We also have 400,000 new recruits coming out of basic and advanced training in two weeks. I move that we send them all to Alaska and begin building up the defenses. We'll also need to move additional mobile laser systems and mobile railguns once the roads start to clear from the snow. These blasted blizzards are really hurting our ability to build up any sort of defenses."

General Rice, the Air Force Chief of Staff, added, "We have 400 fighter drones being delivered from the factory next week. I will order all of them to Alaska. That will bring our manned aircraft to 300 fighters and our fighter drones to 1,100. I know the Navy has been hit pretty hard, but if they can focus their subs in the Alaskan waters, that would greatly aid our defense."

Admiral Juliano knew he had to do something, because his submarine force had been getting hammered. The Chinese had sunk five submarines in the last three weeks in the South Pacific. "I can transfer three subs from the South Pacific, but that's about it. I only have seven operational attack submarines in the Pacific; I've lost twelve subs in the last three months, five in the last three weeks. I can move three of our cruise missile subs, but with the laser defense systems they have, I'm not convinced they'll be very effective. Right now, they're causing havoc, hitting their shipping lanes, which of course are less protected than their carrier fleets."

Knowing he needed to offer more, Admiral Juliano decided this was a good time to bring everyone up to date on a secret Navy initiative to reclaim the waters of the Pacific. Taking a deep breath before continuing, Admiral Juliano explained, "There's a new weapon that we've been developing for some time that we believe could be a game changer. It's our new Swordfish underwater drone, or SUD. It's going to be the first of what we hope to be many UDs we are currently developing—"

The President interjected to ask, "—Is this something that can be deployed in the next thirty days?"

"Yes, Mr. President. We have two of them completed—one of them just finished its test trial and is being moved to Anchorage as we speak."

"I think I was briefed about this when it was still a concept. Can you bring us up to speed on this, Admiral Juliano?" asked the Secretary of Defense.

Juliano opened a file on his tablet and began to play several test videos and demos of how the new weapon would work. "Essentially, the SUD is an underwater Reaper Drone. It has a speed of 70 knots, a depth of 2,000 meters, and an unlimited range. It carries eight of our new advanced antiship torpedoes."

The President raised his hand for the admiral to pause for a second and interpolated, "Tell me more about these antiship torpedoes and how they're different than the ones we're currently using on our submarines."

Having known the President might ask this, Admiral Juliano pulled up the dimensions of the current torpedoes and the new torpedoes. "As you can see, the newer torpedoes are much smaller, about one-third the size of the current torpedoes, but they're significantly faster and have a much longer range. The newer torpedoes have a 60-mile range, giving the attacking submarine, or in this case the SUD, a much higher survival rate. The newer torpedo uses a new detonation chemical component that makes the torpedo three times as explosive. It also uses a much newer AI targeting software, so once the torpedo is launched, it has the approximate GPS and depth of the target it was fired at and proceeds toward it without an active sonar. Once the torpedo gets within two miles of the target's last known position, it activates its sonar, but at that range, it's too late for the target to evade."

"This new torpedo sounds amazing," the President said. "So, how are we going to make use of it now?" asked the President, eager to find a way to employ it quickly.

"We still have a few bugs to work out in the new torpedo. Some of them have been failing to detonate on impact. We're not 100% sure what's causing the failure, but we hope to have it worked out over the next few months. As to why they're not on our current subs, presently the torpedo doesn't fit on them. Our new submarines being built going forward are going to use the newer torpedo, which we're calling the Hammerhead. The SUDs will also use the Hammerhead, and so will our antisubmarine helicopters and aircraft starting at the end of the month. We presently only have a small stockpile, and they've been allocated for the two SUDs that we have," the Admiral said while going over the inventory numbers and the projected monthly delivery numbers from the factory.

"How soon could we retrofit our existing fleet of submarines to use them?" asked General Branson.

"We are already working on that right now. The older Los Angeles attack submarines that we're taking out of mothballs are having their torpedo tubes retrofitted to use the Hammerheads while they're in dry docks getting the rest of their upgrades completed. The timing of this works out well because they needed to be in dry dock to have their sound proofing upgraded, along with their propeller screws. We anticipate having eight of them ready for service starting in June and will have eight more a month coming into service until all forty-four have been brought out of mothballs," the admiral said with a smile.

The President smiled from ear to ear and said, "Admiral, this is great news. Absolutely wonderful. How many of the new SUDs are going to be coming online per month as well?"

"We have the first two right now, and we're supposed to receive a total of eighty of them over the next three years. I'm working with the contracting company to expedite them, but some of the materiel needed for them are also being heavily used by the Pershings."

General Branson jumped in to say, "We will have to stick to that timeline then, Admiral. The Pershings are far too important right now to cut back on their production. The Chinese and Russians both have a new MBT coming online soon that we haven't yet seen."

"I have to agree with the general on this one, Admiral. We'll have to stick to the timeline the manufacturer is giving you then. I'm not ready to shift resources away from the Pershings. We're still working on solving the materiel problem," the President concurred.

The admiral paused for a moment, not sure if he should bring up the following topic or not. "I had heard from one of my science advisors that some of the rare materiel that we use in the new armor for the Pershings can actually be found on the moon in the asteroids. If that's the case, then is there any way we can collectively find a way to acquire more of it? I mean, if this materiel is so rare and yet so vital to our military equipment, how can we obtain more of it so we can ramp up our production?" asked Juliano, hoping he didn't sound crazy.

The President was actually surprised to hear the admiral ask this question and clearly wanted to discuss this more, but his own science advisor wasn't in the room to facilitate that discussion. "You bring up a good point. I believe we'll have to have that discussion at a later date when I can bring in the chief scientist who's leading that effort presently. Professor Rickenbacker is at one of our other facilities right now."

Turning to look at Monty, the President directed, "Monty, arrange for a special science briefing with the professor to bring us up to speed on some of the new technologies they've been working on. Let's see if we can do this sometime next week. Also, gentlemen, this meeting that you'll be invited to will be 'eye's only.' No aides, no notes and no recording devices," the President said secretively.

A chorus of "Yes, Sir" could be heard as the President turned back to General Branson. He wanted to continue with the briefing. "Gentlemen, we have limited resources right now. We need to figure out how we're going to defend Alaska and British Columbia. If the Chinese are able to establish a base of operations and a foothold there, they'll flood troops and materiel in by the millions, positioning them to invade the rest of the country. We need to buy time until we can produce more military equipment and get more recruits through training," the President directed.

General Branson pulled up maps of some different areas in Alaska and began to address the group, saying, "We may need to give ground to buy more time. We can plan on putting up one blistering attack and try to prevent the initial landings, but if they are successful, then we'll need to pull our forces back and try to turn this into an asymmetrical war of attrition. We're building multiple layers to our defensive lines throughout Alaska and British Columbia, but as you know, the blizzards have been hampering this effort a lot.

"One good note—we have the training facilities up and running, turning out a hundred thousand soldiers a month for the South American Expeditionary Force. We anticipate having this force ready for deployment as its own army by the end of summer. If the situation warrants it, then we can use them in Alaska instead of Europe," General Branson said, sounding very optimistic about their chances in Alaska and the overall war effort.

"We still need to make a decision on Europe. Do we continue with our offensive in the spring, or do we continue a defensive action and focus on Alaska?" asked the Secretary of Defense.

The President knew a decision about Europe and the Middle East needed to be made, so he took charge. "I want General Wade to hold off on his offensive. Tell him to hold in place. This will give the EU more time to grow their military and their military manufacturing capability. Use everything we have to hold Germany and keep the Russians at bay. If General Wade believes he needs to launch a limited offensive to do that, then he may, but unless the entire Russian front falls apart, he is to hold Germany and not get sucked into Eastern Europe. Tell General Gardner he is to proceed with his offensive. I want the IR knocked out of the war so we can focus on these other theaters. Once his heavy combat operations are done and it moves to an occupation, we can look to move some of his heavier armor units to Europe and bolster our forces there."

Everyone in the room rose as the President stood up to leave the room and quickly begin putting into motion the plans they had just discussed.

Chapter 22
Operation Red Dawn

Day 122
3 April 2041
Moscow, Russia
National Control Defense Center

The National Control Defense Center (NCDC) facility was just down the road from Red Square. The NCDC was a massive edifice that had replaced the older Ministry of Defense building in the mid-2020s. This center could control all military activities around the globe and run the entire economy and country if need be. Once the world powers had agreed to keep the war conventional, President Fradkov had begun to spend more and more time at the NCDC. The facility boasted a nuclear shelter in the basement and was connected to a number of other critical locations throughout the city via underground tunnels as well.

The war in Europe and the Middle East was going about as well as they had hoped for up to this point. Russia had secured all of its former satellite countries and was devastating the EU. The Americans might have stopped them at the German border, but that would change with the coming summer offensive. In the meantime, the MiG40s were causing havoc among the Allied air forces. The only thing preventing Russia from having full control of the skies was the limited inventory of MiG40s available.

The Allies were slowly figuring out how to track and identify the new MiGs, which had led to several of them being shot down. For the moment, Russia controlled the high-altitude fight—everything above 15,000 feet. Below that level, the Doppler radars the Americans had would guide the laser defense systems or railguns in the area to their location. Fortunately, the MiG could also carry six guided bombs, enabling them to attack Allied laser and railgun systems from a high altitude. If the radars on the lasers or railguns could detect the bomb fast enough, they could engage and destroy it; however, the percentage of successful hits was typically around 30%, still making the effort to attack them more than worthwhile.
****

President Mikhail Fradkov walked into the war room in the basement of the Kremlin to discuss the war effort, the summer offensive and the Alaskan invasion: Operation Red Dawn. "Generals, please be seated. We have a lot to discuss, so let's get to it. How are the invasion plans going with the Chinese?"

General Gerasimov, the head of the Russian military, began his brief. "We have eight additional troop carriers and two roll-on/roll-off transports at our port in Vladivostok. We have 1,800 main battle tanks and 2,400 light drone tanks in port ready to go. The plan calls for the Chinese to conduct a massive missile and air attack for several hours before the invasion starts, in order to pound the American positions a bit before the landings.

"We have 300,000 troops ready to go when the Chinese are ready to move. Operation Red Dawn should start on May Day, the first of May. The Chinese plan on invading at nine different locations along the Alaskan coast, which will draw away most of the American Air Force. We believe we should have the upper half of Alaska secured by the end of summer, before most of it becomes impassable due to the weather. We will also be inserting several thousand Spetsnaz units throughout Alaska to attack their airfields, supply depots and critical communication nodes throughout central and northern Alaska." The general spoke with an air of confidence that bordered on arrogance as several images of airfields and communication targets were shown.

With Operation Red Dawn starting to draw more resources away from the European theater, Sergei Puchkov, the Minister of Defense, needed to determine what they wanted to do in the Middle East. So, he boldly interrupted the discussion. "—Generals, Mr. President, we need to discuss our strategy in the Middle East. Intelligence indicates the Americans are going to start a new offensive shortly, and prior to that happening, we need to determine our strategy. Are we going to send more reinforcements and launch a counteroffensive, or are we going to withdraw our forces and use them somewhere else?"

President Fradkov had initially wanted to destroy the Americans and Israelis, but that had been proving harder to achieve than they had originally thought. The Middle East was turning into a meat grinder, and the question was—how much longer did Russia want to continue to fight in it? If the Americans hadn't committed so many troops to defending Israel, Russia never would have committed so many troops to the Middle East. At this point, the fight was forcing the Americans to battle on more fronts than they were effectively able to do.

"Generals, the fight in the Middle East is a fight we need to stay committed to, as it ties down immense amounts of American resources. These are assets they cannot commit to Europe, or soon to our operations in Alaska. We will reinforce the Second Shock Army as appropriate. Is that understood?" questioned the President.

"Yes, Sir."

Wanting to get back to the European front, the President wished to discuss the new tank that they had been developing and how soon it could be ready for action in Europe. "Minister Puchkov, what is the status of our new battle tank? Is it ready for action?"

Minister Puchkov opened some folders and started displaying some pictures, video and stats of the new T41 main battle tank on the holographic display. "The T41 is going through its trial runs right now. The blizzards have been slowing some of these tests down, but we have determined that the main weapon functions to our satisfaction. The issue we are still trying to work out is the power supply. The T41 is a tank, but it is a very slow and cumbersome vehicle that will rely heavily on other support vehicles around it in its current iteration. Right now, the top speed of the T41 is roughly 22 miles per hour, and it has a range of about 200 miles."

Not happy with these numbers, the President asked, "Why is the vehicle so slow and cumbersome? This is not what was briefed last month. Back then, everyone said this new tank could keep up with our armored forces and would be a good counter to the American Pershing tanks. What has changed since our last discussion?"

"The power generation changed. The tank can fire just ten shots before it needs to idle and recharge for about an hour. Each individual shot requires about fourteen minutes of recharge before firing again. We thought we could get about thirty shots from the battery pack before it would need to idle, but once we started to test the laser against the Pershing's armor, we learned we were wrong. The energy used by the laser needed to be increased by some 300% for it to penetrate the Pershing's armor. This dropped the number of shots the battery could hold. To augment this, we had to build a new, larger power generator, which in turn meant a redesign of the rear mount. All of these changes added an extra ten tons of armor and weight to the vehicle that was not in the initial design," answered Minister Puchkov.

"Mr. President, if I may—I would like to suggest that we send the T41 back to the designers to figure out how they can better integrate these new design changes. I don't want to have some unreliable new tank on the battlefield, or worse, taking up production capacity and materiel," said the Commanding General for the Russian Armed Forces.

"I agree. Let's send the T41 back to the drawing board. I want a new prototype ready in 90 days, something that incorporates these new design requirements," the President said as he ended the meeting.

Chapter 23
Trifecta

Day 125
05 April 2041
Amman
Axis Powers Command Center

The Russian commander for the Second Shock Army was meeting with his Chinese counterpart and the IR military leadership to discuss the pending operation. They knew the Americans were going to launch an offensive soon, and they wanted to launch a spoiler attack to throw them off balance. The challenge was going to be determining how to attack an Allied army that had now swelled to over one million troops with a force close to that same number. When launching an assault, it was best to have a five-to-one advantage, which they clearly would not have.

General Abdullah Muhammed was the overall military commander for the IR in Israel. He knew the Russians and Chinese wanted to launch a new offensive, but they lacked the numbers to make it successful. That meant the IR would have to bear the brunt of the manpower used in this next offensive. "General Lodz, I agree that the Americans are going to launch a new offensive, probably in the very near future. I am authorized to commit up to one million IR regular army forces, but that is the extent that I can pledge. Any more and we lose the ability to even prevent the Allies from invading our own lands."

"General Muhammed, I understand your concerns, and they are valid. We will accept your contribution, but I would like to have operational control over them so that I can coordinate their attacks properly with ours," General Lodz said, knowing this was a bit of a reach.

Having realized already that this request might come, General Muhammed had already made his mind up to agree. The IR had already fouled up the first invasion and lost nearly 1.5 million troops. If the Russians believed they could do better, then perhaps it would be best for them to take the lead. "I am reluctant to agree to this; however, we share the same goals, and I want to see the Allied army crushed before it can gain in strength any more than it already has," General Muhammed responded.

General Fang, the overall military commander for the Chinese First Expeditionary Force, saw this as an opportunity to get some additional forces for his own army group. His reinforcements were still a month away, and the Russians wanted to launch this new offensive immediately, not wait for Chinese reinforcements. "General Muhammed, if I may. China would like to request a much smaller contribution of forces from the IR. We are going to make a push for Southern Israel and attempt to cut them in half, whence we can then take control of the Suez. We would like the IR to commit 200,000 troops to our effort," Fang requested, hoping he could strike a deal, especially since he had asked for one-fifth the number of troops.

"General Fang, the IR appreciates everything the Chinese have done to help us. Because of this, I will grant your request. You will receive 200,000 IR reinforcements and their commanders will report to your chain of command for the duration of the operation," General Muhammed replied, having already anticipated this entreaty as well. The Chinese had assisted the IR tremendously these past four months, so there was no real way he could turn down their invitation and not insult them.

"Excellent, then we will begin to issue orders to the respective units and prepare for the coming attack. The offensive will begin in four days. We need to move quickly, as our intelligence sources say the Americans plan to start their offensive in five. We need to throw them off balance before they are able to get organized into their offensive formations. I also have two additional squadrons of MiG40s en route to our positions in Turkey; they will begin providing high-altitude air cover and precision bombing of the enemy laser and railgun positions just as they have been doing in Europe. This will limit the Allied air support capability and increase the likelihood of our success. My military planners will send the details to your staffs immediately so you can plan accordingly." General Lodz was authoritative as the overall area commander. Muhammed and Fang both nodded in compliance and left for their respective commands.

General Lodz had been General Kulikov's executive officer for several years prior to being promoted and given command of the Second Shock Army. General Lodz was a brilliant tactician and military leader. He had led the modernization efforts to turn the older Shock Army concept into a 21st-century killing machine, heavily incorporating the use of drone tanks and infantry fighting vehicles.

****

The following four days were a flurry of activity as hundreds of thousands of troops began to move to their various jump-off points and the MiG40s arrived. The increased MiG activity had an immediate impact; four MiGs had been shot down during the preparations, but they had shot down sixty-eight Allied aircraft and destroyed five laser defensive sites and twelve mobile railgun antiaircraft systems.

The arrival of additional MiG40s was a complete surprise for the Allies, who had only been dealing with them in limited numbers in Europe, not the Middle East. The Allies' worst fear was starting to come to fruition; enough MiG40s were being produced that the Russians could now field them in two active war theaters in greater numbers. Unbeknownst to the Allies, the two squadrons of MiG40s were actually part of the European group. The Russians had transferred two of their five squadrons to the Middle East specifically to support the upcoming operation. They would be returned to Europe once the campaign was completed. The Russians were still only able to produce thirty aircraft a month, which barely kept up with the losses. It would be another three more months before production levels would reach sixty aircraft a month, and a year before it would reach 120 a month.

The Russian offensive started off like all Russian attacks; there were immense amounts of artillery and rocket attacks, quickly followed by scores of tanks and mechanized infantry in their wake. The MiG40s were in the sky and quickly downing Allied aircraft, trying to attack the Russian armor units and bombing mobile railgun and laser systems as they found them. The goal was to use the artillery and rockets to draw the laser and railgun systems out into the open, then destroy them with direct munitions from several of the MiG40s, which were designated purely for bombing missions, while the other MiGs were hunting for Allied aircraft.

The assault was swift and vicious, as most Russian attacks were, and was followed up by an attack from the Chinese six hours later. The goal was to distract the Allies and draw additional forces to the north to deal with the Russians. Then the Chinese would launch their own attack in the south against a weaker Allied flank.

Chapter 24
Modern Trench Warfare

Day 126
07 April 2041
Near the Lebanon Border

Sergeant Jordy Nelson's company was part of the 1st Infantry Division, 1st Brigade, which had been in Israel since the start of the war. The 1st ID had been involved in every major battle that had taken place, from the invasion of the Jordan Valley and the siege of Jerusalem to the counterattack to retake Jerusalem and the Jordan Valley. After a short break in the fighting, the 1st ID was pulled from the line and given thirty days to rest and regroup as new reinforcements arrived. By the time this reprieve had taken place, the entire division had suffered a casualty rate of 62% either killed or wounded. The division was a shell of its former self and as new replacements arrived, the division would regain in strength and be moved back to the frontlines.

Sergeant Nelson had started the war as an E-5 sergeant. During the reorganization and rest period, he had been promoted to sergeant first class E-7 and given command of a full platoon. They were now assigned to the front lines in Lebanon, facing off against the Russians.

Jordy Nelson had joined the Army after high school, just as his brother had done two years prior. They came from a low-income family with no way to pay for college, so they had joined the military to get the GI Bill and pursue their dreams of college after their four years were up. Jordy had made good use of the college courses being taught on base and nearly had 30 credits completed. When they offered him a $35,000 reenlistment bonus for two more years, he couldn't resist. Knowing a war was on the horizon, most soldiers were reenlisting and taking the money rather than waiting to be called back up from the inactive ready reserves. His brother had already served his eight years and now had a cushy job working for AFC.

As SFC Nelson was walking along the defensive network that his platoon had established, he was impressed with the progress they had made. Their battalion had been assigned to defend this ridge about a month ago, and they had been hard at work ever since. The ridgeline was covered in dense green trees and undergrowth. The valley below it was also covered in the same lushness, and had there not been a war going on, it would have been beautiful. For now, it just presented an obstacle to their defensive effort.

Once they had established their reinforced trench lines, foxholes and machine-gun bunkers, the men immediately began to clear the underbrush and trees for up to four hundred meters in front of their positions. Rows and rows of barbed wire, antitank objects, tank mines and Claymore antipersonnel mines were laid throughout the four-hundred-meter kill zone. They had also preregistered artillery and mortar positions, so if the Russians did advance, they were ready for them.

One of the most unique and game-changing weapons of the war was the railgun. The M5 AIR fired a .25mm round. The venerable M2 .50-caliber heavy machine gun (or Ma Deuce as the infantry called it) was augmented by the new heavier railguns, which fired a 20mm antitank projectile. This round could penetrate armored personnel carriers and all but the heaviest of Russian tanks. Unlike the railguns used by American tanks, these heavy infantry weapons didn't have the barrel length to generate the needed speed to penetrate the heavy armor of Russian main battle tanks. Despite this, they were incredibly effective at blunting an infantry attack. Unfortunately, the railgun itself, the ammunition and the power pack for it were not just heavy but difficult to move, which was why they were used in fixed positions and not carried as a heavy weapon like the old .50-cal machine guns were.

The platoon had established multiple heavy railgun and .50 cal positions aimed at covering their fields of fire and likely armored approaches. Word on the street was that the Army was going to start a new offensive soon; however, their group would not be joining. Their orders were to stay and man the defensive line. If the Russians did get frisky, they would be ready for them.

It was a bright and beautiful day with the birds singing and the smells of spring fresh in the air. One of Nelson's junior NCOs was walking toward him and asked, "Sergeant Nelson, some of the guys just got back with the extra ammunition you requested. They also picked up a few cases of grenades. You really think the Russians may try to attack before the new offensive?"

Thinking for a moment before responding, he replied, "I think it's possible. The Russians aren't stupid. They probably know something's up, and they may try to launch a spoiler attack. I heard those new MiG40s are here now in even greater numbers. If that's true, then you can bet they're getting ready for something." Privately, Jordy thought it was a certainty that the Russians would launch a spoiler attack, just as the IR had done right before the Americans were going to declare war on them last November. He had seen the US do the same thing if they thought it would blunt an enemy attack.

"Yeah, I heard the same thing about those new MiGs when we were back at the supply depot. I suppose you may be—"

"INCOMING, EVERYONE DOWN!" someone yelled.

Within seconds, heard the whistling shrieks of incoming artillery and rockets from the Russian lines beyond the horizon. Everyone dove into the trench lines and prebuilt bunkers as the rounds began to hit all across the ridgeline that their defensive network was built upon.

Round after round thrashed the ridge and the kill zones in front of their positions, turning a beautiful, luxurious valley forest into a moonscape wasteland within minutes. The ground shook with every rocket and artillery round, making it feel as if there was an earthquake. The roar of the explosions and the continuous concussions from the blasts was numbing to the soldiers in the machine-gun bunker Nelson had moved into. After thirty minutes of shelling, the Russian artillery and rockets moved to positions further behind SFC Nelson's position to hit the reserve and follow-on units. That was when the Russian infantry and armored vehicles began to show up.

Sergeant Nelson peered through his binoculars to see wave after wave of armored vehicles, tanks and infantry a couple of miles away, moving toward their positions. He immediately began shouting orders to his platoon and his radio operator.

"Get those heavy guns ready to start attacking those armored vehicles! I also want artillery to start hitting those pre-positioned targets. We need to break up their formations and start to thin them out before they get too close." Nelson had a sense of urgency in his voice. The particular bunker Nelson was operating out of was designated as the company's forward artillery post. They were responsible for coordinating the artillery and mortar fire for the company as they had one of the best vantage points of the trench line and the bunkers.

As friendly artillery impacted in the midst of the Russian tanks and infantry, the projectiles destroyed a number of tanks and other armored vehicles, blowing tracks off the vehicles. Some lucky hits blew the turrets off the tanks. As the rounds exploded, Nelson could see several infantrymen being thrown into the air like ragdolls and others ripped to shreds by shrapnel. Then the heavy railguns opened fire, demolishing numerous light drone tanks and infantry fighting vehicles. Several Russian infantrymen were cut apart by the heavy guns; legs, arms and heads were ripped apart from the soldiers' bodies as the fast-moving 20mm projectiles were devastating even when they did not directly hit a person. Just being nearby when a round flew by at Mach 5 was enough to tear a limb right off the body.

When a 20mm railgun round hit a light tank or light armored vehicle, it created a small entry hole and either bounced around inside the vehicle, killing everyone in it, or, in most cases, passed right through the other end of the vehicle. When it passed through the vehicle, it created a high-pressure vacuum that would crush the lungs of the individuals inside the tank and, in some cases, suck objects out the other end. It was a cruel but effective weapon, and since it emitted no smoke or flash when fired, it made it hard to identify where the rounds were coming from.

For twenty-five minutes, the Russians advanced toward their position under artillery and direct support from their tanks, until they were just about to enter the 400-meter kill box. At that moment, the Russian attack began to falter and then halted all together. It was at that moment the Russian artillery and rockets began to once again rain down on their positions, intermixed with smoke rounds to screen the Russian advance.

Sergeant Nelson had his platoon switch their HUD views so they could see through the smoke. As their HUDs cleared through the smoke, they saw the Russian armor and infantry advancing into their prepared kill zone and begin to activate the various mines.

SFC Nelson began to detonate various antitank mines as he saw armored vehicles either rolling over them or getting near them, disabling and destroying numerous vehicles while injuring the nearby infantry. The sound of the heavy railguns, the M5 AIR and .50-cals could also be heard as the men of his platoon aggressively repelled the invaders. The sound of the battle was deafening.

Despite the "hell on earth" being rained down on both sides, the Russians continued to advance until they were less than 50 meters from the American lines. The fighting was about to turn into hand-to-hand combat as the Russians rushed their positions. Soldiers reached for trench knives and bayonets, killing each other in a very personal manner. It was at that moment that SFC Nelson received a radio call for his platoon to destroy the heavy railguns and fall back to their secondary defensive positions. Next to each railgun position was a thermite grenade. The order was to pull the pin and ensure the grenade was over top of the gun and battery unit. The heat from the grenade would essentially melt the gun and make it unserviceable.

As SFC Nelson made his way out of the bunker and directed the soldiers around him to their secondary positions, he saw a group of Russian soldiers advancing quickly toward them. He raised his rifle to his shoulder and fired several short bursts, hitting several of them, but not before one of them threw a grenade at them. The grenade landed right next to five of his soldiers. One of the new privates who had joined their platoon only four days earlier jumped on the grenade just as it exploded. The soldier died instantly but saved his fellow soldiers. Several of the fighters around Nelson began to engage more and more Russian soldiers as they jumped into the trench line below them. It was time for Nelson and his men to make a break for it back to their secondary fighting position before they were overrun.

After three hours of intense combat, the Allies had to abandon their first line of defense. Within the following hour, they would be forced to abandon the second line as well. An Israeli armored division finally moved forward and engaged the Russians, forcing them to stop their attack. Two more Israeli infantry divisions and one American tank division with Pershings also moved to engage the Russian armored thrust and managed to blunt the rest of their attack.

The Allies had lost eight miles of land and all of their fixed defensive positions, but they had finally stopped the Russian advance. The Reds had hit their line with three armored and five infantry divisions. They had overwhelmed the 1st ID with an eight-to-one ratio, mauling them as they absorbed the brunt of the initial Russian offensive.

Chapter 25
A War of Attrition

Day 126
07 April 2041
2nd Marine Expeditionary Force
Near Hastor Ashbod Airbase

First Lieutenant Thornton's company had been stationed near the Hastor Ashbod Israeli airbase following 75 days of continuous combat. The battalion needed time to decompress, reorganize and integrate their new replacements. Lieutenant Thornton was sitting in the battalion command tent, along with the other company commanders, when word come down that the Russians and Chinese were launching a new offensive. Their battalion had been planning to move to their own jump-off position within 24 hours for General Gardner's offensive when the Russians and Chinese launched their spoiler attack.

Major Lee walked into the tent after talking on a command phone with his own higher-ups. "Marines, as you all have heard, the Russians and Chinese are launching a preemptive attack. Our guys in the north are getting hammered hard by the Russians. The 1st MEF is also getting blasted by the Chinese in the south. We've been ordered to reinforce the Army and the Israelis in the north. I know we're closer to the 1st MEF, but apparently the Chinese aren't hitting them nearly as hard as the Russians are.

"As of right now, the Russians have plowed through our entire defensive line in the north. The 1st ID suffered 30% casualties within the first six hours of combat and has been forced to fall back. Intelligence says the Russians are advancing with their entire force and a group of about one million IR troops as well. You all know the drill—have your companies ready to move within the next two hours. We roll out in support of an armor unit, so be ready. Dismissed." As Major Lee finished his speech, his officers quickly got up and began to head toward their units and infantry fighting vehicles.

The 2nd MEF had been heavily reinforced after their brutal mauling during the first 60 days of the war. They now had 60,000 Marines, along with 300 Pershing tanks and 800 M1A4 tanks. It took the battalion three hours to reach the edge of the battlefield, and what they saw reminded them of the first few weeks of the war. Off in the horizon, they could visualize hundreds of artillery rounds and rockets being destroyed by the railgun and laser defensive systems. Despite the valiant defensive efforts, hundreds of missiles and artillery rounds were impacting the American and Israeli positions. The sounds of tank rounds and the rumbling of explosions was nearly constant. It was a cauldron of death that they were driving into.

"Lieutenant Thornton, this is Echo 1. We are passing through the Israeli forces now and moving along the edge of the ridgeline, Jericho 1," said the lead scout vehicle in Thornton's company.

"Continue to move forward and be alert. See if you can find a defensive position for the battalion to hunker down," Thornton said to his scout leader.

Thornton's company was the lead element for the battalion of Pershing tanks they were escorting. His infantry battalion had been filtered into an armored brigade that was moving to engage the Russian armored units. Their mission was to provide infantry support to the Pershings and act as scouts to find the enemy and identify ambush positions.

The scouts continued to move along the edge of the ridgeline until they spotted half a dozen Russian tanks and dozens of infantry vehicles moving forward. They were currently engaging a dozen or so Israeli tanks that had just passed through ten minutes earlier. The scout leader found a good position, just shy of the top of the ridge, that would give them a clear field of fire without silhouetting them against the top of the ridgeline and making them easy targets for Russian tanks. The scout leader radioed in the position, and the battalion, led by Thornton's company, began to move into their new defensive position and set their trap.

Less than an hour after the battalion set up their positions and kill zones, a column of Russian infantry vehicles supported by some additional tanks made their way toward the Israeli positions, which took them right across Thornton's kill zone. They held their fire until the enemy vehicles had moved to the end of their kill zone.

"Open fire!" ordered Thornton.

The entire battalion opened fire as soon as Thornton's company did…the fight was over within five minutes. Multiple enemy infantry vehicles and tanks were destroyed before they could be pulled back. The

Russians managed to destroy several Marine tanks, including three Pershings, when a pair of MiG40s arrived on scene above their positions. The Russians called in artillery and rockets to pound the battalion positions and hold them in place while another Russian armored battalion maneuvered around the ridge to get behind the Marines. The Israelis, seeing the tank battle taking place not far from their positions, also joined in and began sniping Russian tanks and IFVs as they tried to maneuver around the Marines.

The Marines had anticipated a Russian move like this and had a pair of Razorbacks on standby in case. Minutes later, both Razorbacks arrived on scene and began to engage the Russian tank battalion. In just a few minutes, they had destroyed nine enemy tanks and seven infantry fighting vehicles. Unfortunately, several MiG40s were also in the area and swooped down from their high-altitude perch to launch a pair of air-to-air missiles, destroying one of the Razorbacks and badly damaging the second. A half dozen surface-to-air missiles jumped after the low-flying MiGs, destroying one while the other managed to get away.

After three attempts by the Russians to capture the Marine positions, the battalion fell back to another position that the scouts had found for them. They immediately did their best to disengage and fall back to their next ambush location and repeat the process. They would duplicate this progression four more times before they were relieved and told to fall back deeper into Israel. Their primary objective was to engage and then disengage the Russians, sapping them of their strength and constantly starting and stopping their offensive. As this played out, various IDF and other American armor units continued to maneuver around the Russian flanks, hitting them repeatedly and whittling their numbers down while rotating fresh Allied units into the fight.

Chapter 26
Bloodbath at Megiddo

Day 128
09 April 2041
Damascus, Syria
General Lodz's Headquarters

The Russian offensive was going better than they had anticipated. The arrival of two additional squadrons of MiG40s had made a tremendous difference. They continued to loiter high above the battlefield, and as laser or railgun defensive systems were identified by Spetsnaz units or scouts, the MiGs would engage them with guided munitions, exterminating them. Soon after they were destroyed, attack drones or helicopters would move into the area and attack the Allied armor and infantry positions. It was a somewhat slow process, but it was proving to be very effective.

The Russians had advanced into Israel and were fighting for control of Acre on the Mediterranean and Tiberias on the Sea of Galilee. Their goal was to capture the critical port facility of Haifa, and then the critical road junction at Nazareth. This would put them in a good position to drive down deeper into Israel and potentially capture Tel Aviv.

The Chinese, by contrast, had not broken through the Allied defensive line in the south at all, though they were tying down a lot of Allied forces, which otherwise would have been thrown against the Russians. It was for this reason that General Lodz wasn't furious with his Chinese counterparts for not proving to be better fighters. As long as they continued to hold dozens of Israeli and American divisions in place, those divisions couldn't be used against his own forces.

"Where do we stand with the battle right now?" General Lodz asked the senior IR general on his staff.

"We're close to a breakthrough right now. The problem is, we're grinding through your Russian armor units. I believe it's time to throw in my IR troops and save your reserve forces to follow in behind them," the IR general replied, eager to get the Muslim army involved again.

"Hmm...go ahead and send in eight divisions from your force to hit Acre. I want that city captured and our forces in Haifa by the end of tomorrow. I also want your forces to secure Megiddo as well. It's a critical road junction that we need to control. Is that understood?"

"Yes, General. It will be done," replied the general, immediately turning to issue orders to the officers near him.

In the following days, 160,000 additional IR infantry joined the 260,000 Russians attacking Acre and broke through the Allied positions. The Allies quickly fell back again, this time close to Hadera, to establish their next defensive line. Additional Israeli troops and militia units moved into the area to help the American Army and Marines try and stop the 420,000 troops bearing down on Tel Aviv. The battles around Megiddo and Haifa were turning into a real bloodbath on all sides as more and more troops, tanks, artillery and air support were being poured into the battles.

Casualties once again rose with each new offensive. In nearly four days of heavy fighting, the Americans had suffered 13,458 soldiers killed and three times that number wounded. Israel was once again turning into a meat grinder as the number of Americans killed since the start of the war in Israel now exceeded 100,000 KIAs with five times that many wounded.

Chapter 27
Redirect

Day 130
11 April 2041
Washington, D.C.
White House Situation Room

The President was starting to get worried. The new Russian offensive in Israel had dislodged the Israeli and American positions in the north of Israel, and now they were bearing down on Tel Aviv. The Americans had suffered another 68,000 casualties between those wounded and killed, the Israelis 92,000. The arrival of additional MiG40s in Israel was proving to be disastrous for the Allies. They were losing laser and railgun defensive systems, opening the Allied armored units up to Russian and IR air attacks.

In spite of the battlefield losses, the US economy was finally starting to produce the tools of war in the quantities needed now that they were focusing on one theater of operations and not spread across all three. The Americans were producing 400 Pershing battle tanks a month, and in those numbers, they would have enough to field the entire Army and Marines with them in eighteen months. The vehicle chassis was also being used in two new armored vehicles, an armored personnel carrier that could transport twelve infantrymen into battle, and a light drone tank and antipersonnel fighting vehicle (APFV), or Wolverine as it was now officially being called. The Wolverine was the newest drone vehicle to enter military service and could fight and function alone or in hunter-killer groups, much like the animal it was named after. It had a medium railgun that could take out other enemy tanks and multiple smaller railguns ideal for attacking enemy infantry. The vehicle was still six months away from first delivery but would be a game changer when it does arrive.

On the domestic front, the Trinity Identity Intelligence program had aided in the apprehension of thousands of Russian, Chinese and IR intelligence operatives and sympathizers. This greatly reduced the level of sabotage, assassinations and terrorist activity within the country. From the start of operations in Mexico, nearly 82,300 civilians had been killed by various terrorist attacks and targeted assassinations within the US.

The program also began to work on tackling other areas of high crime in America. This improved apprehension rates of criminals, reducing crime across the country. It also began to overpopulate the American prison system, which ironically provided an opportunity. Nonviolent prisoners were immediately moved into work gangs and began building defensive positions on the West Coast and in the Pacific Northwest, freeing up thousands of military engineers and soldiers for other critical duties.

Despite the war and massive government spending, the seizure of IR, Chinese and Russian assets, properties and businesses was paying for the war. It had also virtually eliminated the national debt. The challenge faced by America now was how to protect the West Coast and win the wars in Europe and the Middle East. The US mainland had 1.3 million soldiers in various units. The military still had another four million civilians to process through basic training, and another five million more that needed to be drafted. Twenty additional military training bases were being opened to increase the training capacity. Wounded soldiers from the various theaters were being reassigned as drill sergeants once they had recovered from their wounds. Then there were the Central and South American multinational armies that needed to be trained and equipped as well.

To further compound the training and equipment problem, the Middle East was once again turning into a black hole for equipment and troops. Every time things appeared to stabilize, a new offensive would start and the losses would pile up. Europe had been fought to a standstill, with horrific losses on all sides until the blizzards forced a halt to the killing. Fortunately, the war hadn't turned nuclear, but how long could that possibly last?

****

As the President entered the Situation Room and walked to the head of the table, he couldn't help but notice the grim faces on his military and civilian advisors. He could tell the state of affairs abroad must be dire.

"Gentlemen, I assume by looking at you that things must be pretty bad," the President said, trying to appear optimistic.

Mike Williams, the National Security Advisor, broke the silence. "They certainly could be better, Mr. President. General Gardner has established a new defensive line, and they appear to have stopped the Russian advance. They took some serious casualties, but so did the Russians and the IR."

"It's those blasted MiG40s. They're chewing our fighters and laser defense systems up," General Branson grunted, clearly irritated.

General Adrian Rice, the Air Force Chief of Staff, jumped into the conversation, saying, "We have a new radar being deployed right now that will change the situation. We're equipping the JF35s, F22s and our fighter drones with them now, along with our air-to-air missiles and the laser and railgun radar systems. It's going to take a few months to get this new piece fielded to every unit and aircraft. However, once it's completed, the MiG40 will show up on radar screens like a commercial airliner would. We *will* retake the skies."

The President had always liked General Rice; he was always optimistic, and no matter how bad the situation seemed to get, he found a way to solve problems. He was also the first Air Force General to rise through the ranks from the scientific track. He wasn't a fighter pilot, though he did have his commercial pilot's license. Rather, he was an Air Force researcher who specialized in drone fighter design and low-earth-orbit spacecraft.

"Excellent, General Rice. You have no idea how relieved I am to hear that we have a viable working solution for countering the MiG40. Soon the Russians will be able to mass produce these aircraft, and if we don't figure out how to challenge them, we're really going to be in trouble." Before turning away from General Rice, the President asked one other question. "Have we found a way to solve our satellite communications problem yet? This constant shooting down of our satellites and drones is becoming a problem."

"We're still working on that. Right now, we're looking at miniature satellites that are the size of a baseball. The challenge we have is that although they are small, they can still be destroyed by a ground-based laser. We're currently designing them to look like the space debris that's already in Earth's orbit, and we've been launching them in mass, using the space debris as a means to hide them," General Rice explained as he used his tablet to bring up an image of what he was talking about.

Mike Williams, the National Security Advisor, let out a soft whistle. "That is an ingenious approach—rather amazing if you ask me. How soon could something like this be in place?"

"We believe shortly, maybe a month. We have our 3-D printers working on them right now. We want to launch them from one of our high-altitude spy planes so that the delivery vehicle won't have far to travel before dispersing them. We hope we can get enough of the satellites dispersed before the Russians or Chinese figure out what we're doing and start to engage the area. To help provide cover for the operation, we're going to launch a couple of missiles at some larger space debris in the area to make the Chinese and Russians think that perhaps we are just trying to clear the debris so we can place a satellite in that area," Rice elaborated.

"I like it, General. Please continue, and keep us apprised. If we can get satellite communications and real-time surveillance operational again, this will greatly aid the war effort," the President said with excitement.

Sensing a pause coming soon, General Branson brought up one more point. "Mr. President, before we break—I would like to bring up the issue of Japan. As of right now, Japan is not going to come to our aid. With that said, I would like to move additional cargo aircraft to Japan immediately and evacuate as much of our critical equipment and personnel to Alaska and British Columbia as soon as possible. There are also three roll-on/roll-off cargo ships in port, not far from our naval station. They are there to move Toyota and Nissan cars from Japan to the US. I would like to recommend that we commandeer these ships and use them to transport a large majority of the heavy armor and equipment that we brought from Korea to the West Coast. We would, of course, compensate the ship owners, but for a short period of time, we would need to take possession of the ships."

"I understand the logic in moving the personnel and equipment, but why do you want to commandeer a ship that you know will cause a political uproar in Japan?" asked the President.

"Right now, we don't have enough of these ships on the West Coast, and frankly, if we don't move those tanks and other vehicles soon, they're likely to get stuck in Japan. The Chinese fleet hasn't sailed yet. Once it does, we won't be able to move that equipment, and chances are the Japanese will look to intern our forces and equipment for the duration of the war," Branson explained.

"Jim, what are your thoughts?" asked the President, wanting to get his Secretary of State's opinion.

"Right now, Mr. President, it's a bit tricky. The Japanese are in a hard spot. They aren't ready to stand up to the Chinese, even with our help. I believe if we act on this, we should let them know so that they don't throw up a lot of roadblocks. They can make a public stink about it to save face, but they will let us do it," Jim replied. He knew that the President wanted to avoid a problem with the Japanese but felt that this could be a workable solution as long as they left them an out.

"Jim, get with the Japanese and make sure this plan will work. General Branson, move forward with your plan," the President directed.

Chapter 28
Chinese Manifest Destiny

Day 140
21 April 2041
Beijing, China
Central Military Committee Command Bunker

The Chinese had consolidated their gains in Southeast Asia, securing Thailand and Singapore. They used these countries as jump-off points to invade Malaysia and the Philippines, further securing their hold on the South China Sea and the Malacca Straits. Prior to the war, nearly 95% of the world's shipping had passed through this region. As the Chinese secured more territory, they established new military bases and defensive networks in order to ensure that China would retain their newly won territories should the US or any other nation try to evict them.

The situation between China and Japan began to heat up once the Chinese learned of the American attempts to move their military force out of Japan to Alaska. The Reds issued an ultimatum to Japan— either intern the remaining US forces in Japan and sign a nonaggression pact, or be prepared to be invaded. Although in the past, the Japanese had been known to be fearsome warriors, they capitulated to the Chinese demands with relatively little resistance, and 11,345 American soldiers, sailors and airman were interned for the duration of the war. Fortunately, before the Chinese had caught on, the US had already moved the majority of their aircraft, naval ships and heavy equipment out of Japan to Alaska. The loss of troops would certainly hurt, but not nearly as much as the loss of equipment would have.

The Chinese continued the preparations for their offensive on Alaska. The invasion force would sail for Alaska on May 1 and arrive on May 15. This would provide the Chinese with the most optimal weather to conduct their assault and complete their objectives before the winter closed in and cancelled any further major offensive operations. Operation Red Dragon was on schedule.

The war in the Middle East was heating back up again. The Russians had made some significant breakthroughs and were pushing forward near Tel Aviv. They had asked for additional Chinese reinforcements to be sent so they could finish the Israelis and Americans off. The PLA agreed to send an additional 300,000 soldiers to the Middle East.

The Reds also sent an additional 250,000 troops to their bases in Africa. The Premier had decided that it was now time for them to exert their muscle in Africa and start their conquest of East and South Africa. The Americans were in no position to stop them, and with the invasion of Alaska happening soon, the Americans would be powerless to stop them. It was time for China to assume its position as the preeminent global superpower.
****

Premier Zhang Jinping gathered with his senior advisors and military leaders in the Command Bunker to discuss strategy. First, he looked to Admiral Wei Shengli, the commander of the PLAN, and asked, "Are we ready to begin the invasion against the Americans?"

"We are ready, Premier. The attack will commence on schedule. We will have six of our seven aircraft carriers with the invasion force. Once we have secured a beachhead and several of the airports, the PLAAF will begin ferrying in thousands of fighter drones and manned fighters."

During the 2020s and 2030s, the Chinese had started construction of six super carriers as they began to build out their blue-water navy. The Russians had provided a lot of expertise in building aircraft carriers, and the Chinese had also stolen a lot of the designs via well-placed spies within the American shipbuilding companies and through the rampant use of cyber-espionage. They had quickly incorporated the latest in American technology into these ships, as well as some of their own. During the fifteen years it took to build their blue-water navy, they had conducted numerous naval training exercises through both the Russian and US Navy partnership programs. Now these bastions of Chinese achievement were going to be put to the test.

"I have 150,000 naval infantry that will secure multiple beachheads for the PLA. These soldiers will be using the new exoskeleton combat suits. This will be our first major use of them. If they work as well as they are supposed to, then we will look at equipping the entire army with them," Admiral Wei Shengli said, confidently showing an image of what the new exoskeleton suits would look like.

General Fang Wanquan, the Commander of the PLA, jumped in at this point to ensure his thunder was not lost. "Premier, I have 4,400 light drone tanks and 3,800 main battle tanks in the following landings, along with 400,000 troops. I have another 1.6 million follow-on forces and 4,000 more main battle tanks that will arrive once we have secured our foothold. We will conquer Alaska by the end of the summer and begin moving down into British Columbia to threaten the American West Coast. During the winter months, we will move another two million more troops into Alaska," bragged General Wanquan, swelling with pride.

For nearly a hundred years, the rivalry between the PLA, PLAN and PLAAF had only grown. Each service believed they were the true protectors of the PRC. Their constant bickering and vying for attention and preference from the Premier was very annoying to their leader. At times, this caused a lot of problems for the PRC as the three groups seldom wanted to work together; this caused a host of coordination and collaboration issues that the Americans seldom had to deal with.

"Before this meeting ends, what was the outcome of the meeting our agents had with their Central and South American counterparts?" asked the Premier.

Clearly, no one wanted to give the bad news to the Premier. General Wanquan stepped forward to give it. "Premier, the meetings did not go well for us. Central and South America, with the exception of Bolivia, have chosen to join the Allies in declaring war against the PRC and have already formed a multinational army, which the Americans are going to train and equip. Our agents were able to estimate how many soldiers will be allocated to this multinational force, and we believe that they have collectively committed one million men and women to this new army, though that number could go much higher, if needed." He waited for the scolding he thought he was sure to get from the Premier.

However, the Premier only sighed before he replied, "It was a long shot getting them to join the Axis instead of the Allies. They already have their Grain Consortium, so it was going to be challenging getting them to leave that in favor of fighting against the Americans."

Jinping continued, "Admiral, I want more of our submarine forces sent to their waters. If they want to be a part of the war, then let's work on sinking their navy and commercial shipping. We may not be able to directly threaten their countries now, but that does not mean we cannot hit them with a few cruise missiles from time to time to remind them they chose the wrong side."

With that, the meeting was dismissed.

Chapter 29
STEM

Day 144
25 April 2041
Northern Virginia
The HIVE, 44th Floor—Science Division

The President had arranged for the Chairman of the Joint Chiefs, his National Security Advisor, and his Chief of Staff to be read into this presidential-level "eyes only" science brief. He needed counsel and advice from his trusted circle on what technology they should pursue and how they could employ it in the war.

All four men arrived by helicopter from the White House and went through several security checkpoints before they arrived at the 44th floor of the HIVE, which was the secured Science Division (SD) floor. This floor and the one above it were where DARPA had some of their greatest secret projects currently in progress. Away from the prying eyes of the public, and with extremely limited access to their floors, let alone the HIVE itself, their work was truly clandestine.

As the President walked up to the final checkpoint, he saw Professor Michael Rickenbacker, the Director of Special Projects. "Professor, it's good to see you. I hope you have some good news for us today," said the President as he shook his hand.

Smiling at the President, Rickenbacker replied, "I see you brought some people with you for this briefing. Are you sure you want to loop them into this?" he asked, a bit skeptical of the guests.

"Yes, I believe it's time for some additional people to be brought into the circle of trust. I need their counsel and advice, and more importantly, I need their perspective on how we can implement these new technologies to help us win the war."

After leading everyone into a small briefing room, the professor sighed for a moment as he turned down the lights and activated the holographic image display unit at the center of the table. "The information and programs I'm about to discuss with you are highly secretive. There are less than a few hundred people who even know about the main project, and less than five people who know about all of the projects combined. We did this for secretive purposes, but also to ensure we had no bleed-over between projects.

"The first project we are going to talk about is a technology called EmDrive." said the professor to the four men in the room. "Have any of you heard of it before?"

The Secretary of Defense looked around the room first before answering, "I believe you're talking about a power or thrust source that uses a resonant cavity to produce thrust without propellant. Correct?"

"That's partially right, yes. We're essentially talking about electromagnetic propulsion. Using an EmDrive device, we make an object float, change directions and accelerate or decelerate very quickly. If the device is built into an aircraft, the pilot would activate its engine and then the plane would start to hover or float. As power would be applied to the engines, the aircraft would begin to move in any desired direction. Using several directional engine ports, the aircraft would be able to climb, descend, accelerate or stop in seconds." Seeing the puzzled look on their faces, the professor brought up the image of a very advanced and futuristic-looking fighter aircraft.

"This fighter, which we're calling the F41 Archangel, leverages an EmDrive propulsion system. It burns no fossil fuels and doesn't emit the type of heat a standard fighter does. It can start, stop and turn on a dime and accelerate to speeds of Mach 10," the professor said with a smile on his face.

"Essentially, you've created a scramjet technology that needs no external fuel source and has one heck of a steering system, right?" asked Erik Jordan, the Secretary of Defense, skepticism in his voice.

The professor smiled at Mr. Jordan. "That's exactly what it can do. But it can do much more than that. We can incorporate essentially this same type of propulsion into virtually all of our current aircraft and increase their speed and maneuverability tenfold. The implications of this technology, just in the transportation sector alone, are amazing. We can also incorporate this into our space program, which is where we would see the greatest advancements," Professor Rickenbacker explained. He didn't get to talk about what he did very often, so he couldn't hide his delight. His face beamed with an almost devilish grin.

General Branson broke into the discussion. He wanted to talk further about the space implementations of this technology. "How else could this be used?" he asked.

"Right now, the Allies, and the world in general, lack a certain type of resource that can really only be obtained from asteroids or other types of space rocks. The specific materiel, Veldspar, has been found in abundance on the moon. When it's refined down, it creates a specialized materiel called Tritium-4, which is what we use in our armor for the Pershings and Razorbacks. Presently, we're creating a synthetic version of this materiel, but it's costly, time-consuming, and resource-intensive. This hadn't been a problem in the past, because we never needed it in the quantities that we presently require." Bringing up a new slide deck with charts and images, Professor Rickenbacker proceeded to show everyone their solution to this problem.

"Mr. President, one thing I would like to gain from you today is your approval to move forward with Operation Pegasus, which is DARPA's and the AFC's lunar mining operation," he requested.

Examining the information, the President asked, "Bring us up to speed on that project again and I will give you a decision. This is going to require a reallocation of some valuable resources, so I would appreciate some input from everyone."

Changing some images, the Professor began, "Operation Pegasus is a lunar mining operation that, frankly, we have been developing for decades. We continue to update it if there is a significant technology change that could make it a reality or lower the costs. The EmDrive and the Angelic power source have made this operation a truly cost-effective reality. Leveraging the EmDrive, the travel time from Earth to the moon would be cut down to two days. That includes taking off and landing on both surfaces."

The National Security Advisor broke in to ask, "Excuse me, you said Angelic power source? Can you tell us more about this?"

"Yes, I call it Angelic as the power source is nothing short of amazing. It's essentially a cold fusion reactor. I'll discuss the reactor in greater detail in a short bit, if we can continue on with Pegasus." He didn't wait for permission but quickly continued.

Showing an image of a spacecraft, he explained, "What we propose is to build a multipurpose ship to initiate the operation. The vessel you're looking at is what we're calling the Hulk. It's 5,100 feet in length, 400 feet in height and 300 feet in width."

The National Security Advisor let out a short whistle, saying, "That's a big ship to construct. Are you proposing to build that in space or here on Earth?"

"We would build the ship here on Earth. Because the ship would use the EmDrive, it would be able to power itself into space without any problem and return to Earth if needed. The intent of this ship is to essentially build a self-contained mining operation. Building the ship would be broken down into several operations. The first would be the cargo bay. This section would carry the equipment and vehicles needed to start the mission. It would also carry with it the equipment needed to build a small modular building and two bio-domes. The modular building would be 200 feet by 800 feet, with an eight-foot ceiling. Connected to this central building would be two bio-domes on either side. The bio-domes would be used to grow food and start to establish some initial food production to support and sustain a permanent outpost. This modular building would be expanded with additional bio-domes, which we would incorporate with each successive transport load from the Earth to the moon." Rickenbacker showed a short video of the process he had just explained.

"The next compartment in the Hulk is the rock crusher. This section can actually be fed externally once the ship has been anchored to the lunar surface. Once the rocks are crushed, they will be separated from the actual ore. The ore will then be moved internally to a small smelter, where it will be melted down into unrefined blocks of Tritium-4. The Tritium-4 will then be loaded onto the transports and sent back to Earth for further refinement and incorporation into our industrial needs. This would effectively solve our Tritium-4 problem and increase our manufacturing capability exponentially. The weapons systems we'll be able to build with this essentially unlimited supply of Tritium-4 would be incredible."

General Branson spoke up first, saying, "I'm not a manufacturing expert, but I suspect this ship of yours, the Hulk—it's going to require a lot of resources that would otherwise go toward our Pershings and Razorbacks?"

"It would require us to suspend production of them for the next six months while we used the synthetic Tritium-4 to build out the ship," Rickenbacker replied, deadpan as could be.

Eric Clarke, the Secretary of Defense, decided to break in. "We can stop production of the Pershings and increase production of the older M1A5s, but we cannot stop production of the Razorbacks. They are more important right now than even our tanks. My suggestion is we go ahead with this project, Mr. President. The gap in Pershings is going to hurt, but like the professor said, having an unlimited new supply of Tritium-4 would, in the long run, change the course of the war. The question is— can we protect this ship during takeoff and while it's en route to the moon and stationed on the lunar surface? Also, can we protect the transport craft that will need to travel to and from the Hulk with the materiel we need?"

The President looked to Rickenbacker for the answer.

"We can, if we time our launches and landings to keep the Russian and Chinese ground-based lasers from optimal attack trajectories. Given that both countries have been working with directional mirrors on aircraft to increase their laser attack capabilities to go beyond the horizon, this could become a problem. But they are still experimental for the moment. The other thing to remember is that the Hulk will be built with a Tritium-4 exterior hull and refractive armor. As long as we know the frequencies their lasers are operating on, which we do, we can modulate the armor frequencies so the laser hits are harmless." The Professor produced another short clip that showed exactly what he had explained and how the entire process would work.

Monty, the President's Chief of Staff and Senior Advisor, praised their presenter. "I am truly impressed, Professor. Every possible question we have asked, you have a ready answer and an illustration to explain it in laymen's terms."

Rickenbacker chuckled before responding, "I gave this brief to the others on this team. We came up with a lot of possible questions and then prepared answers for you.

"Well, gentlemen, not to appear rude, but like I said, we do need an answer on whether to move forward with production immediately."

"Professor, I am impressed to say the least. Unless anyone has an objection, the project is approved and given top priority above all other projects. With the exception of the Razorbacks, the Pershing program will be suspended for the time being until the Hulk is completed. Your AFC LNO will have full authority and support to get production going as quickly as possible, and for all equipment needed to make this project a reality," the President directed.

"Thank you, Mr. President. This is going to require a lot of manpower…we're looking at close to 140,000 people in all to work on the varying aspects of the project. Our AFC LNO said he can shift people around and make it work though," the professor said confidently.

Now that Operation Pegasus had been approved, the professor continued. "The next piece of technology I want to discuss with you is this…"

The professor pulled out a small spool of cabling and passed it to the group. "I would like to draw your attention to this materiel. This substance is twenty times stronger than steel or any other matter known to man. It is also the materiel that is going to make the space elevator a reality. If we are able to establish a platform base in high earth orbit, then we can establish a space lift. This elevator will enable us to move great amounts of materiel to and from Earth; it would be the cornerstone of a permanent base."

Before going down the rabbit hole the space elevator would be, the President wanted to get back to the new fighter design and low-orbit aircraft. "Professor, the space elevator concept is amazing, and I want you to continue to pursue it. However, we have a war we need to win now, so please discuss the EmDrive technology again and how we are going to incorporate it into our current military equipment?" directed the President.

"As you wish, Mr. President. Once we had sufficient supplies of Tritium-4, we would begin to replace our jet propulsion engines with EmDrive propulsion. The EmDrive propulsion uses no fuel and runs purely on hydrogen or water. We simply divert more power from the reactor to increase the speed, and likewise decrease the amount of power drawn from the reactor in order to slow it down. This is a propulsion system that will work in the atmosphere, in orbit and in space.

"The idea of fighter aircraft being able to incorporate this technology sounds incredible. How soon we can get a working prototype going?" the President asked warmly.

"The technology is complex, but something that we have the capability to build. I'd like to be optimistic and say we can have it completed in a couple of months, but it may be closer to a year. It really depends on how much of our resources and manpower is put into it," said the professor.

Monty broke into the conversation saying, "Mr. President, the Boeing plant that Vice President Kern was visiting when he was nearly assassinated could be used. It's a new plant and has increased security."

"Get with the manufacturers and find out if that plant can work. We need to get a working prototype built immediately, and that might be best done at our Skunkworks facility in Nevada. Once the bugs are identified, then we can get it into full production," the President directed.

Eric Clarke, the Secretary of Defense, provided counsel on this subject. "The key to getting this aircraft into production, Mr. President, is going to be not making the structure of it more complicated than it needs to be. We should look at developing two versions: one a pure drone, and the other a manned aircraft. See which one works the best, and then go in that direction."

"Make it happen Eric...please, continue, Professor," directed the President, not wanting to get too far off course from the presentation.

Trying to remain patient, Rickenbacker continued, "There are a couple more inventions I would like to go over with you as well. Two are something we can use now to help us win the war, and the other is something that will enable the US to not just reach for the stars, but to conquer them."

General Branson interjected, saying, "Let's focus on the first couple that can be used immediately. We need to win this war before we can think of anything that could be used in the private sector or to dominate space." Branson did his best not to come off as abrupt or disrespectful.

"Yes, General. The first is, as of two days ago, we successfully tested our first limitless energy reactor. It's essentially cold fusion. This is the Angelic power source I mentioned earlier."

"That is incredible," the Secretary of Defense said, knowing that if this type of technology were miniaturized, it could completely change the battlefield.

"Right now, the device is about the size of a reactor used in a nuclear-powered plant, except that this apparatus could power not just a city but an entire state. We believe we could build a version about three times as large and power a full quarter of the entire country. But this is only half the story. This new technology also gives us the ability to build a fully functional plasma laser. Not only that, we can miniaturize the weapon to fit on the new aircraft we're going to build," said the professor with excitement in his eyes and voice. "The things we will be able to do with this new technology are truly amazing."

The men in the room all generally agreed that this was a stupendous step forward and that the project should continue to be advanced.

General Branson changed the topic. "What about the cybernetics, and this new Raptor combat suit I've heard about?"

Rickenbacker seemed a bit alarmed that General Branson knew anything about the cybernetics or Raptor suit. Those were closely guarded secrets. "I was going to mention those next, but since you've brought them up, the Raptor combat suit is similar to the exoskeleton combat suit our Special Forces and the Chinese and Russians are currently using. The difference between the Raptor and the current models the Reds are using is that our version also incorporates a suite of cybernetic implants. These grafts give the user a host of new capabilities the exoskeleton suits never could hope to achieve.

"Let's start with the suit itself. The ensemble encases the operator in an environmental and bullet proof shell. Each suit is fitted to its operator, so it's nice and snug like a diver's suit. It has its own filtration system that allows the operator to regulate their body temperature, in case they're operating in the heat of the Middle East, or in the tundra and mountains of Alaska. It can also operate in a chemical or WMD environment. It has radiation shielding, which will also make the suit perfect for space operations down the road. In the meantime, one could wear the suit and move through a radiation hot zone and survive just fine.

"If for some reason the armor is penetrated and the person inside is shot, or shrapnel rips a hole in it and the operator is injured, the suit will self-seal up to an inch-wide hole. It will also fill the person's wound with an antibiotic gel that will both stop the bleeding until the injury can be properly addressed and numb the area so the operator can continue to focus on the job at hand without getting distracted by the pain. The suit also has several self-injections to apply, if needed. One is adrenaline—it has up to five adrenaline shots that can be applied and refilled. It also has up to two morphine shots—one to relieve the pain, and a second one in case help is a long way off or if the operator is too injured and wants to self-terminate." The professor showed some videos of the suit in action.

"The suit provides the person inside with the ability to lift up to five times their body weight, run up to 35 miles per hour, and jump as high as 30 feet. The suit weighs 250 pounds and uses a variety of new polymers and nanofiber technology, which gives it flexibility and speed and makes it lightweight. The power for the suit is geothermal, so the body heat and movement of the operator actually regenerate the suit." Professor Rickenbacker was almost giddy with excitement. "This new type of geothermal energy is going to have a host of new civilian applications once the war is over."

Not wanting to miss something, General Branson asked, "Where do the cybernetics come into play?"

"Ah, yes. Well, there are two versions of the suit. The standard issue, which uses no cybernetics, and then the advanced version, which incorporates them. The standard issue can do everything we just talked about and all of the other functions that you see on the display. The enhanced suit that incorporates the cybernetics enables the operator to integrate their mind into the operating system of the suit and the targeting system. Essentially, it allows an operator to see and engage targets faster than someone could without a cybernetic implant. The implant connects at the base of the skull and interfaces with the neurons in the brain that allow a person to process images and threats."

"The implant also allows the operator to push the limits of the suit to the max. Instead of being able to run 35 miles per hour, someone using the implants could easily hit 50 or 60 miles per hour. They can do this because their body becomes completely fused with the suit for the duration that they are connected. We've tested it, and the results are amazing. However, not everyone is able to integrate with the cybernetic implant. Some people's bodies reject it; others are simply not able to control it. So, in this regard, the cybernetic implants are still a little ways off from full implementation."

Eric Clarke, the Secretary of Defense, saw the Raptor suit as a means of being able to even the odds for the American forces, particularly in regard to the troops in Alaska, who would soon be facing an army of nearly five million—and who knew how many of them would be equipped with the Chinese and Russian exoskeleton suits.

"How soon can we get the standard Raptor suit into production and begin training our troops on them?" asked the Secretary of Defense, eager to get a new technology operational quickly.

Rickenbacker handed a tablet to Eric with the full specs needed to build the Raptor and a training program for how to use it. "This should help. It's fully ready to be fielded now. We've actually been working on this project in one form or another for nearly three decades. The exoskeleton the Special Forces have been using was second generation. This is now the fifth generation of that same technology. Where the first two generations were not a fully enclosed system, this is, and that is why this system is going to be so much more advanced compared to anything the Chinese or Russians have.

"You can begin building them immediately, but they will take time. You can construct most of it using 3-D printers, but training a soldier on how to use it is going to be the challenge. There's no way around that particular problem," Rickenbacker explained.

Knowing they had been in the meeting for nearly five hours, the President indicated to the group that their session was coming to an end. "Professor Rickenbacker, you have given us a lot of food for thought and certainly provided us with some new technologies to look at. When we get back to the White House, I'm going to start bringing others into the loop on the Raptor combat suit, the EmDrive propulsion system and the F41. We need to get these three pieces of technology into the war immediately. I want you to be available when the time comes to answer questions by some of the engineers from the major producers in the country," the President directed.

Rickenbacker agreed, and then the men parted company.

Chapter 30
Saving Samson

Day 145
26 April 2041
Tel Aviv
Third Army Headquarters

The Russian offensive had finally been stopped, just south of the city of Haifa at the Carmel Mountain National Park and stretching to just north of Nazareth to the Sea of Galilee. The fighting was nearly constant and intense up until that point; all sides had lost tens of thousands of soldiers a day during the fighting. The Israelis were beginning to consider more drastic measures to defeat the Russians, having decided that if the Russians broke through their last line of defense and reached Megiddo National Park, they would activate their Samson protocol, the use of nuclear weapons. Just as the Biblical character for which this protocol was named had mustered his last bit of superhuman might to push out the columns of a Philistine building and collapse it upon all inside, this maneuver of last resort would destroy the enemy, but possibly also themselves in the process.

The Israelis knew that with modern-day laser defense systems, ballistic missiles would have no chance of hitting their targets. So instead of conventional mines, the IDF had buried dozens of cobalt-laden nuclear devices along the Israeli border and several at key points inside of Israel. If it appeared that the country was lost, then they could detonate these devices and forever eradiate the land. They also had their Jericho bombs, which were smaller nuclear devices in the 1-kiloton to 10-kiloton range. These bombs were buried all across Israel and could be detonated on enemy forces as the IDF continued to fall back.

General Gardner was aware of the protocols and the bombs in play. He had argued for time and patience with the Israeli government to not use such weapons. Entreating them, he pleaded, "The Americans are here in force and are not going to leave. We have time...we could grind the Russians and IR down. The US has already nuked the IR hard, so there is no reason to destroy the Holy Land with nuclear bombs as well."

Ultimately, the IDF commanders heard what Gardner had to say, and he had won the argument, at least for the moment.

General Gardner called this new meeting of his division commanders to hear some ideas from them on how they could push the Russians back. "Generals, as you know, I have called you together to hear some of your thoughts for how we can dislodge the Russian positions. I am handing the floor to you, so please, let's begin," the general directed.

Major General Kennedy, the 3rd Infantry Division commander, was the first to speak. "General, I appreciate the opportunity to share some ideas. As you know, the Russians have dug in pretty good at this point. They made their lunges as far as they could and then settled in while they consolidated for the next attack. I believe we need to find a way to get in their rear area and threaten their supply lines. Once their forces are drawn away to deal with their tail, we can launch our own counteroffensive across the entirety of Israel. We would hit the IR near Amman, the Chinese in the south and the Russians in the north. Then we could throw the entire Axis off balance with an airborne assault." Kennedy had prepared a holographic map of his strategy and displayed it for the room to view as he spoke.

After twenty minutes of discussing the idea, General Gardner said, "I like the thought, but I'm not sure we have enough airpower right now to support that. Plus, the MiG40s are still causing a lot of problems for us. The JF35s are just now starting to take them on with the new radars. I'm concerned that if we sent airborne troops in to attack their supply lines, we might lose a number of transports before they even get over their drop zones. Do you have any ideas on how we make this work without losing a lot of aircraft to the MiGs?"

Kennedy thought for a moment before responding. "Sir, historically, during the invasion of Normandy and other airborne operations, we lost aircraft and men. Despite those casualties, we still managed to land a large enough force that we were able to cause significant problems. Perhaps if we used the Razorbacks instead of cargo transports to do the insertion, we might be able to reduce our losses, at least in the higher-risk areas. If we swarmed the skies with drones and then the Marines joined in to conduct an amphibious assault, we could bring enough force to make a difference."

Major General Lance Peeler, the 2nd Marine Expeditionary Force commander, liked the idea. He put in his own two cents, "Sir, my Marines could make a landing north and south of Beirut and capture the city and the highway leading to Chtaura inside Lebanon. This would place a 60,000 man blocking force in their rear area. If the 101st Airborne is able to land all around the Beirut area, that would cause enough of a distraction that my Marines might be able to capture the area with minimal casualties. Once 82nd Airborne captures Chtaura, then we have them cut off. That places 100,000 troops at their rear that are equipped with armor support."

Before agreeing to move forward with this plan, General Gardner clarified, "Essentially, we'd be launching our own version of MacArthur's Battle of Inchon, where he landed forces behind the Chinese and North Koreans to recapture Seoul and cut them off from their supply lines. Does everyone like this plan, or does someone else have another they would like us to consider?" He looked around the room for any dissent.

Major General Twitty, the 1st Armored Division commander, spoke up. "I like the plan. If the Russians feel they're going to be cut off from their supply lines and encircled, they'll pull back, and perhaps we could even get them to fall back to Damascus. My only concern is that if we do this, we need to see it through to the end no matter how many casualties we take, and we may take a lot. This would be our one big chance to crush the Russians in the Middle East and knock the others out of the war as well." He slammed his fist on the table for emphasis.

"Very well, then. We will move forward with this plan and staff it through the chain of command. I will consult with the IDF and ensure they shift forces around to fill in the gaps as we advance. We will go for broke, gentlemen. Make sure your commanders know that this is it; there will be no second chances. Either we're going to win and finish them off, or this war is going to drag on a lot longer. We may even lose Israel if we take too many casualties and are defeated. I want you all to hit them hard and win. Dismissed!"

With that said, the group broke up and the various generals went back to their divisional commands to begin preparations. The invasion and offensive operations would take place in six days, which was not a lot of time considering all of the moving parts. Fortunately, the Navy had complete control of the waters in this area and had the amphibious assault ships needed already in port. The vessels were only moving about 55 miles up the coast to drop off the Marines, so it wasn't a long jaunt by any means. It was fortunate in this case that Israel was a small country.

It meant that shifting forces and aircraft around wouldn't be nearly as big of a challenge as if they were carrying out the same type of attack in Europe or Asia.

****

Major Lee looked at his company commanders as they stood in a circle under the helicopter flight deck of one of the many Marine assault ships off the coast of Lebanon. Sensing a momentous occasion on the horizon, he began to address them about the battalion's assignment for the invasion.

"Lieutenant Thornton, Alpha and Bravo Company are going to air-assault in and secure the Beirut International Airport. You are the OIC for the airport operation. I want your company to take the terminal, the tower and the main section of the airport. Bravo Company is going to secure the southern end of the airport, which is where the Russians are encamped. Charlie and Delta Companies are going to air-assault into the Golf Club of Lebanon, just north of your position, and secure it for a medical battalion that will arrive in the seaborne invasion group. The brigade is going to set up their headquarters at your location once you have the airport secured.

"I'm going to establish our battalion headquarters initially with Charlie Company and will then transition to the airport once Brigade arrives. Because our two locations are less than a mile apart, Delta Company will be your quick-reaction force if you need additional reinforcements. Charlie Company will continue to hold the golf course and provide security for the medical battalion. Once you have established control of the airport, a few dozen air transports are going to land and offload a company of light drone tanks and infantry fighting vehicles. An aviation battalion will also arrive and get the airport ready to receive and launch a few squadrons of Razorbacks.

"It's imperative that you secure the airport as quickly as possible; those follow-on forces will arrive ninety minutes after you land," Major Lee said, looking Thornton directly in the eyes. "This entire operation is a major risk. We have to secure the city, airport and seaport for the armored forces, or we're going to find ourselves in a world of hurt when the Russians turn their attention toward us. Remember, there are nearly 50,000 Russian soldiers in and around this area and another 150,000 in Damascus, not that far from our objectives."

In addition to doubling the size of the MEF, each company was doubled in size, which meant a company could accomplish a lot more now than they used to. "My men will get it done, Sir. They're pretty wired right now, and I'll make sure they stay wound up. We all know this is the opportunity to knock the Russians out of the war," Lieutenant Thornton said with conviction. The glint in his eyes showed an iron will and no lack of determination.

****

Two hours later, Lieutenant Thornton's company was in the air heading toward the Beirut airport. The Army Rangers were already in the city, securing half a dozen key bridges for the armor units and other strategic targets throughout the city. The 101st Airborne was landing airborne troopers east of the city via hundreds of Razorbacks and was forming up to secure their corridors and targets. The 82nd Airborne parachuted in at Chtaura, hitting the Russian supply depots and blocking any reinforcements from Damascus. With nearly 60,000 airborne troops dropping from the sky and 40,000 Marines assaulting from the sea, this was the largest airborne assault since the Normandy invasion of France during World War II.

Lieutenant Thornton's company came into sight of the airport as they flew over dozens of Marine landing craft and vehicles hitting the beaches below. Dozens of green tracers started to reach out for his Razorback as they continued to fly toward the airport. The pilot took evasive action and counterfired a slew of antitank missiles and rockets at the targets that had been shooting at them. One of the crew chiefs swiveled his mini-gun toward several of the buildings as the aircraft got closer to landing, and he raked the buildings with bullets to keep the enemy heads down while they landed. As they neared the landing zone, the Razorback took several hits, jarring it a bit. Luckily, the Razorback was so heavily armored that the rounds bounced harmlessly off the protective covering.

The Razorback began to flare as it landed. Lieutenant Thornton yelled to everyone in the cabin. "Start identifying targets and take them out fast! Shoot and move, and do it quickly!" he yelled as he readied himself to jump once the craft leveled out.

Within seconds, they were on the ground and coming under heavy enemy fire. One of Thornton's men was hit in the face and fell to the ground in front of him, dead. Seconds later, an antitank rocket flew from one of the nearby buildings and struck the Razorback just as it was starting to gain altitude…it blew up instantly. The explosion threw Lieutenant Thornton to the ground, knocking the wind out of him. He lay on his back for a few seconds to regain his composure and breathe before getting back up and leading a charge with his men to the buildings from where the rocket had originated. They needed to get off the taxiway; they were sitting ducks out in the open like this.

As Thornton ran toward the building, he had his rifle at his shoulder and was firing while moving. His HUD continued to identify new targets as it was able to distinguish friend from foe through the blue force tracker his men used. He continued to fire round after round as he and his men advanced to the buildings and then into the terminals. Once inside the terminal, they began to stack against the walls of one of the hallways. They then cleared the rooms one at a time as the platoons made their way through the terminals, hallways, and other rooms they encountered. Russian soldiers were everywhere.

The control tower had a small hallway that connected it to the rest of the terminal. It also had an exterior exit, which was where the Marine team immediately headed. They wanted to avoid entering it through the terminal, fearing that that entrance might be a trap. As the team headed for the control tower, they were met by heavy machine-gun fire, killing several Marines.

While the remaining Marines were getting into position to breach the tower, a Russian soldier threw a satchel out of one of the windows in the tower toward the jarheads below. The Marines saw the bag charge and immediately scattered, which enabled the Russian machine gunners to once again pummel the American forces. Then the satchel exploded, killing and wounding the rest of the Marines who had been in its vicinity.

The Russians had very cleverly set up several heavy machine guns and a couple of snipers in the tower at various levels. Despite the tower not being a very large structure, it provided the Russians with enough cover to cause the Marines a lot of trouble securing the airport. Having lost nearly two squads trying to secure this one objective, the platoon sergeant had three of his Marines pull out their AT6 rockets in order to destroy the tower.

The Marines were also coming under a lot of sniper fire from buildings next to the airport, forcing them to extend their perimeter farther beyond the airport than where they had originally wanted to attack. The dilemma for the jarheads was that they were operating under a short timeframe to secure the airport. Follow-on forces were on their way, and though the C17s could land under enemy fire, it would be better if they didn't. The Russians were everywhere. They fired relentlessly, killing a number of Thornton's men despite the losses they were taking.

After ninety minutes of continuous fighting, building to building, room to room, and expanding the perimeter beyond the airport, they finally secured the area. Lieutenant Thornton called the battalion headquarters and requested the QRF be sent to his position and for several medevacs. His company had taken heavy casualties capturing the airport, and so did Bravo Company, which had the southern end of the airport, where the Russian Air Force housed its personnel.

In addition to securing the airport and the perimeter, they also had to move numerous destroyed and disabled vehicles from the runway and taxiways. The Russians had moved as many vehicles as possible to prevent aircraft from landing on the runways, in addition to blowing up several large holes in its surface. Fortunately, a couple of front-end loaders from an engineering unit were brought in by helicopter thirty minutes after the first Marines attacked the airport. They immediately began to move dirt to fill in the holes and helped to move the numerous damaged and disabled vehicles blocking the runway, getting it ready to receive aircraft. A few dozen Air Force controllers and other personnel also arrived with the engineers and began to coordinate initial air operations.

Major Lee came on the radio and to give his congratulations. "Lieutenant Thornton, good job on securing the airport. Brigade has twelve Razorbacks inbound to your location, with additional troops and equipment. That flight of transports I told you about is inbound as well, so look for them and make sure nothing happens to them," he said, and he quickly signed off the radio. Thornton could hear a lot of machine-gun fire over the radio and assumed the major was still in the process of securing his own position.

"Sergeant Miller, get on the radio and let Bravo Company know we have transports and Razorbacks inbound. He needs to make sure the runway is secured and protected, understood?" Thornton called to his radioman.

Ten minutes later, several medevac helicopters landed and began to evacuate the dead and wounded. Minutes after they left, twelve Razorbacks joined the tarmac, along with their aircrews and additional equipment. Thornton ran out to one of the Razorbacks and met the brigade commander Colonel Ladd and his staff; they spoke briefly before Thornton pointed in the direction of the terminals for them to head toward. "Sir, we've secured the terminals and the airport, Terminal B is the least shot-up area for you to set up, if you would like."

The colonel nodded as his staff followed Thornton to the terminal. As they entered the corridor, the colonel saw a number of dead Russian soldiers and spent shell casings from a mountain of gunfire. Clearly, this area had been fought over. Within ten minutes of landing, the colonel was in charge and directing operations.

Several Air Force personnel joined the Marine Headquarters group and began to direct several C17s as they began their final approach. The planes were taxiing to offload light drone tanks and munitions for the Razorbacks on one of the taxiways and then preparing to take off again and head back to Cypress to pick up the next load.

Once the light drone tanks were offloaded, they headed toward the base perimeter and linked up with a platoon from Bravo Company, which was going to accompany them to their next objective. It was important to get the light tanks into the fight as soon as possible and get this area of the city and airport secured as quickly as it could be. A lot of aircraft and equipment was about to start moving through this airport.

After the flight crews for the Razorbacks established their own air operations, several of them took off, heading toward the city to provide additional close air support to the Marines, moving their way through it. There was continuous artillery and heavy machine-gun fire emanating from the city center and the east side of the city as the Marines continued to move inland from the various beaches from which they had invaded. The Russians were forcing the Marines to fight house-to-house and were turning the city into a meat grinder.

A fourth wave of Razorbacks landed and offloaded a full battalion of fresh Marines along with a battery of 155mm Howitzers, which immediately began to provide fire support as soon as they were set up. The additional Marines relieved Bravo Company just as Major

Lee and the Battalion Headquarters arrived at the airport. It was now time for the battalion to consolidate and await their next assignment.
****

The sky above Chtaura was abuzz with aircraft activity. Hundreds of drones and manned fighter aircraft were engaged in combat with dozens of MiG40s in an effort to provide cover and protection for the sixty-plus C17s carrying paratroopers from the 82nd Airborne, who were preparing to jump. Private First-Class John Mitchell stood up in the C17, getting ready to jump with the rest of his company, when the aircraft suddenly veered to one side and then descended quickly. The jumpmaster yelled, "Everyone to get ready to jump!"

Then the pilot came on over the PA, and announced, "There are enemy MiGs in the area. Repeat, enemy MiGs are in the area. Everyone is to jump immediately!"

The jump light went from red to green, and then the paratroopers of the 82nd Airborne jumped out of the plane one after the other, passing the jumpmaster at the door.

As PFC Mitchell fell, his parachute opened quickly and he dropped his pack below his feet to dangle until he landed. As the company descended to the airport below, he saw hundreds of parachutes all around him. The C17 his company had just jumped out of had taken a direct missile hit from a MiG, which had blown the left wing clean off. The aircraft caught fire and spiraled to the ground before crashing into the hills below, creating a huge fireball. It didn't look like anyone from inside the aircraft had been able to make it out before it exploded.

While PFC Mitchell descended steadily toward the ground, he grabbed his rifle and took aim at the Russians on the ground, who were now only a few thousand feet away. Several Russian soldiers aimed their heavy machines up toward the paratroopers and opened fire. Suddenly, the sky was filled with green tracers crisscrossing back and forth across the sky.

PFC Mitchell took aim at a cluster of soldiers manning one of the machine guns while he continued to float down to below 500 feet and then opened fire. He quickly dispatched the soldiers he had targeted at the helm of the machine gun, only to be cut apart by a different machine gun crew. His lifeless body continued to drift to the ground until it landed in a heap.

****

The fighting was intense during the first four hours of the battle for Chtaura. The Russians fought hard and gallantly but were outnumbered by the airborne troopers. The M5 AIR and HUD system that the Americans used was perhaps the most superior combat rifle system ever developed. It provided the American soldier with the tactical advantage and gave him a rough average of five-to-one kill ratio. The Americans quickly captured the Russian supply depots and blew them up. They immediately began to establish multiple defensive positions along the major supply routes, highways, and air corridors that the Russian planes and drones were using, making it hard for the Reds to keep their forces in the surrounding areas supplied. They had established their blocking force, preventing Russian reinforcements in Damascus from being able to assist their brothers-in-arms in Beirut.

By the end of the first 36 hours, the Americans had secured an 18-mile-long defensive line from Beirut, Lebanon to Zahlah, Syria. This effectively cut the Russians off from their entire supply line system and blocked any reinforcements they might have been able to receive from Turkey and the Black Sea. As the Americans began to dig in to their new defensive positions, the Russians were left with some hard choices. They already had nearly 300,000 troops in Israel, along with 500,000 Islamic Republic forces. What should they do? If they stayed, they risked being surrounded, but if they fell back to Damascus, where their reserve force was, they would lose all of the hard-fought ground they had gained so far.

With the successful invasion and airborne assault, General Gardner ordered an additional 90,000 soldiers from his reserves to be sent to Beirut, and an all-out offensive against the entire enemy line. The Israelis launched a massive assault from the Jordan Valley, and began to push the IR back toward Amman. The Americans had been equipping the IDF with the same M5 AIR and HUD system that the American soldiers were using, giving them the same tactical advantage that the American soldiers currently enjoyed.

The Chinese were caught off guard by the initial counterattack from the American and Israeli forces. They rushed their reserves forward, believing this was just another defensive ploy by the Allied forces. Unbeknownst to the Chinese, the Americans had cut the Russian supply depots and supply lines off from their main force. They were also unaware that the Israelis were attacking through the Jordan Valley with nearly 600,000 soldiers. However, the Israelis had no intention of attacking Amman directly. Their goal was to cut deep behind the Chinese lines, and then swing south and behind the Chinese forces, surrounding them while they were fully engaged with the Israeli and American forces to their front. At that point, the Chinese would either be forced to surrender or be wiped out. The grand objective was to either capture or destroy the Chinese Army, along with the Russians. Once that was accomplished, they could drive the IR out of Jordan and push toward Riyadh, Baghdad, and Kuwait City. So far, General Gardner's plan was working.

****

The conflict in Mexico was not often mentioned in the media or widely talked about by the average person on the street. With the wars in the Middle East, Asia, and Europe raging on, the people generally didn't have the attention span to think about another potential problem. However, some Islamic Republic Special Forces units were still operating in Mexico, and they were doing a good job of creating chaos whenever possible. By and large, the country's conflict had tapered off. More and more people in Mexico were finding work, and many were being drafted into the American army. The government had already drafted 1.6 million Mexican young men and women, ranging in age from 18 to 38, into the US military. Most of these draftees were being deployed to the conflict in the Middle East and Europe, with less than 200,000 of them being deployed stateside.

More than 70% of the population was on board with being a US territory and enjoyed the benefits of being a part of America. While the conflict was winding down, the military continued to draw down forces and shift them to the other conflicts. The private military corporations continued to stay and provided security for the DOJ, DHS, FBI, and other government agencies as they continued to expand their footprints.

The cartels had been nearly eradicated during this time period. The few Special Forces units still operating in Mexico were hunting them down relentlessly. Plus, the DOJ and DHS had placed a huge bounty on their heads. It was becoming hard for them to continue to hide, let alone run their operations. When it came to dealing with the cartels, there were no rules being followed. Unlike the old Mexican government, which had been powerless against the cartels, or in some cases colluding with them, the Americans hunted them down relentlessly.

****

The war in the Middle East had gone from bad to suddenly great. The Beirut invasion had proved to be a resounding success, similar to MacArthur's landing of troops at Inchon during the Korean War. The Israelis had broken through the IR forces near Amman and swung around behind the Chinese Army to the south. They had cornered the Chinese against the Red Sea and now had them completely surrounded. The Israeli artillery was giving the Chinese the fight of their lives, pounding them relentlessly 24/7. General Gardner believed the Chinese would be forced to surrender within the next day or two, as they had nowhere to go and not nearly enough strength left to fight their way out of their position.

The Russians had initially chosen to keep their army in Israel and drive again toward Tel Aviv, relying on their forces in Turkey to engage the Americans in Lebanon. They broke through the American and Israeli lines once again and came within eight miles of Tel Aviv, but ran out of steam and supplies. Unfortunately for them, while the main army was attacking Tel Aviv, General Lodz, the Russian commander, was seriously injured in an artillery attack. The extent of his injuries was such that he had to be flown back to Russia for medical treatment. The US Navy and Air Force pummeled the army in Lebanon with massive amounts of air attacks, effectively stopping the Russian relief army group that had been attacking from Turkey.

Prior to the MiG40s being rebased to Turkey, they had scored over 253 fighter drone kills and 127 piloted aircraft kills, all while losing only 23 of their own number. Despite the enormous loss in aircraft by the Allies, they were able to destroy much of the Russian armored forces and prevented their relief army from breaking through the American defensive lines. The Russians and their supply lines continued to stay cut off. General Gardner was quick to seize on the tactical defeat of the Russians and absence of General Lodz and moved to encircle the remaining Russian Army.

Chapter 31
Before the Law Takes a Break

Day 150
01 May 2041
Washington, D.C.
White House Situation Room

President Stein was walking toward the Situation Room with Monty, talking about the recent success in the Middle East and concerned with the situation developing in Asia. As the President sat down, the meeting began quickly. General Branson kicked things off.

"Mr. President, I would like to start the briefing by going over the situation in the Middle East first, then transition to Europe and end with Asia."

The President smiled and nodded toward General Branson for him to continue.

"The Israelis have the Chinese Army surrounded, although intelligence shows another large Chinese naval force approaching the port of Kuwait. It would appear they're going to offload another large army group, but they won't be able to form quickly enough to help their comrades. The IDF commander has asked if we may be able to help them by taking possession and control of the Chinese prisoners once they have surrendered," General Branson said as he looked to the President for guidance.

Henry looked up from his notes and said, "Convey to the Israelis that we will take possession of the prisoners, but we request that they provide at least half of the security force needed to guard them. We will look to relocate the prisoners back to the US until the end of the war. I would like Attorney General Roberts to identify suitable locations for us to intern them."

AG Roberts wrote a couple of quick notes before looking up and asking, "Am I to assume I can use them to help build these facilities as well?"

"Yes, use them as you see fit. Let's put them to work on the various projects that need to be done. Perhaps we should use them to help with the salvage and cleanup operations in New York and Baltimore," the President directed.

"Yes, Mr. President. My office will work with the rest of the NSC team to find the best use for them," the AG said, finishing a few notes.

General Branson resumed his brief. "In the north, the Russians are caught between a rock and a hard place. Their supply lines have been cut off, along with the fastest routes of retreat. They have also pulled their MiG40s back to bases in Turkey, so they aren't able to smother our aircraft and the front lines like they had done previously. Our fighter bombers are now going after any and all fuel tankers we can find to further limit their options."

General Gardner, who was attending the briefing via the holograph, interjected, "Mr. President, I am moving the last of my reserves to finish encircling their army. Once we have them surrounded, it will then be a matter of tightening the noose and forcing them to surrender. I firmly believe when the Russians capitulate, the IR is going to collapse quickly. We will finally be able to start to apply more direct pressure to them. The issue we are running into right now, and it is starting to become a serious one, is munitions. We are running out of artillery rounds and heavy machine-gun ammunition.

"Another point of order I need to address is equipment—not for my army group but for the IDF. Reinforcements are pouring into Israel from all over the world; their numbers are really starting to swell. As they finish additional IDF training, they're being filtered into the rest of the line units. However, they don't have the gear that they need. Is there any additional armor, artillery and rifles we can equip them with?" asked General Gardner, looking for support.

Eric Clarke, the Secretary of Defense, spoke up, "We're working on the munition problem right now. We have twelve aircraft that should be arriving from Europe with ordnance, and about ten freighters a couple of days later. That's the best we can do. To address your equipment problem, we're going through the various vehicle and aircraft boneyards, refurbishing everything and getting it combat-ready. Most of the equipment is dated, but it will still work, and it will still kill well enough. As for rifles, we're cranking out M5 AIRs and HUDs at a high rate, so that shouldn't be a problem."

Gardner's face softened a bit, knowing that his needs were going to be met. "Any equipment we can get them, they will use. Thank you for the emergency resupply of artillery rounds."

General Branson regained the President's attention. "I'd like to move on to Europe. As of right now, we have the Russians stopped at the German border and in Austria. They've taken the Czech Republic and the entire Balkan region, with the exception of most of Albania and Greece. It was a real slaughter though in Bulgaria, Hungary, Serbia and Romania—their armies virtually collapsed. The Russians weren't taking a lot of prisoners. We may have to fall back further into Germany if the EU isn't able to get additional reinforcements to the front lines."

The President was curious what the issue was, since the fighting was taking place on the continent and they weren't having to move troops nearly as far as the US was having to. "What's the holdup? Why is it taking them so long to get troops to the front lines?" asked the President.

Branson sighed before continuing, "The issue is, they're keeping a large force near Brussels and the French border. It's as if they're already anticipating losing Germany and are working on their next line of defense."

"General Wade, what are your thoughts?" asked the President. General Wade, the SACEUR commander in Brussels, was also attending the briefing via the 3-D holograph.

"Sir, General Branson summed it up well. The Germans are fighting ferociously to keep the Russians out of their border along with the Dutch, but the rest of the EU forces, mainly the French, Belgians and Spanish, are digging in a secondary defensive line along the German-French, Belgian and Dutch borders. I'm having a hard time getting Chancellor Lowden to release the French, Belgium and Spanish armies. They're also holding the Spanish forces in northern Italy, despite their needs up north."

"What about the British? Are they able to commit any forces to the continent?" asked the President curiously.

General Wade sighed again and said, "Unfortunately, no. They have already committed three armored divisions with 70,000 troops. They have 25,000 soldiers in Iceland right now, and their main focus is on protecting the North Atlantic Greenland-Iceland gap. The Russians have made numerous naval attempts to break through, but thus far have been repulsed. Their ground force is only about 250,000 soldiers. They have another 250,000 in training, but it will take time before they are ready. Right now, their main concern is defending their island and the fighting in Norway—not the continent."

President Stein had known this was going to be a problem long before the war had started. "Generals, we knew this was a possibility. The EU Army does not have a history of working together or being ready to defend their homeland. General Wade, how long can your forces hold out?" asked the President.

"If the Russians don't push hard, we can hold for a while longer. The problem we're facing is that the warm weather of summer almost certainly signals a new Russian offensive; once that happens, we'll most likely have to fall back. I believe we can make a stand at the French border, but there's no way we can hold all of Germany if the Russians really come at us," General Wade responded, knowing this might not have been the answer the President wanted to hear.

"Thank you for your candor. I'm going to place a call to PM Bedford and see if I can convince him to commit some additional forces to help you out. In the meantime, I want you to plan on a delaying defensive action if you do have to retreat through Germany. Make sure they pay for every yard, and then hold the line in France if that's what it comes down to. As you know, we have millions of men and women in training. We will have the force necessary to recapture whatever they take in time. I also want you to try and override the Chancellor and get those French and other forces into the fight. Remind them that they are part of NATO, and those forces fall under NATO command and control, not national command and control," said the President forcefully. "If I have to get involved, I will, but I would like this to get sorted out at the NATO level without me having to threaten them in order to get them involved in the war."

General Branson saw the President was clearly getting incensed with the EU Chancellor and wanted to change topics quickly before the President went down one of his anti-European tangents. He quickly changed the holograph maps to display the North Pacific, with a number of areas highlighted on it.

"Mr. President, moving to Asia—the Chinese are nearly ready to make their move on Alaska. The intelligence from our sources and drones in Japan has identified six of their supercarriers and hundreds of additional ships and transports. At this point, it's only a matter of time before they set sail for Alaska. It's about a two-week journey by sea once they leave. At present, the Navy has strung some of the approaches with mines, and we're mining all of the potential harbors and landing zones."

The invasion of Alaska was a near certainty; the question had been when it would occur. It now appeared that the invasion would take place sometime in May of 2041, which meant that the Chinese would want to try and complete their operation before the end of the summer season. The President knew that if the Chinese were able to establish a secure foothold throughout the winter, then they would use it to launch their next offensive down into the rest of the country in the spring of 2042.

The President had ordered nearly 400,000 troops to Alaska over the past four months to get them ready for the invasion. "What is the status of the defenses?" asked the President, curious to know how ready the army was.

"We have a two-pronged strategy for our forces in Alaska. The first is to meet them at the beach. As we identify the shores they will hit, we will shift forces to meet them. We're already readying the potential landing locations and fallback positions. This first strategy will bloody them and prevent them from having an easy landing. We'll give them a warm American welcome. The likely beaches are already being fortified with defenses, which will be heavily reinforced once it becomes clear where the Chinese are going to commit their forces," Branson said while showing various images of the defenses under construction.

"The second strategy is for us to fight a continued delaying action of attack, a counterattack strategy. We'll stay in near constant contact with them but continue to fall back. Our units will rotate troops in to the frontlines and various fall back positions, allowing them to gain some rest while the enemy is constantly having to fight. We're going to bleed them dry in Alaska," General Branson said as he read off the talking points from his tablet.

"When the winter comes, we'll continue to fight. The war will turn a bit more asymmetrical during the winter, and we'll employ a lot more sniper operations, but they'll get no reprieve during the winter. The guys at DARPA have come up with some sort of new sniper drone we plan to test in Alaska. I only bring it up because if it works, this will be a great addition to every infantry company to have on top of the existing surveillance drones. Come spring of 2042, we will have one million more troops ready, another 3,600 Pershing tanks, and an additional 2,500 Wolverines."

"Don't forget the new Raptor suits—those are going to make a huge difference for our guys," the President said, eager to start getting more of the newer tech involved.

General Branson added, "We take possession of the first 50,000 Raptor suits in June. We have the troops identified and are starting their initial training. These troops will be ready for combat in August."

Director Rubio of the CIA interjected, "It's going to be a tough fight, Mr. President. The intelligence we're getting from those mini satellites is really starting to pay off. We're seeing a massive troop movement in Russia as well; they're moving their invasion force into position. It truly is disappointing that we don't have the naval power to go after these fleets. There are hundreds of transports and other ships involved in this invasion, and we just don't have the naval capabilities to attack them."

Admiral Juliano, the Chief of Naval Operations, spoke up. "I've ordered nearly all of our submarines to the North Pacific. The British are sending four submarines as well. Everyone knows the Swordfish drones are still in production. There's only so much the Navy can do right now. The Swordfish drones we have are already proving to be worth their weight in gold, but we only have two. We have three new attack submarines being completed in July, and we'll have another five completed by the end of the year. We have to remember, it takes close to two years to manufacture a submarine." The admiral spoke in a defensive tone.

The President let out a slow sigh. "The issue always comes back to not having enough ships, submarines, cruise missiles, tanks and so on. The de Blasio administration and others really screwed up our military and our ability to defend the country, haven't they?" said the President with a bit of despair, speaking to no one in particular.

"They certainly didn't help, but just like America of 1941, the economic giant of America has been awakened. We need a bit more time to ramp up production, and in time, we're going to crush them," replied Eric Clarke with defiance in his voice. "We may not crush the Chinese or Russians this year, Mr. President, but by God we will crush them."

Stein knew everyone was nearing the end of their ropes, and the pressure just kept on coming. "All right, let's move to domestic matters. John, can you go ahead and give us a quick update?" asked the President.

Attorney General John Roberts was exhausted—his department had been working feverishly to stabilize Mexico and to bring law and order back to so many small and large cities in America. The integration of the Trinity Program into everyday counterterrorism efforts had greatly increased the FBI's effectiveness in identifying and preventing acts of terrorism and sabotage. However, it had also created an enormous backlog in both the FISA courts and the regular judicial court system. Tens of thousands of cases needed to be brought before a judge, and there was a critical shortage of justices.

Between the Russians, Chinese and the IR, they had really done a number on the American civil service sector with their targeted assassinations and killings. It was fortunate the Trinity Program identified these individuals quickly so they could be stopped, but the initial damage had been done. Aside from identifying, nominating and appointing new judges, his office also had to help the White House identify candidates for the Supreme Court. It was imperative that the country's judicial systems get back up and running as soon as possible. The President was adamant about the country returning to a constitutional republic. His detractors had been likening him to a dictator or king because of the extraordinary actions he had taken as of late. However, in all fairness, all the actions the President had been taking were authorized under the various defense authorizations, acts, and existing laws; very little had been done through executive order.

John Roberts rubbed his temples, trying to wake himself back up after a long couple of months of long hours. Having mentally prepared himself, he responded, "Yes, Mr. President. As you know, the Trinity Program has significantly reduced crime across the country. The issue is judges. We have been identifying and nominating magistrates as fast as possible. Next week we will be sending your office five candidates for nomination to the Supreme Court," AG Roberts said with as much energy as he could muster.

The President saw his staff was tired and realized this was going to lead to mistakes. They needed rest. "Listen, I know there's a lot of work and we're all under immense amounts of pressure. However, you all need to take care of yourselves as well. I want everyone to find a way to take a 48-hour break. I don't care what you have to do to make this happen, but you all need sleep and some downtime. We're going to start making errors and bad decisions if people don't start to get rested. So, consider this an order," the President said as he dismissed the meeting.

Chapter 32
Armageddon

Same Time
Megiddo, Israel
1st Infantry Division

SFC Nelson's company had been reinforced with forty-eight new replacements and was sent right back into the meat grinder that was the front lines near the city of Megiddo—or, translated into English, Armageddon. The fact that one of the major battles was taking place at this historical end times location wasn't lost on the men and women fighting there either. The Russians were putting up heavy resistance, moving hundreds of tanks and armored infantry fighting vehicles into the area.

A flight of five Razorbacks swooped in from behind the American lines and let loose a barrage of hellfire antitank missiles at the incoming tanks. As the Razorbacks flew in for a second pass, a Russian antiair laser system zapped one of the Razorbacks, cutting a hole right through it before the aircraft exploded. Within seconds, two more Razorbacks were shot down. The other two got away. Despite the loss of three critical aircraft, they had accomplished their mission of stopping the Russian armored advance by destroying more than sixty armored vehicles.

As SFC Nelson looked over the battlefield, all he could see was the burning husks of what had once been fearsome Russian battle tanks and infantry fighting vehicles. Thousands of Russian soldiers were still intermixed with the destroyed vehicles firing at his battalion. Their objective was simple: advance across the battlefield and make direct contact with the Russian infantry. The American counterattack was now in full swing. It was now time to tie the Russian units down while other armor units advanced around their flanks and closed off any chance of retreat.

As Jordy Nelson advanced, he saw hundreds of red and green tracers flying back and forth between the two opposing groups. Soldiers on both sides were being hit, some dropping dead before they even knew what happened to them while others fell to the ground languishing in pain, screaming for a medic or their mothers. The slow whistle of artillery could be heard, and he wasn't sure if the rounds were friendly or incoming. Nelson knelt down next to a rock and a tree stump while he took aim at the enemy and began to engage them.

The built-in HUD and targeting system with the M5 AIR were amazing. With the 5x zoom he could see targets up to 250 meters away and engage them easily. There were hundreds, perhaps thousands of Russian and IR soldiers, frantically digging foxholes and firing back at his soldiers and the rest of his battalion.

Within ten minutes, Nelson had gone through two 250 round magazines. His power pack was at 47%—still good for at least another magazine and a half. Checking his HUD, Nelson saw his platoon had seven KIAs and thirteen WIAs. The medics were working on the wounded guys, pulling them behind cover and then moving them back to the rear area, where they could be medevacked to a hospital.

SFC Nelson switched his radio frequency from the company net to his platoon net and addressed his group. "Everyone, listen up. That Russian gun emplacement has been causing us a lot of grief since we got here. It's time we take it out. First and second squad are going to provide covering fire while third and fourth squad advance. We're going to move forward to that debris pile about 20 meters in front of our current positions. I want heavy suppressive fire when we move, understand?"

"Sergeant, how close do we need to get before we can just use our AT6s and take that position out?" asked one of the soldiers in the platoon.

"We need to advance at least 50 meters before we use them. I want us to get close so that once it goes down, the platoon is ready to advance on that trench line," SFC Nelson responded.

Captain Chantilly came over the company net and said, "Everyone, the artillery guys are about to drop a few rounds on the enemy. I want everyone to be ready to advance to the enemy trench line once the barrage ends. Battalion wants us to go on the offense for a while. Be ready to advance."

Dropping to the First Platoon net, Captain Chantilly spoke to the platoon and SFC Nelson, saying, "I heard your plan to engage the enemy gun position, and I agree, we need to take that thing out. I wanted to let you know that I called in the artillery to assist you guys, and the rest of the company will follow your lead. Good initiative, First Platoon! Out."

Smiling, Nelson was happy that someone had recognized the need to take that gun position out. Finally, the Company would be going on the offensive rather than sitting still and getting shot at. "All right, everyone, you heard the captain—same plan as before. We just wait for the barrage to finish and then we advance."

The artillery continued to whistle overhead as it flew through the air, this time impacting all around the enemy gun positions and defensive trench line. A mixture of ground and airburst rounds could be seen and heard as they hit all along the Russian positions. Nelson could only imagine how many soldiers were being killed or maimed by this barrage. As soon as the bombardment started, it ended. That was when the platoon, and then the company, advanced.

Within seconds of advancing, the remaining Russians in the defensive line began popping up from their foxholes and trenches to engage the Americans. Nelson could hear bullets zipping past his head. He quickly hit the dirt. Immediately, he brought his rifle to bear and quickly identified a soldier in a foxhole, shooting away at his platoon. He took aim and fired, hitting the soldier in the face and turning his head into a bright red mist.

Checking his HUD quickly, he saw his platoon had taken a couple of casualties but was advancing in good order. Within a couple of minutes, they had moved forward to within 30 meters of the Russian defensive positions. Soldiers on both sides began throwing grenades at one another. Then the captain came over the radio and ordered the entire company to charge the positions immediately and overwhelm them. Everyone stood up and began to yell as loudly as they could, charging into the enemy positions. In seconds, Sergeant Nelson was nearing a foxhole with two Russians in it. He fired a quick burst from his gun, killing both men. He jumped into the foxhole with their dead bodies. Bullets could be heard whistling overhead, and others were slapping the dirt around his position.

Nelson took a second before popping his head up to see where the firing was coming from. He saw three other Russians in another foxhole about 20 meters to his right. They were now focused on some of his platoon mates to their front, so Nelson grabbed one of the grenades from his vest, pulled the pin and threw it in their direction. He quickly grabbed a second grenade and threw it at them as well. The first grenade landed a little short of their position but caused them to duck. The second grenade landed near the edge of their foxhole and went off just as two of the enemy soldiers had poked their heads up to begin firing again. Nelson took aim with his rifle and took the third soldier out. In seconds, his platoonmates had made it to the position and jumped in for cover.

The company had pushed the Russians back, forcing them to give up their defensive positions. The ground around the area was littered with dead American and Russian soldiers. The wounded began to cry out for medics and help. Medics and doctors began to move from one wounded soldier to another, triaging to see which ones they could help, and making comfortable the ones that were too far gone.

The Russians, unlike the IR, made the Israelis and Americans pay in blood for every inch they gave. The Israelis were probably the most fearsome fighters out of all the countries in the battle, and why shouldn't they be? This was their country, and they knew that if the Arabs won, their families would be killed. The Arabs had already killed hundreds of thousands of Israeli civilians during the first days and weeks of the war. It was wholesale genocide. In response, the Israelis were taking no prisoners in this war. The Americans had been abiding by the rules of the Geneva Convention, until hundreds and then thousands of American prisoners and wounded soldiers had been crucified on crosses and the IR had nuked New York and Baltimore. It was then that the Americans had thrown the rule books away, and it became a very dirty and brutal war of either life or death. Surrender was not an option for either side.

Chapter 33
Alaskan Blues

Day 152
03 May 2041
Nome, Alaska
Nome Airport

Private Lopez hated Alaska. From the first day they had arrived in Nome two weeks ago, it had been miserable. It was cloudy, raining most of the time and the temperature stayed in the mid-fifties. The weather had finally started to get better, but all they had done since they'd arrived was dig trenches, build bunkers and prepare machine-gun nests. Now his platoon was working on building several antitank ditches and wiring them up with explosives.

Word had it a Russian invasion force had already set sail for Nome and was expected to arrive within the next two weeks. Their lieutenant kept telling them they had to hurry, that they did not have much time left to get the city and airport ready to defend, but Private Lopez wondered what the point was. This was a small airport in the middle of nowhere Alaska. The real fight was going to be down near Anchorage.

Chapter 34
Stronghold

Day 152
03 May 2041
Anchor Point, Alaska

Sergeant Paul Allen had been transferred to the 12th Infantry Division, XI Army Group, Second Army, in Alaska after he had recovered from his wounds a month ago. He had been part of the 1st Infantry Division and had been wounded during the battle of Jerusalem. After taking several bullets to the chest and surviving, he had been promoted to sergeant and transferred to a brand-new infantry division, the 12th, to help form the new NCO cadre and bring some combat experience to the group. Close to half of the NCOs and officers had been previously wounded in the Middle East or Europe, and rather than being transferred back to their old units, they were becoming part of the nucleus of the new infantry divisions being formed in the US.

Anchor Point, Alaska, was a small town, but it controlled the inlet leading to Anchorage, making it a critically important area to defend. If the Chinese wanted to secure Anchorage by sea, then they were going to have to dislodge the American positions at Anchor Point and Homer. The engineers had been building numerous reinforced trenches, bombardment bunkers and gun emplacement positions for the 20mm heavy railguns. These railguns were going to be the primary land-based weapon in preventing the landing craft from getting ashore.

Two kilometers behind the primary defensive positions at the beach was a secondary defensive stronghold. The engineers were building defensive positions that were between two and four kilometers apart. They were ensuring the Chinese infantry would have to fight every position, one at a time, in order to clear the peninsula to get at Anchorage. The fight for Alaska was going to be a bloody one. If the Chinese and Russians thought they could invade America and find a weak and defenseless population, they were in for a real surprise. Dozens of civilian militia units had also formed and were being armed by the military as well. They were being given specific hit-and-run targets to go after, while the regular army focused on the main enemy units. With tens of thousands of US soldiers arriving in Alaska a day, this fight was shaping up to be one of the nastiest of the war.

Chapter 35
Quadrant Identification

Day 152
03 May 2041
Joint Base Elmendorf-Richardson, Alaska

General Tyler Black, the Commandant of the Marine Corps, stepped down from his duties at the request of the President to take over command of the newly minted American Second Army. He would now become the overall commander of the defense of Alaska and the West Coast. General Black had been in Alaska for four weeks, preparing the defenses from Nome, the Yukon Delta, and the Aleutians Island Chain, to Kodiak Island and the more densely populated areas of the mainland such as Homer, Seward and Anchorage. It was a daunting challenge considering more than 40% of his army was still on paper and not a reality yet.

When General Black arrived four weeks ago, there had been 160,000 troops currently in Alaska. Nearly 600,000 additional troops had been assigned and ordered to Alaska but still hadn't completed basic combat training. Convoy after convoy of troops, infantry fighting vehicles, tanks and light drone tanks were constantly arriving in Anchorage from Seattle. Twelve thousand, five hundred troops were arriving by air via commercial charter and military transports daily. Anchorage was becoming an enormous military encampment. Many of the Marine and Army divisions were still being formed as soldiers and Marines continued to arrive daily from basic training and advanced military training schools.

The next challenge, aside from the forming of the numerous divisions, was transportation and logistics. Moving divisions and their equipment to—in some cases—extremely remote locations throughout Alaska was proving to be a challenge. Ensuring those units were supplied and properly equipped was going to be the enduring logistical nightmare, especially once hostilities began. Intelligence said the Chinese fleet had set sail, meaning he had less than twelve days to finalize his troop deployments and prepare for what would be a truly enormous defensive effort.

General Black broke the Alaskan theater down into three quadrants. The top half of Alaska, which included Prudhoe Bay, Fairbanks and Nome, was quadrant one. Quadrant two included the entire Yukon Delta National Park and the Aleutians Island chain, including the Kodiak Islands. Quadrant three included everything from Homer to Denali National Park, and the eastern half of the state.

Quadrant one was being run by a major general with three divisions. 85,000 troops spread through a myriad of fire bases and combat outposts guarding strategic locations and infrastructure. Quadrant two was being managed by a major general as well, and had five divisions, or 150,000 troops. This group had the most actual land to defend, and the most beaches to have to repel the invaders from. They also had Kodiak Island to protect, which was a key strongpoint at the mouth of the inlet leading to Anchorage. Quadrant three was commanded by a lieutenant general and eight divisions, with 235,000 troops altogether. This was the most populated area of the state and had the most critical infrastructure, such as road and rail networks, to defend. It was also the key to gaining access to the rest of the Canadian States and the lower half of the US. Additional troops from the rest of the country would continue to arrive even after the invasion started, but this would be the starting American defense force for the Russian/Chinese invasion of America.

Chapter 36
Rescuing Berlin

Day 155
06 May 2041
Berlin, Germany
Field Marshal Dieter Schoen's Headquarters

Major General Dieter Schoen had been promoted to Field Marshal, giving him his fourth star as a general. His defensive efforts in Poland had bought the German/EU and Allied armies the time they needed for the American Fifth Army to assemble and engage the Russians. It was the emergence of the Fifth Army that ultimately stopped the Third Shock Army from capturing Berlin. The Allies were now trying to determine if they were going to fight for Berlin and turn it into a bloodbath like it had been during World War II, or if they were going to declare it a free city and hope that the Russians occupied it peacefully.

Marshal Schoen's army had been reinforced with an additional three hundred main battle tanks, bringing his total Panzer force up to 680 again. He had also been given a full battalion of Pershing battle tanks, which was really giving his army a big boost. Berlin had been turned to rubble during the Second World War, and turning it back into rubble wasn't something anyone in Germany wanted to have happen again. The new plan General Wade was promoting was for Schoen to pull his forces back to Brandenburg, west of Berlin. The hope was that this would draw General Kulikov's Third Shock Army around Berlin to the open flat country near Rathenow, Germany. In these flatlands west of the city, they might have a better chance in a tank battle of either seriously hurting the Russians or stopping their attack.

If their initial attack failed, then the fallback plan was to regroup at Stendal on the west side of the Elbe River and make their stand there. With nearly three million Russian troops invading Germany, and two and half million soldiers attacking through Southeastern Europe, the American and European armies were starting to buckle under the pressure. After significant pushing and outright threats from President Stein, Chancellor Lowden had released control of the rest of the EU and national armies and allowed them to be controlled by NATO. The bulk of the forces were being sent to the mountains of Croatia, Slovenia,

Austria and the German Alps to block the Russians from gaining entry into Southern Europe.

The Allies controlled the Mediterranean and the Adriatic Sea, preventing the Russians from conducting a direct seaborne landing. The Reds could and often did parachute small numbers of forces into Italy to conduct raids and guerilla operations, but they lacked the capability to conduct a large-scale airborne assault as the Allies had done.

The Russian offensive in Europe was coinciding with their attack in the Middle East and their massive invasion fleet's movement toward Alaska. Their operations in Europe were going well, with the Allies having been pushed back to the outskirts of Berlin. Operations in the Middle East had started out great, and they had nearly broken through to Tel Aviv before the Allies launched their surprise airborne and seaborne invasion of Lebanon. The Second Shock Army had a reserve contingent in Damascus and Aleppo, but both forces had been defeated by the Allied blocking force. Now the Russians had to make a hard choice: they could either give up the gains they and the Islamic Republic had made in capturing most of northern Israel, or they would face the real possibility of being surrounded and completely cut off from any reinforcements.

General Lodz was a dynamic Russian general, and his loss was felt immediately. His deputy commander took over, but he either ignored the intelligence of the Allied strength at his flank or thought he could go for broke and end the war. Either way, he decided to advance when he should have retreated. Now the Second Shock Army was in danger of being surrounded and cut off. If that happened, then chances were they would be forced to surrender—but not before they ran out of ammunition. They would bleed the Americans and Israelis before they had to throw in the towel.
****

With the Allied decision made to declare Berlin a free city and withdraw, Marshal Schoen began the immediate work of moving his forces west of Berlin. His new post was in an area that he had identified to be a good location for one of the decisive tank battles of the war, a nice flat patch of land with the River Elbe to his back. The American Fifth Army had 620 Pershing main battle tanks and 2,800 of the older venerable M1A4 MBTs. Couple that with a fighting force of nearly

760,000 combat troops, and they were a superior force, despite being outnumbered nearly four-to-one.

The advantage the Russians had was in their MiG40s, which were still wreaking havoc on the Allied air forces and their drone tanks and infantry fighting vehicles. The Russian drone IFVs were particularly nasty. The Allies called them Lemmings because they were small, about the size of a Ford F-150, and traveled in small packs, typically following a lead drone. They were lightly armored but carried two 7.62mm machine guns mounted on a lowered armored turret and an upper turret with a single 30mm gun used for destroying light armored vehicles. They ran somewhat autonomously of their owners, in that the drone pilot would program in the directions of where to go, and the drone would drive itself to that location. If it encountered resistance along the way, it would either stop to engage the opposition if it was substantial, or it could drive right through it. The drones had an automated targeting system that leveraged cameras, motion tracking, body temperature and a sophisticated AI that assisted the drone pilot. Typically, a drone pilot could manage three to five drones fairly easily, which was another reason why they were often referred to as Lemmings, blindly following their masters.

Drones and the use of AIs in the drones was really changing the way wars were being fought. The Americans held a slight advantage in fighter jet drones, railgun technology and the infantry railgun rifles and HUD systems. Where the Americans were behind was drone tanks, IFVs, manned fighter aircraft, additive manufacturing, shipbuilding and an industrial network that had been on a war footing for years. The American and EU governments and economies were behind the eight ball; neither economy was on a war footing and it was going to take time to convert. Both militaries were also behind in recruiting and training the needed force to challenge the Axis powers of the Islamic Republic, Russia, and China. At this point, their adversaries had had both their economies and their military forces on a war footing for several years before the conflict of World War III had even begun.

Chapter 37
Smile for the Cameras

Day 165
16 May 2041
Washington, D.C.
Rose Room, the White House
Fox News Interview of President Stein

After months of requests by the networks for a one-on-one interview, the President finally agreed to a two-hour interview with John Blume of Fox News. John was a well-known journalist who hosted *Special Report* on Fox. Fox News *was* probably one of the friendlier networks to the Stein administration, but that wasn't why the President agreed to talk with him. The President knew an interview like this would be a chance for him to continue to make the case for the Freedom Party as the party of growth, and to assure the American people that the war was winnable and progressing well, despite the losses occurring in Germany and the Middle East.

"Good evening, this is John Blume, and I'm here with President Henry Stein to discuss domestic and overseas issues in this special segment of *Special Report*," John said as opened the show.

"Mr. President, under your leadership, the US economy has made quite a turnaround. The country had gone from twenty percent unemployment or higher to less than three percent, and essentially there is now a critical shortage in labor, particularly with the current draft going on. Do you attribute that growth to the war, or to something else?"

President Stein responded, "I attribute the economic growth to a government functioning within the guidelines of the Constitution. The Freedom Party stands for just that—freedom to choose to be who you want to be in this country, and freedom to work for yourself if you choose to. For decades, our country had been saddled with regulations and rules that made it impossible for an entrepreneur to succeed. The bulk of American corporations had their headquarters overseas because of taxes and regulations. This was killing our economy. We also needed tax reform, a remonetizing of our currency and a reform of our social programs to make them financially viable.

"The unemployment really began to drop once we began to put people to work through the Reconstruction and Modernization Act of 2037. Millions of jobs were created through this program and the America First Corporation. People were suddenly getting hired, or in some cases, receiving multiple job offers. AFC has proven to be an incredible boon for the American people, not just because of the jobs it provides but also the revenue it has generated for the federal government. It has made Social Security solvent, and we've even been able to increase Social Security payments to ensure that every American retiring through it will receive a minimum yearly retirement of $40,000 if they retire at sixty-seven and $52,500 if they retire at seventy-three."

John countered, "I would like to go back to the remonetizing of the debt. Some would identify your remonetizing of our currency as one of the reasons we're at war with China. How do you respond to that?"

The President replied, "This war is about power, resources and land. It has nothing to do with our monetary policy. China wants to conquer Asia, and as we can see, they are in the process of conquering Africa as well. Russia wants to occupy and control the EU. Their empire would stretch from the Atlantic to the Pacific, and place over 750 million people under the rule of the new Communist state they have established. The Islamic Republic wants to impose Islam as the dominant religion across the world. They conducted a genocide of the Israeli people, as well as anyone who did not agree with their brand of Islam. As we have already seen, they have killed nearly one million Jews in Israel alone. They crucified over 3,000 US servicemen and women and cut the heads off our dead soldiers and placed them on pikes. They are barbaric. This war is about tyranny. Will we stand by and let the forces of evil in this world prevail, or will we stand up, united by freedom to do something about it?"

John Blume seemed a little taken aback by this answer. He continued, "The United States has already suffered the loss of over 200,000 men and women killed. How many more losses do you believe the American people will accept before they demand an end to the war?"

Without missing a beat, President Stein replied, "You mean how many more casualties will it take for America to surrender? That's essentially what you are asking."

Obstinately, Blume retorted, "I didn't say surrender—I just said an end to the war."

President Stein smiled at the lack of logic in his counterpart's response and explained, "The Axis powers will accept nothing less than our complete surrender. Some will argue that that isn't true, but let me ask you this. Are you willing to give up our Constitution for the sake of peace? As long as I am President, America will never surrender. To capitulate means to give up our rights as Americans. It means we give up our Constitution, and I will not allow that to happen. I will also not sacrifice our Allies and all of Europe for the sake of appeasing the political left in our country. This war is barely six months old, and already people on the left are wanting to give up. Let's not forget that our country was savagely attacked. Our soldiers were being crucified and their heads cut off and placed on spikes. We were further nuked, killing nearly six million civilians…and people want talk about ending the war? We will end the war when we have won it. Mark my words, the American manufacturing and ingenuity has only just awakened. Our economy, and our military, will see this war through to victory."

Changing topics, John continued, "It would appear that Alaska is about to be invaded by the Russians and Chinese. What are you doing to ensure we don't lose one of our states? This is, after all, the first time America will have been invaded by a foreign power in force since the War of 1812."

The President replied, "I assure you, and the American people, the military is doing everything they can to protect this country and Alaska. As the commander-in-chief, I am working to ensure our military has every resource they need to win this fight. I have the utmost confidence in our generals and military commanders—"

Blume interrupted, "—Even General Gardner? The general who destroyed the Al Aqsa Mosque?"

Stein didn't get flustered. He calmly responded, "I did not agree with, or authorize, General Gardner's destruction of one of Islam's holiest sites. That said, General Gardner has done a superb job of defending Israel and moving us that much closer to defeating the Islamic Republic, the country that nuked New York and Baltimore."

The President continued, "I also want to release a new piece of news. As of an hour before this interview started, the Chinese Expeditionary Force in the Middle East has officially surrendered, and so has the Second Shock Army. It won't be long before our armies are driving through Riyadh. We have General Gardner and the US Third Army to thank for that, along with our ally, the Israeli Defense Force."

The interview went on for some time as the President continued to assure the American people that the war was moving in the right direction. The bottom line was that the country was recovering from the nuclear attack, and the economy was stronger than ever. At the end of the day, most Americans were going to be content with the fact that they had decent jobs and money in their pockets.

Chapter 38
The Invasion Begins

Day 180
31 May 2041
Nome, Alaska
Operation Red Dawn

As the Russian fleet approached the city of Nome, Alaska, they encountered the Navy's new Swordfish underwater drone for the first time. The drone was able to launch four torpedoes before the Russians even knew it was in the area. It sank a troop carrier and damaged one of the two Russian carriers. The other two torpedoes hit an ammunition ship and a troop transport, sinking both ships.

The Russian fleet began to launch a massive missile barrage in coordination with the carrier air wings, heavily damaging the airport and city of Nome. While the bombardment was underway, hundreds of smaller amphibious landing craft were making preparations for the first Russian seaborne invasion of America.

While the amphibious landing was taking place, the sky was being filled with drones and aircraft vying for control of the battlespace. Dozens of transport aircraft were dropping thousands of Russian paratroopers deep behind enemy lines to sow as much confusion and chaos as possible. As the first wave of infantry hit the beaches, they met heavy resistance from the American positions near the coastline. The battle for the beach raged on for nearly three hours. It wasn't until the Russians landed their third wave of forces, intermixed with tanks, that they broke through the American positions.

The shore and several hundred meters inland were littered with the dead and dying. Hundreds of bodies could be seen floating in the water and crashing against the shore as the waves continued to push their lifeless bodies against the sand and rocks. The water became red from their blood.

Once the beach area was lost, the Americans began a quick retreat to their secondary positions. The troops returning from the coast were exhausted, beat-up, dirty, and low on ammunition. They passed through the secondary defensive line and the troops assigned to defend it, giving them as much information about the oncoming Russians as they could before they were loaded into waiting vehicles and driven to the third line of defense, where they would re-form and prepare to meet the Russians once again.

Chapter 39
Clash for the Kodiak

Day 180
31 May 2041
Kodiak Island

The massive Chinese fleet began their final approach to Alaska, with their next stop being Kodiak Island. A smaller PLAN fleet and landing force were securing the Aleutian Island chain and peninsula, while the main fleet sailed closer to Kodiak and the inlet that would lead them to Anchorage. The goal was to secure Kodiak Island and turn it into a land base and logistical hub for the main invasion of Alaska. They needed to secure the city and the airport nearby; then they could move on and capture Shuyak Island State Park, Ushagat Island in the center of the channel, and Kachemak Bay State Park. Once these locations had been secured, the Chinese Navy would begin to ferry in millions of PLA soldiers and equipment. From there, a gravy train of supplies and troops would be sent from China directly to the front lines.

As the fleet moved closer, the five Chinese supercarriers began to launch their air wings of drones and manned fighters to begin battling for control of the skies. While the fighters were mixing it up in the air with the Americans, the Naval Task Force began a massive rocket and missile barrage of the entrenched American positions throughout the state parks, islands and Anchorage itself. Hundreds of amphibious landing craft were disembarking from their motherships and began heading toward the beaches and various landing sites in a massive and well-orchestrated invasion.

As the landing craft neared the city of Kodiak, they started to receive enemy fire from numerous heavy railgun positions. Short-range rockets and mortars were starting to be launched by the hundreds as the invaders continued to get closer and closer to the shoreline.

Corporal Chang stood in the leading vessel, wearing his specialized exoskeleton combat suit. He was ready to kill Americans. This was Chang's first time using this new combat suit, and he was eager to see if it lived up to its reputation. It was also his first time facing the Americans. From everything he had heard, the Americans fought like men possessed by devils. He had been told this would not be an easy landing, and that he should not take the Americans for granted as an easy foe to defeat. They all knew the First EF had been defeated in the Middle East—no one wanted to repeat that history.

The PLAN infantry had been given priority to receive the suits first, since they would be leading the amphibious assault against America. The suits gave their users an incredible advantage over their adversaries. Aside from being able to run at close to 30 mph and lift nearly 2,000 pounds, the suit's wearer was sheathed in the newest generation of Dragon Skin body armor. This was the same body armor that the American soldiers used. The blueprints had been stolen years ago, and the Chinese had seen no need to change the name. The name fit its design. The Dragon Skin was essentially bulletproof against all modern-day assault rifle ammunition, with the exception of the Americans' new M5 AIR. The soldiers' arms, legs and necks were still somewhat exposed, leaving the suit vulnerable in certain areas.

As Chang's landing vehicle got closer to the targeted site, they began to take heavy enemy fire. Dozens of bullets bounced off the armored shield on the front of the landing vehicle; the craft itself was bounced around by artillery and mortar rounds landing nearby. Geysers of water spouted and soaked the troops on the landing vehicles from nearby misses. Fire and shrapnel would consume others who weren't so lucky. Chang looked through one of the bullet proof window slits in the landing craft to catch a glance at the shore. What he saw was nothing short of spectacular horror.

Tracer rounds could be seen crisscrossing between the landing craft's heavy weapons and those of the Americans entrenched near the shore. It was like watching a laser show, with the sheer volume of terror being unleashed between the two sides. Rockets continued to hammer the American positions while heavy mortars and artillery continued to land amongst the amphibious fleet that was nearly to the shore now.

A voice came on the radio, barely audible over the growl of the engines and machine-gun fire, to let Chang's squad know they were about to make landfall and that they should be ready to exit the rear of the vehicle quickly because they wouldn't be sticking around very long. The landing vehicle needed to head back to the mothership and pick up the next wave of soldiers. Suddenly, the vessel hit the gravelly beach, and the back door dropped down for Chang's ten-man squad to exit the vehicle and make for their objectives. Chang's squad had been assigned three gun emplacement positions to secure before moving inland to engage other targets.

While they were exiting the rear of the vehicle, a mortar round landed nearby and exploded. It knocked Chang off his feet and threw him a couple of feet back into the water. The rest of his squad began to fire their rifles at the American positions and advanced in good order, just as they had been drilled and trained to do. Chang quickly got to his feet and ran after his squad. Just then, the landing vehicle began to back up where Chang had been just seconds earlier. The roar of all of the machine guns and explosions was almost deafening. As Chang neared a disabled Chinese tank that his squad was using for cover, he ordered them to advance to the first gun emplacement 100 meters to their front. Two of the soldiers in his squad moved forward ten meters while the remainder of the squad provided covering fire.

When the first two had moved ten meters and found cover, they dropped down and began providing covering fire along with the rest of the squad as two more advanced. Within seconds, the American gunners quickly saw what was happening and turned their machine guns toward Chang's advancing squad. While Chang's crew was advancing toward the gun emplacement, four other squads began to advance as well. The machine-gun crew was manning a .25mm machine railgun, spitting out nearly 600 rounds a minute. They swept their gun back and forth between the advancing groups, hitting some while missing others. Other men in the trenches were also sending tremendous volumes of fire in their directions as well.

Several of Chang's men along with men from another squad got within 30 meters of the gun emplacement and the trench line. All of a sudden, a massive explosion occurred and blew eight Chinese soldiers apart. The Dragon Skin armor generally did a good job of protecting the core of a soldier's body; however, the explosion ripped their legs and arms right off. The screams they made as they thrashed around on the ground, calling for help, were horrendous. The Americans had detonated three Claymore landmines they had put into place earlier. A nearby lieutenant ordered everyone in the area to advance at once toward the gun emplacement and try to overwhelm the defenders.

As the soldiers in the area rose to advance, the machine railgun came alive again, cutting dozens of soldiers down. The exoskeleton suits enabled the Chinese soldiers to advance quickly toward the American lines. As they got within 20 meters of their positions, the Americans triggered another series of Claymore mines, killing and maiming dozens of additional Chinese soldiers. In seconds, Chang was in the American position and found himself face-to-face with an American soldier. Chang quickly brought his gun to bear and was able to shoot the American in the face, exploding his head before he was able to use his M5, which would have cut through Chang's body armor.

Chang called out to the others in his squad to form up around him as they continued to clear the trench network they were currently in. An American jumped out from one of the bomb bunkers and threw a grenade toward Chang and his men. Without thinking, one of Chang's soldiers jumped on the grenade just as it exploded. The soldier died immediately, but he had saved half a dozen of his fellow soldiers. One of Chang's men charged the American bunker, while another soldier shot his grenade gun into the entrance. A small explosion could be heard, along with the quick bursts of several machine guns from both Chang's men and the remaining Americans in the bunker. In less than a minute, the conflict was over, and Chang's men began to shift their focus to their next objective.

Chapter 40
Drone Attack

Day 180
31 May 2041
The Sky Above Anchorage

Lieutenant Daniels was a drone fighter pilot. He had just been transferred to Eielson Air Force Base near Fairbanks after completing drone flight school four days earlier. Daniels was controlling an F38A fighter drone, and his squadron was tasked with providing cover for the F38B ground attack drones that were supporting the infantry as they tried to repel multiple landing invasions.

Daniels heard his squadron commander sign in and began to give them a quick message before the squadron moved as a group to engage the hundreds of fighters heading in their direction. "Men, listen up. I know most of you are fresh out of flight school and this is your first real combat mission. It's OK to be nervous and doubt yourself, but trust your training, and remember, this is the real deal. There are tens of thousands of soldiers on the ground depending on us to succeed so our ground attack planes can provide the close air support they desperately need. Remember your training—I cannot stress that enough. Your preparation works, and so do the tactics we're about to employ. If your fighter is shot down, I want you to grab another and get back in the fight."

As Lieutenant Daniels's squadron headed toward Anchorage, they began to detect hundreds of enemy fighter drones and manned Chinese aircraft. "All right. Our squadron has been directed to engage the fighter drones. One of the other squadrons is going to engage the manned aircraft. We'll be in range to launch our AMRAAMs in three minutes. Everyone is to launch your missiles, one after the other, and then accelerate to get into knife range and engage with your sidewinders. Once we go weapons free, you and your wingmen are on your own, understand?"

"Yes, Sir," they all replied in unison.

The pilots continued to position their aircraft to engage the Chinese. Daniels's squadron consisted of twenty-four drones. Each pilot had three spare drones at the base, ready to be moved to the runway as soon as the pilot was ready to use it. The F38A was a powerful fighter drone; without having to worry about the survivability of a pilot, the aircraft was able to incorporate some incredible new designs that allowed the aircraft to maneuver on a dime. It had a range of 520 miles, could travel at speeds of up to Mach 3, and carried a 20mm railgun for air-to-air combat. It was armed with six AMRAAM air-to-air missiles, which could engage an enemy aircraft as far away as 90 miles at a speed of Mach five. It also carried six Sidewinder 4 short-range heat-seeking missiles, which had a range of 15 miles. The aircraft had an advanced suite of electronic countermeasures and defensive systems to assist in its survivability.

The squadron was engaging about 80 Chinese drones that were trying to secure the air over Kodiak Island. Daniels's aircraft came into AMRAAM range just as his squadron began to release the first volley of missiles. Daniels toggled a couple of switches and released his six missiles toward their targets, when all of a sudden his warning alarms went off. His aircraft was being targeted by multiple enemy drones, who simultaneously fired their own missiles at him and his squadron. His aircraft now had five enemy missiles heading toward it. He hit the afterburner, bringing his aircraft to its maximum speed as his wingman maneuvered to stay next to him. The two of them were going to bring their aircraft up to maximum speed and then begin to jink and pull a few other maneuvers as they closed the gap between themselves and the Chinese.

As Daniels followed his training, he was surprised to see that all of the missiles that had been fired at him had missed when he'd conducted the series of tight turns and jinks designed to make it impossible for a missile to continue to track his aircraft, especially in light of his suite of countermeasures. Suddenly, he was within 15 miles of the remaining Chinese aircraft, and he began to cycle through his last remaining missiles. Just as Daniels's last missile left his aircraft, he was hit by machine-gun fire from a fighter that had somehow gotten behind him. In seconds, Daniels's fighter drone was ripped apart by bullets, and at the speed it was traveling, it lost control. He immediately disconnected from the drone and activated another that was now leaving the secured bunker and moving toward the runways.

After less than sixty minutes in the air, nearly all 24 of the drone fighters in Daniels's squadron had been shot down, but not before shooting down 73 enemy fighter drones. Most of the pilots were in the process of piloting their second drone out to the runways or just taking off when the building's alarms went off. A loud explosion could be heard nearby, and suddenly, a lot of machine-gun fire. It sounded as it if it was coming from the floor above them, which was the operations room, where a lot of the analysis and fighter operations were conducted.

A guard ran into the room and shouted to everyone, "Russians have infiltrated the building! They're on the floor above! Everyone, get your sidearm ready!"

BOOM! An explosion could be heard just outside the secured door, and suddenly, several objects flew into the room. Daniels had just enough time to realize the flying circles were hand grenades before one bounced off the wall near his pod, exploding and killing him instantly.

A 90-man Spetsnaz team had infiltrated the base perimeter and begun to attack several buildings before the base security knew they had penetrated the boundary defenses. Another team of Spetsnaz rained down 120mm mortars on the runways, which were now lined with fighter drones being prepared for takeoff. As the rounds landed amongst the drones, they started a chain reaction, causing numerous secondary explosions. Their ordnance started to add to the chaos. The Russians knew exactly where the fighter drone pilots were operating from; they had long ago stolen the blueprints of the building from the contracting company that had built it. They had painstakingly planned and prepared their mission around accomplishing two main tasks: disabling the runway, hopefully for 24 hours, and attacking and killing the various drone pilot squadrons.

They were going to attack all eight squadrons' worth of pilots and destroy the equipment. One after another, each building was successfully penetrated; the people inside were killed and then the buildings were destroyed. With the attack a success, the Spetsnaz teams were done and began to exit the structures to head toward the base perimeter and the safety of the surrounding woods, where they had staged the attack. Unexpectedly, several Razorback helicopters arrived on the scene and engaged the Russians. The quick-reaction force quickly wiped out the attacking group, which had very little in the way of cover to hide behind and no heavy weapons or missiles capable of disabling or destroying the armored helicopters.

In the thirteen-minute attack, the Russians had lost all but four members of the Spetsnaz team but had killed the pilots and operational staff for all eight drone squadrons on the base. They had also substantially damaged the runway, making it impossible to use for at least a half day. This would prove disastrous not just for the American fighter drones in Alaska, but also for the manned aircraft. Most of the pilots flying over Alaska had originated from this airbase. The Russians had nearly neutralized the American airpower in the first day of the invasion.

Chapter 41
After the Shock and Awe

Day 180
31 May 2041
General Black's Headquarters

General Black was sitting at his desk, looking at a tablet with the losses from Eielson AFB, and he couldn't believe his eyes. The Russians had somehow snuck a large enough attacking force through the base defenses and, knowing exactly where the drone pilots were operating from, had shut down the whole fleet. They had taken out the guards and destroyed the entire facility in less than fifteen minutes. General Black had specifically selected Eielson to be the primary launch point for the drone squadrons because it was far enough away from the invasion fleets that it wouldn't come under direct enemy missile attacks.

The next report was from sector one, in Nome, Alaska. The Russians had busted their way off the beaches, and it looked like they were about to break through the second line of defense. Reports were showing that a limited number of Russian soldiers were using the new exoskeleton suits. Of course, the entire Spetsnaz team that had attacked Eielson was using them. Reports of Spetsnaz teams popping up all over Alaska were starting to come in. He had to get in touch with his Special Forces commander and have him assign the appropriate teams to hunt them down. He couldn't have dozens of Russian Special Forces operating in his rear area.

Putting one tablet down and picking up another, General Black began to look through the battle report from Kodiak Island. In less than four hours, they had secured twenty miles inland from the beach and might have the rest of the island secured within the next four to five days if they continued advancing at their current pace. General Black had a message sent to the commander on the island to have his men try to hold out longer. The more time that passed with the Chinese invasion fleet this close to the coast, the more danger they were in from land-based attacks. The Navy was now starting to hit the Chinese with hundreds of smaller attack craft that would swoop in swarms and launch a volley of antiship missiles. The goal was to overwhelm the carrier defenses with antiship missiles while coordinating the attack with land-based aircraft and short-range land-based antiship missiles. The beach areas needed to hold the line for 48 hours to give the Navy and Air Force enough time to coordinate a massive strike against the fleet.

General Black's Chief of Staff, Major General Cooper, walked into the general's office and said, "General Black, the Eielson base commander is on the line when you're ready."

General Black sighed and motioned for MG Cooper to take a seat. His JAG and J3 also walked into the room and took a seat at the round table in the general's office. "Brigadier General Miller, we'll keep this meeting as short and to the point as we can. I want to know how in the world a ninety-plus man Spetsnaz team was able to penetrate so deep into your base, identify the drone squadrons and wipe them out without alerting your security forces," Black said in his gruff Marine style.

"Sir, we're still trying to determine how they were able to identify the drone squadrons so quickly. From the time the base perimeter sensors went offline until the time they attacked the squadrons was less than five minutes. We immediately scrambled our QRF to the location. Right now, we're working on the assumption that either someone gave them the location, or they acquired the blueprints from the construction company who built it. We were made aware that that company had had a cyber breach about fifteen months ago, when we began building the location."

He continued, "The Russians were using those new exoskeleton combat suits, which is probably how they were able to move so quickly and carry those weapons and explosives. At first, the QRF was concerned with neutralizing the mortar team that was hammering the airfield. By the time we received the notice that the squadrons were under direct attack, the QRF was already engaging the mortar teams. We released the second QRF team, but when they arrived on scene, the damage to the squadrons had already been done."

"General, this is simply unacceptable. I cannot, for the life of me, fathom how one of our most important assets to this war was left so undefended that a Spetsnaz team was not only able to gain access it, they were able to slaughter all the pilots, staff and destroy the facility within nine minutes of entering the base." He took a deep breath to calm himself before continuing, "Brigadier General Miller, I am relieving you of command, effective immediately. I have your replacement inbound as we speak, along with several additional SF teams which will begin to hunt down the rest of the Spetsnaz teams operating in your AOR."

"Sir, I understand your frustration, but losses happen in war. The Russians got lucky—it wasn't incompetence," BG Miller protested, clearly taken aback that he was being relieved of his command.

"General, I comprehend your shock and frustration. However, you were charged with guarding one of the most important pieces of our national defense, and you failed to protect it. Perhaps it was luck on the Russians' part, but it happened on your watch. You are being reassigned back to the Pentagon. Please do not take this as a slight against you. We're giving you the opportunity to redeem yourself in D.C.," the general said, trying to lessen the blow to BG Miller, and ended the call.

"Well, that went well. Hopefully, he'll do better at the Pentagon," said MG Cooper.

Looking at General Cooper, General Black said, "Cooper, I need a frank assessment from you. How are things shaping up in sector one?"

Pulling some information up from his tablet, Cooper said, "Shaky, but as expected. Aside from the debacle at Eielson, everything is turning out about as well as we suspected and planned. They hit us hard today. What we didn't anticipate was how many Spetsnaz teams they would be able to infiltrate behind our lines. The same goes with Chinese SF units. The Chinese and Russians hit us with those new exoskeleton combat suits with their first and second wave of landings. We weren't surprised by them, but their performance was incredibly effective. Most of our forces are fighting in their third lines of defense; once they lose those lines, the next lines of defense are typically fifteen to twenty miles further back."

"Do we know when they are going to make their main landings near Homer and Seward?" asked General Black.

"Probably in the next three to five days. We believe they want to fully secure their current gains before advancing again," said MG Cooper.

General Black thought for a moment, trying to determine if they needed to adjust their strategy yet, or if they should continue to stick to the plan for the moment. "Gentlemen, I have a video call with the national security staff and the President in ten minutes. I would like you to sit in as well, in case I need you to provide some information. Please

take a few minutes to get any new updates you need, and be prepared to brief it should I call on you," Black directed before dismissing his inner circle to prepare for the presidential briefing.
****

President Stein walked into the Situation Room and saw the entire staff was already there and ready. He signaled for one of his aides to bring him a fresh Red Bull; the President was beginning to live on these things with all the long hours he had been working since the start of the war. His doctor said he was going to have a heart attack if he didn't cut back on the caffeine, but this was one vice he simply couldn't give up given the current state of affairs.

Stein took his seat at the head of the table and signaled for the briefing to begin.

General Branson stood up and walked over to one of the monitors and began his brief, "Mr. President, we are now nineteen hours into the invasion of Alaska. The Russians have successfully landed around 38,000 troops in sector one, and they have also parachuted around another twelve thousand paratroopers all across sector one. Right now, they have several dozen or more Spetsnaz teams running around in central Alaska, causing all sorts of problems with our logistical networks. General Black sent a few dozen of our own SF teams to try and hunt them down.

"Sector two has been hit hard; we have lost most of the Aleutian Island chain and the rest of the Peninsula. General Black doesn't expect to hold them for more than a few more days. We never really had any intentions of being able to stop them there. It was really only meant as a defensive and asymmetrical fight to tie down Chinese forces. Unfortunately, it does look like they're going to capture Kodiak Island a lot sooner than we had hoped. Our goal was to hold the island for at least a month, tying down nearly a hundred thousand soldiers—"

The President interrupted to ask a question. "—What happened? Why are they not going to be able to hold the position for much longer?"

General Branson brought up various drone feeds showing the fighting on the beach. Images could be seen of hundreds of PLAN infantry moving from their landing vehicles and quickly sprinting across the shore right into a number of American defensive positions. "They move so fast," commented Director Jorge Perez, the DHS Secretary.

"The PLAN infantry received priority status for their new exoskeleton combat suits. As we can see, these suits really provide their soldiers an advantage. They can advance and move quickly, making them harder to shoot. They closed the gap between their positions and ours fast. They were able to move through the first line of defense rather hastily. They slowed down a bit at the second line of defense, and have been stopped at the third for the time being."

General Branson continued, "We've slowed them down by using sheer numbers. So far, they haven't landed enough soldiers yet to be able to punch through our third line of defense. That will change in a day or so, once they start to land their light drone tanks and IFVs. I also have a piece of bad news to report." Branson had some trepidation about this next part—he knew the President was going to be livid.

"A Spetsnaz team was able to penetrate the base perimeter at Eielson AFB and attacked the drone squadrons. Unfortunately, they destroyed *all* of the drone piloting pods and killed all the pilots. We also lost nearly two-thirds of all the fighter and bomber drones at the base. We're sending new pilots and additional drones and piloting pods to Eielson. It's going to be a couple of days until they're operational again. In the meantime, we're going to be focusing on our manned fighters for the time being to provide the bulk of the air cover over Alaska."

The President put down his Red Bull mid-drink and said, "How in the world did they penetrate the base defense and wipe out eight squadrons of pilots and equipment? That's a lot of critical people they killed in one swoop." From his tone of voice and facial expressions, he was clearly beyond angry.

"The base commander has been relieved of command, Mr. President. It would appear they gained access to the designs, and thus the location of the site, through a cyber-attack that was conducted against the contracting company that built it. Once they had the blueprints, we suspect it wasn't hard for them to build a replica of it somewhere in Russia and train for it like we would have," Branson said, hoping his answer might diffuse the President's anger a bit.

"This is a colossal screw-up, General. How bad is this going to hurt our efforts in Alaska?" asked the President.

"It's going to stifle our efforts a lot. Right now, most of our airpower in Alaska has been taken offline. The runways have been repaired, and we have limited manned flight operations, but the loss of eight fighter drones' worth of pilots is going to hurt. We're moving drone pilots from all across the US to Alaska right now to fill the gap. It's going to leave us shortchanged in a lot of other places," the general explained.

The President shot back, "Get this fixed, General Branson and General Black. We need to do better in Alaska or we are going to have a serious problem on our hands."

With that, the meeting ended.

Chapter 42
Field of Blood

Day 181
01 June 2041
Kodiak, Alaska

General Jing Zhu stepped off the landing craft on the beach near the city of Kodiak, Alaska. What he saw made his stomach churn. The water around the shore was still red with blood, and gore soaked the beach. Bodies could be seen floating in the water and strung all along the coastline for as far as they eye could see in both directions. Clearly, the Americans had fought hard for this section of land, and the Chinese had paid dearly to capture this beachhead. Off in the distance, General Zhu heard the rumble of artillery fire and the continuous cacophony of machine-gun fire as both sides tried relentlessly to kill each other.

Overhead, the screams of aircraft could be heard as Chinese drones and manned fighters continued to fight for dominance of the skies. General Zhu turned his head slightly and watched as a group of eight attack helicopters headed toward the front lines. Then he saw a large landing craft drop its front ramp; a large main battle tank came to life and rumbled off the landing craft, heading toward the front lines.

"General Zhu," an aide said, interrupting his thoughts. "The command post is over here. The rest of your staff is ready."

As General Jing Zhu entered the half-blown-out town hall that was now serving as the command post for the ground operations, he saw the commander of the PLAN infantry, along with his army commanders.

He smiled as he began, "Generals, Operation Red Dragon has been a huge success. For the first time in modern history, a foreign army has invaded America. Today marks the end of America and the rise of the Dragon…"

From the Authors

Miranda and I hope you've enjoyed this book. We always have more books in production; we are currently working on another riveting military thriller series, The Monroe Doctrine. If you'd like to order Volume One of this action-packed page-turner, please visit Amazon.

If you would like to stay up to date on new releases and receive emails about any special pricing deals we may make available, please sign up for our email distribution list. Simply go to https://www.frontlinepublishinginc.com/ and sign up.

If you enjoy audiobooks, we have a great selection that has been created for your listening pleasure. Our entire Red Storm series and our Falling Empire series have been recorded, and several books in our Rise of the Republic series and our Monroe Doctrine series are now available. Please see below for a complete listing.

As independent authors, reviews are very important to us and make a huge difference to other prospective readers. If you enjoyed this book, we humbly ask you to write up a positive review on Amazon and Goodreads. We sincerely appreciate each person that takes the time to write one.

We have really valued connecting with our readers via social media, especially on our Facebook page https://www.facebook.com/RosoneandWatson/. Sometimes we ask for help from our readers as we write future books—we love to draw upon all your different areas of expertise. We also have a group of beta readers who get to look at the books before they are officially published and help us fine-tune last-minute adjustments. If you would like to be a part of this team, please go to our author website, and send us a message through the "Contact" tab.

You may also enjoy some of our other works. A full list can be found below:

Nonfiction:
Iraq Memoir 2006–2007 Troop Surge
Interview with a Terrorist (audiobook available)

Fiction:

The Monroe Doctrine Series
Volume One (audiobook available)
Volume Two (audiobook available)
Volume Three (audiobook available)
Volume Four (audiobook still in production)
Volume Five (available for preorder)

Rise of the Republic Series
Into the Stars (audiobook available)
Into the Battle (audiobook available)
Into the War (audiobook available)
Into the Chaos (audiobook available)
Into the Fire (audiobook still in production)
Into the Calm (available for preorder)

Apollo's Arrows Series (co-authored with T.C. Manning)
Cherubim's Call (available for preorder)

Crisis in the Desert Series (co-authored with Matt Jackson)
Project 19 (audiobook available)
Desert Shield
Desert Storm

Falling Empires Series
Rigged (audiobook available)
Peacekeepers (audiobook available)
Invasion (audiobook available)
Vengeance (audiobook available)
Retribution (audiobook available)

Red Storm Series
Battlefield Ukraine (audiobook available)
Battlefield Korea (audiobook available)
Battlefield Taiwan (audiobook available)
Battlefield Pacific (audiobook available)
Battlefield Russia (audiobook available)
Battlefield China (audiobook available)

Michael Stone Series
Traitors Within (audiobook available)

World War III Series
Prelude to World War III: The Rise of the Islamic Republic and the Rebirth of America (audiobook available)
Operation Red Dragon and the Unthinkable (audiobook available)
Operation Red Dawn and the Siege of Europe (audiobook available)
Cyber Warfare and the New World Order (audiobook available)

Children's Books:
My Daddy has PTSD
My Mommy has PTSD

Abbreviation Key

AFC	America First Corporation
AG	Attorney General
AI	Artificial Intelligence
AIR	Advanced Infantry Rifle
AMRAAM	Advanced Medium-Range Air-to-Air Missile
AOR	Area of Responsibility
APFV	Anti-Personnel Fighting Vehicle
BDA	Battle Damage Assessment
BH	Battle Helmet
CENTCOM	Central Command (located in Tampa, Florida, covers the Middle East AOR)
CG	Commanding General
CIA	Central Intelligence Agency
CO	Commanding Officer
CP	Company Post
COG	Continuance of Government
COMSUBLANT	Commander Submarine Force Atlantic
CONUS	Continental United States
DARPA	Defense Advance Research Projects Agency
DHS	Department of Homeland Security
DIA	Defense Intelligence Agency
DoD	Department of Defense
EAM	Emergency Action Message
EF	Expeditionary Force (Chinese)
EFP	Explosively Formed Penetrators
EMP	Electromagnetic Pulse
EMT	Emergency Medical Technician
EU	European Union
FBI	Federal Bureau of Investigation
FEMA	Federal Emergency Management Agency
FISA	Foreign Intelligence Surveillance Act
HEAT	High-Explosive Anti-Tank
HUD	Heads-Up Display
ICBM	Intercontinental Ballistic Missiles
ID	Infantry Division
IDF	Israeli Defensive Force

IFV	Infantry Fighting Vehicle
IR	Islamic Republic
JSTAR	Advanced Medium-Range Air-to-Air Missile
LNO	Liaison Officer
LT	Lieutenant
MANPAD	Man Portable Missile
MBT	Main Battle Tanks
MEF	Marine Expeditionary Force
MIRV	Multiple Independent Reentry Vehicles
MLRS	Multiple Launch Rocket System
NAD	New American Dollars
NATO	North Atlantic Treaty Organization
NCDC	National Control Defense Center
NCO	Non-Commissioned Officer
NSA	National Security Agency
NSC	National Security Council
OCONUS	Outside Continental United States
PE	Private Equity
PLA	People's Liberation Army (Chinese Army)
PLAAF	People's Liberation Army Air Force (Chinese Air Force)
PLAN	People's Liberation Army Navy (Chinese Navy)
PM	Prime Minister
PMC	Private Military Corporation
PRC	People's Republic of China
QRF	Quick-Reaction Force
RA	Royal Army (British)
RAF	Royal Air Force
RFID	Radio Frequency Identification
ROK	Republic of Korea (North Korea)
SACEUR	NATO Supreme Allied Commander
SAEF	South American Expeditionary Force
SAM	Surface-to-Air Missile
SCZ	Suez Canal Zone
SecDef	Secretary of Defense
SD	Science Division
SF	Special Forces
SFC	Sergeant First Class

SLBM	Submarine Launch Ballistic Missile
SSBM	Nuclear-Powered Ballistic Missile Submarines
SUD	Swordfish Underwater Drone
UD	Underwater Drone
XO	Executive Officer (second in charge)
3C	Command, Control & Communication

Printed in Great Britain
by Amazon

23287594R00129